The Scorpio File

A Novel

Author World Wide Web site address is
www.falconagency.com

First Edition Print 2004
ISBN: 1-59113-602-4

Printed in the United States of America

The Scorpio File

A Novel

By

W. Robb Robichaud

Acknowledgements

There are those who are always giving me
the encouragement to keep writing.

Friends and associates who
give me the inspiration:
Pat, Karon and Tom.
Thank you, all.

To a special person whose editorial
help is totally appreciated.
Thank you, Karen D.

And to Roseann,
my best friend and confidant,
for her encouragement when
I was off track, her patience,
positive advice and endurance.

Thank you for always being there.

W. Robb Robichaud

Dedication

Dedicated and in Remembrance
to the members of the
United States Military Forces
who are serving, have served,
died or sustained injuries during
their service and sacrifice
to our country.

God Bless America.

Table of Contents

Author's Message

"We as human beings have unlimited,
untouched powers within ourselves.
There will come a day when mankind
will understand. The movement toward
utilization of these hidden attributes
has begun and it all starts with
knowing you."

W. Robb Robichaud

Chapter I

Unification of Intelligence

In 1996, a government liaison officer who answered only to the President of the United States walked into the White House oval office. His power and authority, second only to the Commander-in-Chief, were not abused. He sat down in the seating area and was joined by the president. The meeting was the highest of top-secret meetings and, as far as government records were concerned, it never took place.

International terrorism was on the rise. One organization of terrorists had stepped up their training campaign in remote areas of third world countries. The training consisted of military- style exercises and those who exhibited excellence were sent to advance training in the field of terrorist infiltration and assassination. The top graduates of advanced schooling were considered the elite and assigned missions in selected countries that were considered the power countries in the world.

The Arab leader of the organization was once a Saudi Arabia citizen. In the early 1990's he was stripped of his citizenship and was persona non grata in his birth country. He traveled to the Sudan and set up his terrorist organization. After being asked to leave the country, he relocated to Afghanistan where that country's leadership welcomed him with open arms.

Usamah bin Laden grew his terrorist group into a worldwide, network, terrorist organization called al Qaeda (the base), which eventually became a name recognized throughout the world. Al Qaeda had been expanding its forces and network since the early 1990's and had success in bloody assassinations and bombing government entities throughout the world. No country's facilities in foreign continents were immune to the possibility of being attacked.

The president understood that unless something was done soon to counter al Qaeda and Usamah bin Laden, there would be no stopping the escalating, terrorist devastation. He had sent bills to Congress asking for additional funds to form a secret assassination squad to circumvent Executive Order 12333, Part 211, which banned any member of the government, including American military forces from committing assassinations. Congress and the Senate had always voted against the bills.

Frustrated with the situation, the president decided to take matters in his own hands. The Washington, DC bureaucracy and red tape had reached the pinnacle of incompetence. A close friend, who had spent years in the intelligence arena, was also frustrated with the situation. Each agency within America's government that specialized in the gathering and the dissemination of intelligence had become an empire within itself. Egos of the top agency directors became over- inflated with their agency's abilities and each separate division considered themselves in competition with other agencies. The two major bureaus that wouldn't share information were the CIA and FBI.

The president decided that something had to be done, and soon. He had two meetings with David Pauls and today was the last one before a final decision was to be made between these two men.

After an hour meeting, the decision was made to recruit a group of highly-trained, ex-military civilians to secretly complete missions against al Qaeda. Pauls had four individuals in mind. The men were all ex-Navy SEALS, extremely successful in civilian life, and had no reason other than hating terrorism to accept the job.

Over the next two years, the group called the International Covert Enforcement Team, acronym I.C.E., was successful in operations in Europe, Asia and Africa. In 1998 I.C.E. had grown to five of the most dangerous, covert killers in the world. Their vicious, blood curdling killings of low-life scum, put the terrorist world on notice. Any attack against American citizens or property, would be answered with extreme prejudice.

Pauls was their control contact and assigned the missions and funding for the assassins was set up through several dummy corporations all over the world. The ability to trace the executive in control of the funds, David Pauls, was virtually impossible.

I.C.E. was dissolved in 2000 and christened with new name. Falcon Agency eventually became a full-fledged, government entity after 9-11 and answered only to the Commander-in Chief.

The top executives of Falcon were the original members of I.C.E. Daniel White, an ex-professional, all-pro linebacker and successful multi-millionaire, was the Director and his two Assistant Directors were Merlin Miles (the Wizard or Wiz) and Raul Estavam. This threesome, along with their Operations Coordinator Kathy Starley, successfully unified the CIA, FBI, NSA and Secret Service into one cooperating intelligence unit. Each individual agency maintained anonymity but now, there was complete cooperation between every entity.

After 9-11, it was proven that all the different intelligence agencies had bits and pieces of information and if they had shared it with their "competitors", the president firmly believed there was a strong possibility the devastating attack could have been prevented.

That is when Falcon Agency became the legal, right hand intelligence organization of the president. The government's bureaucracy had been circumvented. Falcon's function was to gather all intelligence information and disseminate it to the other agencies. If the CIA, FBI, NSA or Secret Service discovered any information that could affect the security and safety of the United States, they were to turn it over to Falcon. For the first time since computer technology was incorporated into America's government, all agencies computer systems were networked into one group and all shared the common intelligence with each other. The agency that provided guidance to the whole operation was the elite, Falcon Agency.

In 2003, the unification proved successful. Falcon along with the FBI, CIA and NSA stopped a biological terrorist attack against the United States one day before the spreading of the chemicals was to commence in the major cities of America. In order to prevent hysteria amongst the citizens, the attempted attack was kept secret and would be for the next twenty years. In keeping with their tradition of extreme prejudice, twenty-six members of the terrorist cell had been wounded or killed by the Falcon team during the attack. The president signed an irrevocable Executive Order guarantying that the secret would not be released to the public.

In the summer of 2004 evidence of an attack that would be the most devastating atrocity ever in United States history was uncovered. The president asked Falcon Agency to investigate.

Chapter II

The Escape

September, 2001

*I*n *a dark, cold cave deep in the granite mountain, a feeble,* wounded al Qaeda terrorist was lying on the floor that was layered with plywood and covered with beautifully decorated and brightly colored Persian rugs. The only light emitting in the dark cavern was from two candles that were flicking their dim glow against the cavern's walls from their resting place on the metal table against the wall. It was deathly, eerie quiet, so quiet that the only audible sound in the grotto was the terrorist's labored, heavy breathing. He was the only survivor from the devastating slaughter in the cave. His two close associates bodies, riddled with bullet holes by the American soldier's AK-47 Russian Kalashnikov automatic rifles, were lying in a bloody heap on the other side of the room.

The terrorist knew he had very little time left to escape. He had heard bombs exploding outside the room and in other parts of the cavern earlier during the assault. The Arab heard the final order given by the lead American to his team of assassins as they were leaving.

"Set the detonators to the other bombs."

Time was running out fast. His body was weak from weeks of sickness that had wracked his frail, thin body and now the bullet that had left a bleeding, gaping wound in his thigh. He knew the wound wasn't serious but it would need attention soon. The tall man didn't have the time to tend to it. Escape from the enclosed death trap was his first priority. The wide cot he had been laying on when the American had shot him was above. He reached for the canvas bed, while feeling the floor beneath him shake from bombs exploding against the mountain range outside. For two days American military jet bombers had been dropping their destructive payloads of explosives against the mountain range. They were determined to eradicate the Taliban and al Qaeda who were hiding in the many impenetrable cave complexes.

The floor continued to shutter and shake as he used what little fading strength he had remaining to push the cot over onto its side. The bed tipped over, making a thud, and he crawled forward, dragging his wounded leg, while depositing a trail of fresh, smeared blood on the rug. The candles didn't provide much light as he struggled to pull back the colorful, thick carpet. Once he had removed the rug and exposed the plywood beneath, he reached for a wooden handle that was bolted to a piece of thin, metal sheeting. The terrorist pulled on the handle and the metal slowly slid towards him, exposing a black hole in the floor. He and his other two associates were the only ones who knew about the escape hatch and his partners were now dead three feet away.

Crawling toward the black opening, he moved his legs forward so they dangled down into the abyss. Searching with his good leg, he felt a rung of the hidden ladder. More explosions outside rocked the granite walls and floor. The bombs were very close to his cave complex and with each barrage seemed to be getting closer. The aircraft bombs wouldn't do any interior damage because the hide-a-way was too deep in the mountain. He sat up and let his one good leg bear the load of his body as he stood. Using both arms and hands that were positioned on each side of the opening, he gradually lowered himself down the hole. When his head was even with the edge, he reached for the metal cover and pulled it over the round hole in the floor, sealing the gap in the floor.

Struggling with all his remaining power, the Arab lowered himself down the twelve foot ladder to the rock floor below. It was pitch black inside and he felt around for the cold granite walls to maintain his balance. He knew there was a natural rock shelf close by which held a nine-volt flashlight. Feeling with his soiled hands against the moist, cool walls that were vibrating from the 500 ton bombs explosions above, he felt the shelf. Sliding his hand forward, he located the flashlight, flipped on the switch and the bright light illuminated the tunnel that appeared ahead of him. His strength from the climb down was all but used up and he collapsed onto the rock-dirt, dropping the flashlight to the floor. It didn't break and he let out a sigh of gratitude between pain spasms.

Retrieving the flashlight, he began to crawl forward. It was hard to move because of his wound and lack of strength, but the Arab knew that the explosives the Americans had left behind, twelve feet above his present position, were about to detonate. His assumption was right and he heard the first one explode. The noise was deafening and very close. His adrenalin kicked in. Shining the flashlight beam ahead, he crawled forward, away from the opening that led up to the cavern. Dust and dirt fell from the ceiling of the small tunnel as he moved painfully forward. At this moment, he didn't care. At the present, he was relatively safe and in another ten feet he would be secure in his secret abode. More explosions continued to rock the cave over his head. The room he was in five minutes ago was now almost filled with debris, boulders and covered the secret, protective metal cover.

Pushing the flashlight forward and then crawling, it took him two minutes to get to the room's opening. At the entrance, he shined the light around. He was familiar with the surroundings, having hidden there many times before. In anticipation of an attack from the Americans, he and his two dead associates had stocked and furnished the hideout with nonperishable supplies six months ago. The penetrating beam of the flashlight flashed across the dark room and stopped when its ray of white light shined on one of the beds. The Arab painfully crawled to the resting place and using his remaining strength, climbed onto the blanketed cot. The mountain was being pummeled by explosions, but he didn't care. He needed rest and once he'd made his way to the sitting position on the bed and removed the thick quilt blankets, the terrorist laid down. Covering himself with the quilts, he switched off the flashlight that was at his side under the covers. The bullet wound was still seeping blood, but the terrorist didn't care. His last thought was that he had fooled the American Satan again and smiled at the thought as he fell into a deep, comatose sleep.

Chapter III

Visitor

June, 2004

*D*aniel White, the Director of Falcon Agency, was busy scanning over intelligence documents strewn on his Washington executive office desk. Iraqi Freedom had been underway for thirteen months and the search for Saddam Hussein's group of sympathizers was still underway. Hussein had been captured with the help of Falcon Agency intelligence. His two sons, Qusay and Uday, were dead and a number of the most wanted Iraqis in the fifty-two card deck were now captured and in U.S. custody or had been killed. Even with Saddam in prison, along with twenty-one of his senior cadre, the noose of military coalition forces was still tightening on those that were still on the loose. Daniel was sure that over time, the rest of Saddam's senior staff would be captured.

Under the directive of the president, all intelligence data from the CIA, FBI, NSA and Secret Service agencies was delivered first to the Falcon Agency, where it was reviewed and then sent to the appropriate agency. Due to the current circumstances in the Middle East, Falcon Agency was forced to expand and was now staffed by 132 highly-trained personnel. The agency was led by Daniel and his three close friends and associates, Merlin (Wizard) Miles, Raul Estapham and the operations coordinator Kathy Starley.

Daniel was reading a detailed report from a CIA operative in Iraq. The agent had compiled a dossier from his investigation in Saddam's home town of Tikrit, north of the capital city of Baghdad. Daniel had additional information from two undercover Iraqis who were working for the United States in the war-torn country. Also on his desk were reports and files from interrogations of captured Iraq senior staff. Combining all the data, Daniel was hoping to discover pieces of intelligence that would lead the coalition forces to the remaining Hussein's senior staff's locations.

Grabbing his telephone, he hit the intercom button.

"Kathy," he said into the speaker.

A few seconds passed and then there was an answer.

"Yes Daniel."

"Kathy, could you get a hold of Bill Angus and Merlin and coordinate a time when they can meet here in my office this afternoon?"

"As a matter of fact, Director Angus is here in Merlin's office right now. Do you want me to send them in?"

"Great. Ah ... give me five minutes."

"Okay. Anything else?" Kathy asked.

"No, that's it." Daniel disconnected the intercom and smiled.

He had just found some interesting information that might lead the military to a couple of Saddam's top cadre's locations.

The President of the United States needed a break. As he sat at his desk in the oval office reading an intelligence briefing from the Homeland Security Director and the FBI, he became increasingly disturbed about the shooting deaths of two senators who sat on the Armed Forces Committee. Both were killed during the past month outside their homes by a sniper who hadn't been caught. The reports he had read from the FBI stated there currently weren't any leads as to who the assassin or assassins were. He had also read in the newspapers stories of eight prominent executives of companies, who were major suppliers and vendors for the government that were assassinated in the similar manner.

The president decided he needed to go for a walk and clear his head. The walks always helped and he enjoyed strolling around the beautiful White House grounds in the summer. The trees and gardens were in full bloom.

Putting on his suit coat, he left by the outside oval office exit. When he was on the veranda, three Secret Service agents assigned to the Commander-in-Chief followed him at a safe distance. They were used to their leader deciding unannounced to escape the confines of the office and gave him ample distance to be alone, while still under their protective guard.

After ten minutes meandering around the gardens, the president strolled toward the building adjoining the White House, where the vice president officed. He wasn't going to visit the VP but another trusting person he admired. In the same building that housed the vice president, was Falcon Agency's headquarters. The president had never been to Falcon's new office since it relocated there seven months ago. He would surprise them and he also wanted to talk to Director Daniel White.

The president and his three guards entered the building from a side door. Two Secret Service guards were inside the entrance and seeing who had entered, snapped to attention.

"Good afternoon, Mr. President. Can I announce you to …. ?" one guard began to ask, a little unnerved by the unannounced president's visit.

The president interrupted the guard while holding his hand in the air. "Good afternoon. No, I'm just going to Falcon Agency's office. I want to surprise them so please don't announce me."

"Yes, Mr. President. Falcon's offices are on the second and third floors. The executive offices are on the second floor. Do you want to take the elevator in the lobby, sir?"

"No, thanks. I'll just take the stairs. I need the exercise," the president said smiling.

The American leader and his trailing security team climbed the two flights of stairs and entered the second floor entrance. Again, they were met by two Secret Service agents at the door. The guards were also surprised by the sudden appearance of the president. The president gave the same response to their query and asked for directions to Daniel White's office.

After receiving directions, the foursome walked down the quiet, wide, dark blue carpeted hallway. The area was not overly decorated and yet gave the feeling of warmth. The walls and offices had dark, highly polished wood. Evenly spaced on the walls, the president recognized pictures of early Washington, DC buildings.

The president looked in offices as he passed. Some were occupied and the occupants of others were absent. The offices were also very neat and orderly, maintaining a professional impression. He said hello to those who were in their offices. Shocked at seeing the president, the staff members jumped to their feet and were nervous. He laughed, told them to relax, said a few kind words and then put his finger to his lips.

"Shhhh ... don't let anyone know I'm here."

Each answered in the affirmative and the president continued down the soft carpeted hall. As he neared the lobby area he noticed the Falcon Agency seal imbedded in the polished marble floor. He had personally given instructions to have it installed when the renovations were planned, wanting the Falcon Agency members to feel the pride that they were part of the government.

He looked into a much larger office that had a conference room adjoining it. Inside the beautiful office were the Senior Deputy Director of Falcon Agency, Merlin Miles aka "Wizard" and CIA Director Bill Angus, deep in conversation. The president walked into Merlin's spacious, well-decorated office.

"So, this is where all the smart people hang out. Nice," the president said with a big smile.

Both Bill and Merlin didn't hear him enter and when the words were spoken, both looked at the source of the compliment.

"Holy shit," was Merlin's immediate response. "Err … I'm sorry sir. Mr. President, how are you?" Merlin asked a little rattled, while rising from his leather executive chair.

"Fine … just fine, Wiz. Bill, how are you?" the president said, with a big smile and walking up to the two senior government officials. They all shook hands.

"What a surprise, Mr. President. You really caught me … us off guard," Merlin said in a shocked voice. "So, to what do we owe the pleasure of this visit?"

"I was just out walking and decided to come over and see your new headquarters. I never saw it finished. It's really nice. I also wanted to talk to Daniel. Is he here?"

"Thank you, Mr. President. We're really proud of it. Yes, sir, Daniel is here. I'll take you to his office if you want," Merlin offered.

At that moment, Kathy walked into Merlin's office.

"Merlin … Bill. Daniel …. Oh my! Mr. President. Excuse me, sir. I didn't know you were here. They didn't announce you," she said shocked, like all the rest.

"It's okay, Kathy. Come on in. I wanted to surprise everyone and I gave the orders not to be announced. Your security agents are not at fault," the president said, extending his hand to shake hers.

"Continue on with what you have to say, Kathy. It's me who is interrupting government business."

"Thank you, sir. Ah … Daniel wants to see Director Angus and Merlin in his office," she answered, still a little rattled with the honored guest's presence.

"Oh, this is great," the president said with a mischievous smile.

He then planned with the two Falcon and the CIA executives on how to surprise Daniel.

Daniel was at his desk with his head down reading a document when Kathy walked in.

"Excuse me, Daniel. Merlin and Director Angus will be here in a few seconds. Are you ready for them?"

"I'm always ready to see Bill, but the Wiz is another story," he said laughing. "Tell them to just come in," Daniel said without looking up.

Kathy left the office and when she walked into the hall, she smiled at the waiting dignitaries.

"He said to just walk in," she said laughing quietly.

Merlin, being the bigger of the two strolled in first. After entering, Bill walked to Merlin's left side. Hidden behind the duo was the president.

"Hey, Daniel. You wanted to see us?" Merlin asked.

"Wiz, you're not going to believe this," Daniel said not looking up. "I've got a pretty good idea where Tahir Jalil Habbash and Zuhayr Talib Al Naqib are."

"Well, it's about time you found them," the president answered, still hiding behind Merlin and Bill.

Daniel heard the somewhat familiar voice, but knew it wasn't Bill's or Merlin's. He looked up with a confused look on his face and as he was staring at his two guests, Merlin and Bill parted, exposing the president.

"Mr. President! Welcome to Falcon Agency, sir," Daniel said rising out of his executive chair.

"Thanks, Daniel," the president answered laughing.

"Wow ... man what a pleasant surprise sir," Daniel said with a big smile and shaking the president's hand. "No one announced that you were coming or here."

"I needed a break from the oval office and went for a walk. I decided to surprise you and see your new offices. They look real nice. How do you like it?"

"They're awesome, Mr. President. Everyone on both floors are really proud of it. We're filling up fast, but right now, we still have extra space upstairs. Would you like a tour?"

"I would, but maybe another time. Do you gentlemen have some time to talk? I have something I would like to discuss with you."

"Yes, Mr. President," Daniel answered for the group.

"Good. Let's sit down," the Commander-in-Chief answered, while leading the way.

The men all sat down in Daniel's office lounge area and as they were sitting, Kathy left and quietly closed Daniel's office door behind her.

"So, where are these clowns?" the president asked Daniel.

"I'm not positive, but I've got it narrowed down, sir. We just missed them by a day or so when they were in northeast Baghdad a couple of weeks ago. I just finished reviewing recent intelligence reports and two significant items popped up from different sources. I think they are hiding around the southern end of Tikrit. We have a report from an Iraqi, which has been substantiated, that two men matching the descriptions of these guys were seen five times in that specific area.

The other item of real importance is there has been an unusual, large influx of new American hundred dollar bills, circulating recently in that particular area. The money hasn't come from us and Hussein had been known to have bundles of cash stashed away in secret locations. We've still got some work to do before we turn this information over to the pentagon. I'd say that within three days we should have enough verified data together to present to Director Angus and Admiral Boryla."

"Good job, Daniel. Keep me updated please. I want all of them locked up or dead. It would relieve a lot of pressure on our forces and the Iraqi citizens knowing they have been captured or proof that they have been removed. There are a bunch of Hussein sympathizer terrorist cells scattered all over Iraq and, like you had said in the report a month ago, these two are the leaders.

What I want to discuss with you is a subject of a different nature. You've heard about the sniper assassinations of the two senators," the president said, pausing to look at each official.

"It's pretty sad, sir. I haven't followed it close because of the Iraq situation. I assume that the FBI and Homeland Security are heavily involved with the investigation," Daniel answered.

"We have a unit also that is helping out," CIA Director Angus added.

"So far, nothing has turned up and from what I've read in the reports, there isn't much to go on. There is another fact that many aren't aware of. Over the past four months, eight executives of companies, who are government vendors, have also been shot. They lived in Texas, Seattle, Silicon Valley, Kansas City, and Virginia, Boston, Detroit and the last one in Boulder, Colorado.

With the exception of the two senator's deaths, these other attacks and deaths have been only reported in local newspapers. That's ten unsolved murders that have no motives and no leads.

For some reason, I have a gut feeling that they're tied together. I don't have any proof but intuition tells me something is up," the president stated.

"Do you want Falcon to look into it, sir?" Merlin asked.

"I know you people have your plate full right now, but if you can spare some time, I would appreciate it. It's not an order, just a favor. Would you get the directors of all the agencies together, Daniel, and find out what you can?" the president asked in a quiet soft tone.

"Sure, Mr. President. I'll tell you what. I'll get a meeting together this week and, after it, I'll report the results to you personally. If I see that maybe Falcon can help, I'll let you know also.

Bill, can you get me a complete, updated report from your agency on exactly what the CIA knows? I'll also request the same from FBI Director John Lambert." Daniel asked.

"Done! You'll have it on your desk tomorrow morning, Daniel."

"Thanks, Bill. Anyone have any ideas right now? You're unusually quiet, Wiz. What's up?" Daniel asked.

"It is a funny thing. I've been following these sniper shootings and one of our agents, Chuck Phipps in Seattle, called me a couple of weeks ago. He said the same thing as you, Mr. President. He thinks there is a connection to all the shootings. I'm going to get all the ballistic reports from the sniper attacks. Maybe they will tie all or some of the shootings together. Funny … this has been bugging me for the past couple of days," Merlin said.

"I better get back to the White House. They probably have an APB out on me by now. I didn't tell anyone where I was going," the president said with a grin. "Thanks for your time, gentlemen, and I look forward to hearing from you tomorrow, Daniel, or whenever you get something solid. Thanks again."

"Anytime, Mr. President. It was a pleasure," Daniel answered while rising from his chair.

The group all exchanged handshakes with their boss and the president left Daniel's office.

Kathy walked in after the Commander-in-Chief left.

"Do you gentlemen need anything?"

"Please, close the door, Kathy. I need you to do something for us," Daniel said to Falcon's OPS coordinator.

Chapter IV

One Shot ... One Kill

*D*aniel *and his senior Falcon Agency team had concluded* their meeting with the heads of the CIA, FBI, NSA, Secret Service and Homeland Security agencies. They were gathered at their Falcon's conference room to debrief. Present in the room were Daniel, Raul, Merlin and Kathy.

"So, what did you think of the meeting?" Daniel asked the group.

"An interesting scenario. After hearing what the directors had to report, I think there is a centralized conspiracy going on from some type of terrorist group. It smells of al Qaeda," Raul stated.

"If it is al Qaeda, then they have taken a different tactic to attack the U.S. Their modus operandi has been to inflict as many casualties as possible when they've attacked before. I don't see them assassinating individuals, unless it was a single opportunity. What do you think the motive would be to use snipers to kill?" Merlin asked, directing the question to the group.

Daniel cleared his throat and gave his input.

"Good question, Wiz. All the targets are high profile individuals. Maybe they are trying to create a panic situation within the corporate and government community. Knocking off senators and corporate heads has definitely rocked Wall Street. The market dropped a couple hundred points the past two weeks. At one point it was down eight-hundred points. That is one hell of an impact. Kathy, what do you think?" Daniel asked, looking directly at his OPS coordinator.

"What I got out of the meeting is no one has any idea who is doing this. All I heard is speculation. Maybe it is renegade individuals like the Washington snipers a couple of years ago or someone who has a vendetta against the government."

"Good point. Wiz, did you ever get the ballistic results from all the assassinations?"

"I've got five so far and the other five should be here by tomorrow. I looked over the reports I have and there is no match. All the bullets were fired from different rifles. The only consistent items are the bullets are 7.62 mm. None of the striations matched. Only two casings were recovered and neither firing pin impacts matched. Once I get the other reports, I'll let you know if we have a match," Merlin answered.

"So, we have five different weapons so far which leads me to believe we have a group of people or someone with a bunch of rifles that fire 7.62 mm," Daniel said while thinking.

"Do you think it might be a terrorist cell here in the U.S.?" Raul queried.

"Could be ... different targets all over the U.S. ... killed by different weapons. Let's set up a time chart when each person was assassinated. Wiz, let's use your office and, Kathy, would you get our profiler, Mark Reilly, to join our team? I have the feeling that there is a big piece of the puzzle missing. Right now, I don't think we have a serial killer here. It's too much territory to cover. Let me know when you have everything set up, Wiz. We have another asset we could use."

"What's that, Daniel?" Merlin asked.

"Xi Xeng (Chi Cheng). He never misses," Daniel answered. "I'm going to get him here if he can get away from the resort."

Xi's friendship with the Falcon team and especially Daniel was unwavering. Previously, terrorists had attacked

Daniel's estate in Colorado and Xi had saved Daniel's life. He had also taken part in all of Falcon's previous missions to Afghanistan and Iraq. Xi's special mystical gifts made the Chinese man a valuable asset.

"It won't hurt. Looks like we could use as much help as possible," Raul added.

"Okay, let's get on it. If you need anything, let me or Kathy know. The president wants this moved up to top priority and Falcon is heading up the operation. I've got to go brief him now and I'll be back in about forty-five minutes. When I get back, Kathy, would you get Xi on the phone for me, please?"

"I will, Daniel," OPS answered politely.

The meeting adjourned and Daniel left for the oval office.

"The president will see you now, Mr. White," the president's appointment secretary Jennifer York said to Daniel, who was seated in the reception area.

"Thank you, Jennifer," Daniel answered following Jennifer into the oval office.

"How's it going today, Daniel?" the president asked rising from his desk.

"Same as usual, Mr. President."

"Have a seat. How did the meeting go this morning?"

"Well, there were a lot of smart people in the room, but no concrete answers. We're all in the speculation mode right now. We don't know if it is a group, an individual, foreigners or citizens who are committing these killings.

I'm setting up a command center at Falcon Agency and calling in our profiler to help. There haven't been any other killings for two weeks now and the chatter around the terrorist world is normal.

What I did find out though, was the chatter, which normally escalates before an occurrence happens, wasn't evident prior to any of the murders. That tells me it might be an isolated group of individuals. But, we're not ruling out the usual suspects like al Qaeda or Saddam Hussein's people, sir."

"What's your gut feeling on this, Daniel?" the president asked.

Daniel paused for a few seconds.

"Mr. President, at this point I don't really have a solid one. I don't think we've seen the end of it. Whoever is doing this is smart and I don't feel that whoever it is has retired. Maybe they are just taking a break and planning another one.

One thing you can be assured of, Mr. President. We will find them eventually. But, what I'm worried about is how many others will be killed before we do get them. I'm calling in a special person who may be able to give us a different perspective."

"Who's that?"

"Xi Xeng. Xi has special powers and maybe they will help us."

"I like that man. Something special and unique there."

"I know, sir. Xi and I are very close. He saved my life when my place in Colorado was raided and he knew it was going to be hit a day before it happened. It's as if he can see into the future at times. Maybe he can see who these people are."

"Let's hope so, Daniel, for everyone's sake. Thanks for coming over and keep me updated."

"I will, Mr. President."

Daniel rose and left for his headquarters. He liked that Falcon Agency's offices had been relocated close to the White House. It was a short walking distance and saved him a lot of time since he didn't have to drive across town.

Two days later, Merlin had the conference room adjoining his office converted into a full- scale command center for this specific project. The Falcon team was gathered for an update meeting by Merlin. A special guest was present in the room. Seated at the table was Mr. Xi Xeng.

"Here is what we have. The first four assassinations happened over four consecutive days and the last four killings did also. There was a week break between each set of killings. Now, the last two murders were three weeks ago and were spaced out by one day. That sets a basic pattern.

Next, I received all the ballistic reports. There were two more casing reports with them. Each casing and bullet was fired from a different weapon. The firing pin impressions were different and all bullets' striations were also. So, we're looking at ten different rifles being used which fired 7.62 mm bullets. Each victim was killed by one shot. These people are good.

There were only two witnesses and neither one heard a gunshot or saw the assailants. All victims were assassinated either at dusk or dark, and eight of them were gunned down outside their homes. One witness was the wife of a victim. She went outside to greet Senator Johnson at their home in Georgetown. As she walked toward the senator, who was getting out of his car, she saw him slump and fall to the driveway.

At first she thought he tripped or stumbled. As she approached him, he never moved or tried to get up. She rolled him over and then saw he was bleeding from his head. He was dead. One shot … one kill.

The other witness was the neighbor of Jonathan Gray, the Chairman of the Board of Gray Technology in Dallas, Texas. As you know, Gray Technology is a major purveyor of military technology and has been instrumental in development of new weapons we've used in Afghanistan and Iraq.

The witness report is almost identical. The neighbor, who lives across the street, was out on his front lawn and saw Gray's car pull into the drive. He waited until Gray was getting out of his vehicle to say hi. Gray got out and then fell to the ground. He didn't get up. Sensing something was seriously wrong, the neighbor ran across to help.

When he got there, he saw a bullet hole in Gray's head. He checked for a pulse and there wasn't any. Again, one shot … one kill.

Neither witness heard a gunshot. That means these snipers are sophisticated pros and are using silencers. There wasn't any unusual activity in either area.

As far as the other eight assassinations, there were no witnesses either and the victims were also shot in the head. Six were found outside their homes and the other two outside their offices in the parking lots near their cars.

In every situation, the investigators used angle analysis to determine where the shooter was. The locations were found in every case. The sniper was hidden either in bushes near houses or buildings, or in the woods. All were shot from a distance of 200 to 335 yards."

Daniel interrupted Merlin. "Yards or feet?"

"Yards, Daniel."

"Damn," Daniel whispered to himself.

"These snipers are really good. Based on all of this data we have now, and this is all we have, I'm still not convinced that we are dealing with a group of people or an individual," the Wizard concluded.

"Each victim was shot once in the head at dusk or early evening. That means the shooters are possibly using night-scopes. Any reports of large thefts or purchases of rifles or night-scopes recently?" Daniel asked.

"Bill had his people check that out and there haven't been any large thefts over the past three years. The last major theft of rifles was down at Ft. Stewart, Georgia, three and a half years ago, and they got the culprits and recovered all the weapons, which were M-16's. Nothing else was found as far as thefts and no large purchases from registered individuals or stores. I had my people check that out also," the Wizard added.

"How about internationally?" Raul asked.

"Bill also had his people check that avenue. Nothing," Merlin answered.

"So, maybe we are dealing with a government entity. That's a bunch of different weapons and governments have them," Raul said.

"Terrorist organizations do also," Daniel added.

"How about the airlines?" Kathy asked.

"I had the FBI and Homeland Security gather all the computer info from the airlines and they are crosschecking for anyone who flew to major airports close to the victim's homes or businesses. That's a lot of data to sort through. There are millions of people who travel to those destinations daily and then there are the connecting flights. It will be at least a week before we have those results," Merlin answered.

"And then, the snipers could live in each one of those areas or close by … close enough to drive," Daniel said.

The group remained quiet for thirty seconds or so, thinking of what to do or another angle to approach.

"Man, this is a tough one. What's the story on intelligence chatter, Wiz?" Daniel finally asked, interrupting everyone's thought process.

"It was normal in every situation. No unusual activity."

"What do you think of this, Xi?" Daniel asked his Chinese friend who was quietly and carefully listening to every word spoken by his fellow compatriots.

"Not sure. Big mess. I think maybe one or two person."

"Why's that, Xi?" Raul asked and the others turned towards him with curious looks on their faces.

"Think people killed by only one sniper. Not many people that good shot. If there be one miss or one shot in body and not head, then maybe more than one or two. But, Wizard say all shot in head. "One shot ... one kill." Xi don't think eight different people kill victim. Think only one... maybe two, not more than three for sure."

"Good point, Xi," Merlin answered.

The rest of the group agreed.

"So, let's assume that there is only one sniper. Ten different weapons were used. How did he ship ten rifles or get them on the plane? I mean, we are talking about victims in Seattle, California, Kansas City, Detroit, Texas, Boston, Virginia, Colorado and the two here in the DC area," Raul asked the group.

Excitement was brewing amongst the Falcon team. It always did when they thought they were beginning to solve a problem and this was definitely a major one.

"Maybe he isn't using ten different rifles. Ballistics are on the casings and projectile. That means the firing pin and barrel. What if he exchanges the pins and barrels?" Daniel asked.

"Are you saying he carries a different barrel and pin to each location? What about the rest of the rifle?" Kathy asked.

"He could break it down and ship it to an address where he is going to strike next. Maybe a hotel or motel where he has reservations. Once he arrives, all he has to do is reassemble the body of the gun and insert a new pin and barrel. When he is done killing, all he does is overnight the body of the gun to his next location and trash the used barrel and pin," Merlin answered with a smile.

"So, the only parts he has to worry about initially, are the barrels and pins, which he could have in the package. I don't think he could get them through airport security. Too much metal. Now we're thinking like assassins. I wonder how that came about," Daniel said laughing.

The rest of the group joined in the laughter reflecting back on their assassination missions. It was a good brainstorming session and they weren't done yet. After the laughing break, Daniel continued.

"Good job, people. Maybe that is why he is killing four in a short period of time. To throw everyone off, he then kills two and disappears for a while. If he is shipping the gun overnight with barrels and pins, the package wouldn't cause any undo suspicions due to the weight. Anyone know how much an M-16 weighs?" Daniel queried the group.

"Ah, now you are pushing my memory. An M-16 ... bare bones ... is 8.3 pounds and with a twenty round, fully loaded magazine and a good scope, you're looking at eleven to thirteen pounds. How'd I do, Raul?" Merlin asked his ex-Navy SEAL buddy?"

Smiling back at his friend, Raul answered.

"As usual, right on the mark. Those SEAL instructors did a good job of imbedding those numbers in our heads. Each barrel weighs 4.8 pounds. So we'd be looking at around a thirty pound package."

"That's if he were using an M-16," Merlin added. "There are many different other good rifles out there and, if I were to pick the best, it would be the Heckler & Koch HK PSG1 rifle with the permanently-mounted Hensoldt 6 x 42 scope that has the lighted ranging sensor."

"Damn. You still keep up with that stuff?" Raul asked smiling.

"It's a hobby. I've always appreciated a good rifle. If I were a pro sniper, that's what I would chose. There is one draw back of the HK. They are a lot heavier than the M-16. I think with the scope and a full clip, you're looking at around 21 pounds. Add another four barrels at six pounds each: with the packing you're now looking at a forty-one to forty-five pound package. It's still feasible to ship and the rifles break down into smaller components."

"Okay, people. Let's check out who has a supply of these Heckler-Koch rifles and see if we can find a trail," Daniel said rising from his chair.

"I'll get on it, Daniel, and give the information to Bill Angus," Merlin answered also rising from his chair.

"In the meantime, while we're waiting for the rifle and airline information ... Raul ... get the staff upstairs on the hotels located in the areas where the ten killings took place. See if any packages were sent to the hotels for guests that were going to arrive around the dates of the killings. Also, check with the major overnight freight companies like UPS and FedEx for shipments.

What do you think, Xi?" Daniel asked.

"Think good idea what you say here. But, Xi think something missing. Too easy right now. I think some more," Xi said smiling.

"What do you think is missing, Xi?" Daniel asked.

"Not sure yet. Xi think more."

"Okay. Anyone have anything else to add?"

No one had anything.

"Let's get on it. Kathy, help Raul with getting everything organized upstairs. I want them on this quick. If we can find out who he is, then maybe we can prevent another assassination."

The meeting broke up and everyone left the room at a brisk pace. Something was happening and when it did, the level of excitement in Falcon Agency's headquarters reached the apex of stimulation.

Chapter V

Sniper

Three weeks prior

*I*n an upscale subdivision outside Montreal, Canada, two individuals sat in the living room of an expensive, lavishly furnished 5,500 square foot home. The topic of their conversation was the elimination of future targets in the United States. The heavily built mid-eastern looking man giving the instructions to the sniper, whose home they were in, was speaking in a quiet voice.

"You have done very well on the other assignments. Our plan has worked well. They have no idea who has killed the senators or the company executives.

Now, here is a list of new targets. There are thirty-two with addresses, companies and phone numbers and all the other information you requested on the other shootings. It's complete and it is up to your discretion as to whom and when you eliminate them. We would like it finalized within four to five months," the man said in a whisper, while handing a thick manila folder to the assassin.

"You can talk in a normal voice. There isn't anyone here in the house, and I have it screened every week for bugs." the sniper said in a normal tone.

"Good. I'm just used to having people around. It's a force of habit. You never know who may be listening.

You and I, along with our friend in Iraq, are the only ones who know who you are. We're going to keep it that way. You are to contact only me for anything you need and I will have everything in place."

Looking over the list the liaison man had given the sniper, the assassin paused and looked up.

"This is an extensive list of prominent individuals. I recognize some of the names as government people. I see the names of senators, Congress people and other officials. Right now, I think I should stay away from them until everything calms down in Washington, DC.

It will take me a day or two to plan out a schedule. These targets are located all over the United States," the assassin stated.

"I realize that and it is all in your hands. I have people standing by all over America ready to assist whenever I call them. Just let me know what you need and where you want it delivered. Just remember, any supplies you need must be placed at locations where you won't be seen picking them up."

"That won't be a problem. I'll give you a list of cities where I will strike and it will be in the order of the attacks. That way you can be prepared for what I need and get it to the locations I specify," the sniper said.

"Good. If you give me a detailed list, we should only have to talk once or twice more. I like that.

Now, eight-million American dollars has been transferred to your Swiss account. Here is the confirmation of the transfer, but I know you. You'll be verifying it as soon as I leave," the liaison individual said smiling.

"You are correct. I will verify it."

"That is all I have. Do you have any questions or requests before I leave?" the liaison man asked.

"No. Everything is clear. I will contact you in a few days."

Both stood up and shook hands and the liaison left the executive-style house.

The sniper immediately went to the phone in the cherry wood office and dialed the bank in Zurich, Switzerland. The eight million dollars had been deposited twelve hours ago. The assassin then left the house.

Over the next two days, the trained killer put together a detailed plan and itinerary for the upcoming elimination of the prominent targets that supported the attacks against Afghanistan and Iraq. The main items needed to accomplish the missions were twelve Heckler & Koch HK PSG1 rifles, with a permanently mounted Hensoldt 6 x 42 with lighted ranging sensor for distances up to 600 meters. The sniper knew they are the best sniper rifles in the world and, at $10,000 each, the most expensive. Each rifle would also need an individual, custom made silencer adapted to the barrel and twenty 7.62 mm hand-loaded, hollow point rounds. The illegal silencers were already being hand made using a special technology never used, by a contracted gunsmith in Toronto who did other illegal work for the killer.

In addition, twenty-four special accessories would be needed and were added to the list. The cost to accomplish the mission was very expensive, but according to the liaison visitor, money and expenses were not a problem and he would pay them with no questions asked. The sniper had earned his respect.

Trained in sniper tactics in Afghanistan and advanced sniper training in Germany, the assassin was the most deadly, unknown killer in the world. There was one more person's name added to the list. The liaison contact that was coordinating between the sniper and those willing to help in the United States would have to be eliminated. The man had no inkling that the assassin had received a special message stating to eliminate the contact. He was the only person who could identify the assassin. All the contact wanted was results and, after ten assassinations over the previous months, the sniper had proved to be deadly and up to the task. Providing that all the requirements to accomplish the mission were delivered and ready, the killer would commence the assassination missions in three to four weeks.

After delivering the itinerary and list of equipment needed to the liaison contact, the killer decided to take a vacation to Washington, DC. The trip would also provide a good cover to do research and recognition of the future targets in the area. This one would be different and based on the information provided by the liaison, a different approach would be needed to kill the unsuspecting civilian. The killer also needed to meet with a secret partner.

Chapter VI

Awaken Terrorist

September, 2001

*T*he *Arab terrorist woke up in the pitch black room. Not* moving on the cot, it took him a while to realize where he was. When he remembered, he searched the cot for the flashlight. His body ached from the sickness that wracked his frail body and when he moved his legs, a sharp pain reminded him of the American who had shot him in his thigh. He found the flashlight and flipped the switch on. Shining the light around the room, he familiarized himself with his surroundings for a few minutes.

Fighting off the pain, he slowly rose from his bed and swung his legs over the side. The terrorist knew he had to get up and move around. His wound had to be tended to. The beam of his flashlight shone on the medical supply cabinet. Next to the metal storage bin was a table that had several candles on it. Struggling to his feet, he stood there gaining his balance and flashed the light down to his leg. The brown pants he wore were stained burgundy from the dried blood that had flowed from his bullet wound. There wasn't any fresh blood visible.

Testing his legs, he took one small step toward the table. It hurt, but he knew he could make it to the candles. Taking small steps, he made his way five feet and lit seven candles with the matches on the table. The inviting light helped illuminate the large room. Seven feet away was another table with additional candles and the Arab hobbled cautiously to it and also lit those. The room was now dimly lit and he made his way toward the medical cabinet. It was then he realized how quiet it was in the cavern. The Americans weren't bombing the mountain range.

He sat down on a cushioned chair next to the cabinet and opened it up. Inside was a fully- stocked supply of drugs, ointments, bandages and swabs. Against the metal wall were surgical instruments. He reached for a set of scissors and cut the dried blood part of his pants away, exposing the bullet wound on his thigh. The blood had dried and created a large scab. It wasn't as deep as he thought it would be. For the next ten minutes he treated the wound.

Satisfied with his medical treatment, hunger pains started to set in. He had no idea how long he had been in the grotto. Looking at his watch, he realized it was a day later and thirty-two hours since he had escaped from the certain death trap twelve feet above his current position.

Looking around, he saw where the food and water supplies were. There was enough in the cache to sustain a single person for at least six months. He decided he wanted to clean up first. His body was now adjusting to the hurt in his torso. The two morphine-based pain killers he had swallowed without any liquids were starting to take effect.

Over the next hour he cleansed his body, put on clean, warm clothes and ate cold soup out of the can. Cold or not, the nourishment felt good. Feeling somewhat satisfied now, he started to set up the room. He lit two kerosene lanterns, which gave the room much more light, and extinguished the candles. The candles would have to be saved for emergencies. A kerosene heater was tucked away in a corner. He placed it near the center of the cave and ignited the burner. It wouldn't totally heat the cavern but it would remove some of the cold chill.

Carefully, he walked around the cavern and, when he got to the west side, paused and stared at a narrow tunnel that led to the outside.

"Should I go and look?" he thought.

Curiosity got the best of him. He got the flashlight and started down the tunnel. The tall Arab was able to walk upright due to the tunnel ceiling being seven feet high and the corridor three feet wide. The pathway was twenty-two feet long and when he reached the end, the light's beam reflected against a large pile of rocks. Near the top of the pile was a small dark opening. He sat down on a larger boulder, reached up, removed two stones, stood and peered through the opening. The aroma of cool, fresh air smelled good. It was dark outside, but he could see rain mixed with snow falling from the cloudy sky. Extending his hand out the opening, he felt the sensation of cool moisture falling on his hand. It was a welcome feeling.

Not wanting to take any chances of being discovered, he placed the rocks back, resealing the hole in the exit. The terrorist returned back to his home. He would remain in seclusion for the following sixteen weeks. If he was to continue on with his mission of jihad, the Arab needed to heal his body and mind. As of this moment, most of the world didn't know if he was dead or alive. He wanted to keep it that way. The American government officials would be informed by those that assaulted the cave complex that he was sealed in the cave tomb, more than likely dead. Well, let them think it. It would work to his advantage in the future, he thought.

He sat down on his bed and began to read the Koran. Suddenly he was startled by a bomb exploding outside against the mountain and then a continuing barrage. Looking around the room, he didn't see any interior impact or damage. He felt safe for the time being as the explosions sent shock waves throughout the granite complex.

Ten minutes later, he said his Islam prayers while American bombs rained down on the Tora Bora White Mountain range. The tall lanky Arab laid down and fell asleep. Usamah bin Laden was still a threat to the world.

Chapter VII

He or She

Washington, DC

*I*n *the Falcon Agency's large mahogany conference room,* the directors of the intelligence agencies had gathered. Daniel, along with Merlin, Xi, Raul and Kathy were sitting side by side. Across the table were the directors of the CIA, FBI, NSA, Secret Service and Homeland Security. They also had their assistant directors with them.

"I guess we have everyone here. It's been two weeks since we combined our efforts in finding those responsible for the sniper killings. I'll let Merlin brief you on our latest information. Wiz, the floor is yours," Daniel said looking at Merlin and taking his seat.

"Thanks, Daniel," Merlin said while rising from his chair. "Results are in from the airlines. All their computer records have been sorted and filtered for five days prior and after the ten killings. A list of two-hundred and fifty-six people has been gathered of individuals who had flown into at least two of the cities during those time frames. Right now, agents from Falcon, the FBI and CIA are personally checking out those on the list and we have it narrowed down to thirty-two people. Those left are all business men who travel extensively. It's not looking good, people. That's all I have."

Everyone just sat there. It was something they were not familiar with. Usually when they had meetings on developments, there was a bundle of information to review. Today, there wasn't much.

Looking around the large polished table at the guests, Daniel spoke.

"Has anything unusual happened within the past twenty-four hours?"

"One of our agent's body was found dead outside Montreal yesterday," Bill Angus said. "He was shot in the head."

"What was he doing in Montreal?" Raul asked.

"We're still trying to find out. His name is Kyle Peterson and has been with the agency for twenty-eight years. We reassigned him back to Langley from Afghanistan about three months ago. He needed a break because his personal life was in shambles. Peterson's wife had filed divorce papers about seven months ago while he was overseas. He had no idea that she filed. He ended up losing everything.

Kyle and I were close friends. We went through training together when we first joined the agency. It was one hell of a shock when I found out," Bill said in a somber voice.

"I'm sorry, Bill. Do you see a connection between the sniper killings and Peterson's?" Daniel asked.

"We're still investigating. From what I've learned so far, he wasn't assigned to any case in Canada. We gave him a break to get his head together. After the news of the divorce, he came unglued and lost his composure. They had been married for twenty-five years and have a daughter and son.

It was a messy situation in court. Katy, Kyle's wife, told the court that his family didn't matter to Kyle. All he cared about was his job with the CIA. This happens a lot in our community. The demands of the job are sometimes too overwhelming."

"Do you think it was suicide?" Merlin asked.

"No. He was found on a deserted roadside and was shot in the back of his head. They found his rental car at the hotel he

"Any idea where the shooting and explosion will happen?" Raul asked with deep concern.

"Not sure. Shooting in warm place. Explosion in big area near land."

"What do you mean near land, Xi. Are you talking about a shoreline or beach area?" Daniel asked.

"Don't see water. See big explosion in air ... near land. Fire close to ground."

"An airplane maybe?" Merlin suggested.

"Not sure. Make Xi mad not knowing. I try hard but no come."

"It's okay, Xi. What you told us at least gives us a warning," Daniel kindly answered his friend.

"I try more. Maybe dream tell who and where. Maybe. Answer always in dream."

"Thanks, Xi," Raul said with a comforting tone in his voice.

"Before we leave here, I have one more question. Anything from the profiler?"

"I talked to him yesterday," Kathy answered. "He just finished reviewing all the dossiers on the killings and seems to think it is one person also. He will have a complete report for us tomorrow. I'll get everyone a copy."

"Okay. Anyone have anything else?" Daniel asked his team.

No one had any.

"I've got to leave for awhile. Susan and the kids are going to Wisconsin for a week to see her parents. I'm seeing them off at Dulles. I'll be back in about an hour and a half," Daniel said and they all left the conference room.

Chapter VIII

Intuition

Life at the old Naval Observatory was good for the White family. It brought a sense of peace and safety. Susan and the children adapted quickly. Her only objection, which was minor, was the Secret Service security team assigned to them for their protection, was always close by. At times she felt that the family's privacy was being violated. They weren't visible when Susan and the children were on the compound, but she couldn't leave the protective environment without the four assigned agents.

"It's a trade off, Susan. Safety is our priority and that means that we do have to make sacrifices," Daniel had told her.

"I know. I'm just venting. I'd rather have the children safe and I know the trade off is worth it," she had answered.

When Susan said she wanted to visit her parents for a week, Daniel made arrangements to charter an executive jet for them. The security agents would accompany his family on the trip and be close by during their entire stay in Wisconsin. There were two Falcon Agency bullet-proof suburbans waiting at the airfield in Milwaukee that would be the transportation while they were on their hiatus.

Daniel arrived at the compound and Susan had all the bags packed. The agents loaded them into a suburban and the White family entered the limousine assigned to Daniel. They left the Naval Observatory, with the security team leading the way and another team in another suburban following closely. The vehicle's blue, red and white lights were flashing as they drove to Ronald Reagan International airport's corporate jet center. The trip took twenty minutes. When the vehicles arrived at the corporate aviation center's guarded entrance, Daniel noticed two men standing approximately two-hundred feet away from the gate. One of the Middle Eastern looking men was talking on a cell phone and, as the vehicles approached, he lowered the phone and stared at the limousine as it passed. Daniel looked over his shoulder at the suspicious men once the vehicle had passed them and saw the man raise the cell phone to his ear and begin talking in an animated state. An uneasy feeling overcame Daniel as the vehicles passed through the gate.

The procession drove to the white corporate jet waiting on the ramp where the uniformed captain of the Lear 45 was waiting to greet the VIP passengers. Daniel asked Susan to remain in the vehicle with their children, Lance and Allison.

"I'll be right back. I want to make sure everything is in order," he stated.

He exited the limo and the Secret Service agents were standing guard outside the vehicle. Daniel glanced back toward the gate where two uniformed guards were standing. Something didn't feel right. He casually walked up to the head of his security team and motioned to the Lear captain to join him.

"Ron, did you notice those two Arab looking men outside the gate when we drove in?" Daniel asked the security chief, Ron Foley.

"Yes, I did. They were acting a little suspicious. I'm going to send two of my men over to check them out right now."

"Good. I don't feel right about this situation," Daniel said while turning toward the jet's captain as Ron left to give orders to two other Secret Service agents.

"Hi, I'm Daniel White. Captain, have you noticed anything suspicious?"

"Hello, sir. I'm Tom Ren. No, I haven't seen anything unusual. We've been waiting for about a half hour here on the tarmac. When we arrived at the jet center about an hour ago, the Lear was parked here and we did the preflight. Is there something wrong Mr. White?"

"I'm not sure just yet, captain," Daniel answered looking back toward the gate. He saw two agents walking briskly out the gate and they disappeared behind a building.

Ron Foley walked back to Daniel's position. "What do you think, Daniel," he asked.

"Ron, I got a bad feeling and I don't like it. I'm thinking of canceling the flight. My intuition is telling me there is danger here. I can't put my finger on exactly what it is, but it isn't good. Here come your guys. Let's see what they have to say."

The two agents were jogging toward the group gathered near the Lear's steps. Once they arrived they had Daniel's attention.

"We didn't see them. They disappeared and we looked all around. I did see a car speeding out of the parking lot but it was too far away to get a license plate number," the agent said between breaths.

Daniel looked at Ron and then Captain Ren. "Sorry, captain. I'm scrubbing the flight. Ron, I'm going to tell Susan and then I want her and the kids returned to the compound immediately. Get a couple more cars to meet you here."

Agent Foley immediately got on his secure radio and made the request while gathering his team together. When he finished the transmission and was addressing his group, they all removed their automatic rifles from the vehicles.

In the meantime, Daniel got back into the limo and explained to Susan the situation.

"What's going on Daniel? Is there something wrong?" his curious wife asked.

"I'm not sure, but I've cancelled the flight. I gave the agents orders to take you and the kids back to the Naval Observatory. We're waiting for a couple more cars with agents to arrive. They should be here shortly. I'm going to go back to the office in another car."

"Should I call my dad and tell him we're not coming?"

"No. Let me call him from a secure phone. I know you're disappointed but I have the feeling something is not right. I'll call you from the office when I get back. Okay?"

"This is scaring me," Susan answered while looking into Daniel's eyes.

"You'll be alright. I just don't want to take any chances."

Susan leaned forward and kissed Daniel. Daniel then explained to the children that the vacation was cancelled. They seemed okay with it.

Daniel kissed Susan again and got out of the car and walked up to Ron.

"Three vehicles with six agents based here at the airport will be here anytime, Daniel."

"Thanks, Ron. I need a ride back to my office."

"I'll stay with Susan and the kids and have one of the others take you there. I also called in a report and they are sending out a team to check out the jet center. Just a precaution. The captain called the hangar and they're sending a tow vehicle to take the jet back to the hangar."

"Okay. Looks like our support team has arrived. What vehicle do you want me in?"

"Jump into the lead suburban. I'm sending a trail team in another suburban as a back up."

"Fine. Let's get rolling," Daniel answered as he walked to his ride.

Ron met with the new arrivals and briefed them. Quickly the vehicles left the area and proceeded to their respective destinations. As Daniel's vehicle was exiting the gate, he saw the jet's tow vehicle hooking up the tow bar to the Lear.

Twenty minutes later, Daniel arrived at Falcon Agency headquarters. As he walked into the third floor reception area, he saw his good friend Xi Xeng sitting there.

"Hi, Daniel. Susan and children gone?" Xi asked.

"No. I cancelled the flight," Daniel answered.

"Oh, something wrong?"

"I'm not sure my friend. Just a gut feeling. What are you up to?"

"I wait here to talk to you when you not busy."

"Okay. I've got to make a call to Susan's dad first. Come on into my office."

Both men walked down the hall and as Daniel entered his office, he saw Kathy Starley, Falcon's OPS coordinator inside waiting. Her face was ashen.

"Hi Kathy, what's going on?"

"I just got a call from Ron Foley," she answered in a trembling voice.

The tow vehicle driver had just finished hooking up the tow bar to the Lear jet's front landing gear, raised the steps to the executive aircraft and closed the door. The flight crew was disappointed about the cancelled trip and the captain and co-pilot were walking across the tarmac back to the charter center operation's office. They had been Daniel's crew of choice in the past and enjoyed previous trips to Wisconsin. To them it was a weird situation. Daniel had never cancelled a charter before and, if it would have gone as planned, they would now be ten-minutes into the flight. They continued walking toward their office and heard the tow vehicle start up.

The driver put the vehicle in low gear and engaged the clutch. Slowly the Lear began to move. Standard procedures when towing an aircraft was to move at a slow pace, thereby ensuring that no accidents would occur. The jet had slowly moved approximately one-hundred feet when the tow vehicle operator heard a large explosion behind him. Not having enough time to react, a ball of fire encompassed the jet and moved forward, wrapping the scorching ball of fire around him and the tow vehicle. The driver jumped off the burning inferno and ran. His clothes were on fire and he rolled onto the cement surface. Yelling, he continued rolling on the ground trying to extinguish the fire. In his panic, he hadn't disengaged the tow vehicle's transmission and the jet continued to roll forward.

The Lear's captain and co-pilot were almost to the hangar's office when they heard a large blast. Turning to see what it was, they saw a huge ball of fire rising from the corporate jet they piloted. The tow driver was on the ground rolling around. Seeing the dangerous, life-threatening situation, both men dropped their flight cases and sprinted toward the raging inferno and driver rolling on the tarmac.

They arrived quickly as the fire engulfed the rolling jet and, while he was running, the captain took off his suit coat. Upon arriving at the screaming driver's side, he wrapped his coat around the driver and started slapping at the flames burning the trousers. The flames slowly were extinguished and the driver's face, though scorched like a severe sunburn, looked up at him as the burning jet continued to move away from them.

The co-pilot ran straight to the tow truck that was still moving forward, pulling the jet that was now totally engulfed in flames. Upon reaching the vehicle, he grabbed the stick shift, yanked it to the neutral position, reached for the emergency brake and gave it a pull upward. The truck came to an immediate halt. Off in the distance, sirens wailed their high pitch scream as the airport's fire rescue emergency response trucks sped towards the burning jet that had towering flames and black smoke surrounding the charred aircraft.

Daniel looked at Kathy. "And?" he asked.

Kathy was a little hesitant. "He said there was an explosion at the airport after you left there. The jet Susan and the kids were to fly on exploded on the tarmac as it was being towed back to the hangar."

"Shit... anyone hurt?"

"The tow driver has second degree burns, but according to the report Ron gave, he'll be okay. No one else was injured."

Daniel was stunned and sat down at the conference table. "Kathy, get Merlin please?" he said quietly.

"I'll be right back, Daniel." Kathy quickly left Daniel's office.

Xi sat down opposite of Daniel at the conference table. "I not see this, Daniel."

"I did Xi. I had a feeling that something was wrong when we got to the airport. Damn. They almost got Susan and the kids. Those son of a bitches."

"You know who?" Xi asked.

"No, but I will find out and they will pay for it."

Just then Merlin burst into Daniel's office. "Kathy told me what happened, Daniel."

"Wiz, get a team of our people to the airport and, under my authority, they are to take charge of the investigation. Also find out who will be agent in charge from the FAA."

"Do you want me to head it up?"

"No. I've got something else for you to do. I want you to take Falcon I to Milwaukee and pick up Susan's father and her two sisters and bring them back here. Get hold of our agents in Milwaukee and brief them on what has happened. Then have them pick up Susan's family and take them to Mitchell Field's Air National Guard's facilities. They'll be safer there than at the jet center. I'll call her dad, Scott, and let him know what is going on.

Then I want the Milwaukee team to check out Scott's house, just in case."

"What are they to look for?" Wiz asked.

"Anything … bombs … booby traps. Just tell them to be careful," Daniel answered, still upset that he almost lost his family.

"Okay. Anything else?"

"No. That'll do it for now. Let Kathy know what you are up to and tell her I want security in place when you get back here with the Gallagher family. Have a fully-armed escort team ready when Falcon lands at Andrews. I want everyone with an armed escort until further notice. You start packing a pistol also."

"I always do. But, I'll be carrying more ammo."

"Good. Before you leave, get a hold of Ron Foley and have him assign an agent to Raul and Kathy also."

"What about Xi?" Merlin said while looking at their Chinese friend.

"Xi and I will be together. He's my guard and I'm his. Okay, Xi?" Daniel asked with a smile to his friend.

"Best team. Okay, Daniel," Xi answered and smiled back.

"If that's it, I'm out of here," Merlin said walking to the door.

"You better put your guards on high security notice at your home also," Daniel suggested.

"I already did when Kathy told me what happened. Adios."

Daniel was quiet for a few moments, contemplating what had happened. He then got up and went to his desk, sat down and called Susan's father, Scott Gallagher. After he had a detailed conversation with Scott, he hung up and looked at Xi, who was still sitting at the conference table. Xi saw Daniel looking at him and rose from the chair and walked to another across from Daniel's desk and sat down.

"This bad Daniel, but good family okay. Xi and Daniel must talk alone."

"I know. I've got to tell you something also. But, first I've got to call Susan and let her know what is going on and then I've got to call Bill Angus at CIA, FBI Director Lambert and then the president. Then we'll talk."

"Good. Xi wait. Much important what Xi must tell Daniel."

Chapter IX

The New Master

*A*ll *the government's intelligence agencies had been* informed on what had occurred at the airport and all went on high alert under direct orders from the president. As Daniel finished up his phone calls, he noticed a large manila envelope in his "inbox" on the desk. He removed it from the basket and looked at it. All mail entering government facilities had to be scanned and screened at the postal facilities for contents. This action was the result from the mail incident where an envelope containing anthrax was sent to a government office right after 9/11. After the screening process was complete and the mail was cleared, the inspectors stamped the envelopes as cleared. Daniel saw the red stamped bold letters "CLEARED" on the envelope.

"So, we need to talk, Xi," Daniel said while opening the envelope.

"Yes, Daniel. Important what Xi have to tell Daniel."

Daniel reached into the manila package and pulled out a single piece of paper. Xi watched Daniel's face as the paper emerged and then saw Daniel's face turn red and anger appeared on his close friend's face.

"What matter, Daniel?" Xi asked.

Daniel didn't say a word and held up the paper. Xi could see writing on the back side that was facing him. It was in Arabic. Daniel then turned the paper around so Xi could see what he was looking at. It was a picture of a person dressed in Middle Eastern clothing standing in what appeared to be a dark room or cave. Xi moved closer to get a better look. There was no mistaking who it was.

As Xi was looking at the picture, Daniel noticed the writing on the backside. Since learning how to speak Arabic, Daniel had also learned how to read the language. He read the short paragraph quietly to himself. Xi had read it and knew the contents.

"You thought you had removed me from this world but Allah protected me. By now you know that your wife and children are dead. It is time for you to suffer in the world of hell."

It was signed, Usamah bin Laden. While Daniel was reading the note, Xi was looking at the picture of bin Laden.

Both men remained quiet. Daniel carefully put the photograph back into the envelope and then called Kathy on the phone, asking her to come to his office.

"Yes, Daniel," Kathy said entering the executive office.

"I need a large envelope that I can put this into," he said holding up the mail. "Then I need one of our agents to get this to the CIA's lab and have it analyzed for prints, writing and any traces of any substance. I'll call Bill Angus and let him know what is going on. This is top priority, Kathy."

"Okay, can I ask what it is?"

"It's a picture of bin Laden. There is a note on the back of it. Now I know who is behind the bombing of the corporate jet. It's that fucking asshole Usamah bin Laden and al Qaeda. He didn't die in the Tora Bora cave. Damn! I knew I should have blown his damn brains out."

Kathy quickly left the room and returned with a very large envelope. Daniel slid the manila package into it. His would be the only fingerprints on the picture.

As she was leaving the office, Daniel said, "I don't want to be disturbed for awhile unless it is priority or an emergency."

"Usamah bin Laden," Daniel said quietly to himself.

"We talk now, Daniel," Xi said, after giving Daniel time to reflect back to Afghanistan.

Xi's voice snapped Daniel out of his thoughts.

"Yes, we can talk now my friend."

"It long time ago, but not that long, when Daniel save Xi family. Since that time, Xi and Daniel become very close friend."

Daniel was paying close attention to Xi. He could see the expression change on the kind Chinese man's face and what he was saying was very important to his close friend.

Xi continued.

"When Daniel find out that Xi have special gift, Master gift, Daniel very interested. Interest not for money but for making Daniel better man. Xi also see inside Daniel and see a special person. See kind man who don't want see others hurt. If hurt, show master skill to make right. In time of war, have good mind to finish objective. Nothing more. Nothing less.

When Xi training as Master in China, teacher tell me that not all people can be Master. Must have special heart and mind. He tell me always look for person who have kind heart, smart mind and one who help others with no want for ... ah ... how say ...."

"Repayment?" Daniel said.

"Yes. No care for repayment for help. Thank you. Xi also tell Daniel long time ago that teacher tell Xi I meet you in far away place. Now know that here in America.

When Xi meet you Daniel, I know you special. See in Daniel's eyes, heart and soul. I know my job to teach you ways of Master and you listen. We start with Kung Fu and

Daniel now Master for Kung Fu. Then I teach some of Master skill with mind. You listen very well. Daniel know most important thing for Master. That is Daniel know "you"."

Daniel had a confused look on his face after Xi's statement.

"Hmm ... I don't quite understand what you mean, Xi ... know you?"

"Sorry. Xi know that ... boy this hard to explain. Daniel know who he is. You know "you". You know mind, body and soul of Daniel. You understand?"

"Yes, I understand now. I know myself well ... right?"

"Yes. Most important that know self. That only way to be Master. Once know self, have balance in life. Have control of own life. Daniel now has all that.

For Daniel to become true Master, Xi tell final secrets. This not take long and, Daniel, what Xi tell you now must never tell to other unless they ready for last lesson. You promise Xi?" Xi asked, looking sincerely at his friend.

Daniel was captured by what Xi was saying. "I promise," Daniel answered sincerely.

"Good. When Xi in hospital in St. Louis, Daniel learned what special power Xi have when bullet come out of me. Special power come from mind, body and soul. You know mind and body. Soul is God inside you. Daniel has God inside him and understands.

When have God inside, God is ultimate, supreme master of spiritual enlightenment. You ready for last step in journey. When done this journey, begin another spiritual one.

Now I teach you how to use special power. You now ready, Master Daniel, and you need special powers to help stop terrorism."

Both men remained quiet for quite a long while. Then Daniel spoke.

"Yes … I am ready, Xi," Daniel whispered.

For the next hour Xi gave Daniel his final instructions in the ways and teachings of the Masters. Daniel never spoke a word unless requested to do so.

"Daniel ready," Xi said after the instructional period. "Now, Daniel please stand here by Xi."

Daniel rose from his chair and walked around his desk to Xi's side.

"Daniel, kneel down and face Xi."

Daniel knelt and as he was lowering himself to his knees, Xi did also. They were an arms length apart, staring into each other's eyes.

"Take off shirt," Xi ordered.

Daniel loosened his tie, unbuttoned his shirt, removed it and let it fall to the floor.

"Look at Xi's eyes and don't stop."

As Daniel stared into Xi's almond shaped eyes, Xi raised his right arm and placed his open hand against Daniel's chest.

"Push body against Xi hand."

Daniel leaned his body hard against the strong hand.

Xi then closed his eyes and Daniel, still staring at Xi's closed eyes, suddenly felt a warm, and then a burning sensation penetrate his chest. It was a feeling he had never experienced before. The burning grew and spread throughout his body. He wasn't scared and enjoyed the feeling. Then the enjoyment of love encompassed his mind and all thoughts departed his brain. His eyes, still looking at Xi's closed ones, lost focus and Daniel then couldn't see anything.

Still kneeling, Xi kept his hand firmly on Daniel's chest. To Daniel it felt that they were now as one. Xi's thoughts entered his brain. After forty-five seconds he felt the burning heat begin to subside and turn to warm. The whole ceremony lasted a little over one minute but it was the most important minute in Daniel's life.

"Daniel, open eyes," Daniel heard the Master say. He hadn't realize that he had closed them.

Slowly, Daniel's eyes open and when they were fully opened, he smiled, but didn't say a word. He felt like he never felt before and knew he was a Master.

Xi removed his hand from Daniel's chest.

"You now Master Daniel. You same as Xi," he said smiling. "Xi give Daniel all power of Xi. Daniel can do same now to other people. Stand please, Master Daniel."

Both men stood up and faced each other. "One more thing must do now," Xi said as Daniel reached down to the floor to pick up his shirt.

"Leave shirt on floor." Daniel dropped it.

Reaching into his pants pocket, Xi removed a small, dark, royal blue box and held it in his opened hand.

"To remember this time Master Daniel, Xi have gift. Not just gift but gift with special power. You never take off and when time to go to other world, you take with you. Daniel understand?"

"You mean when I die, this gift goes with me, right?"

"Yes. You not give to anyone. Only for Daniel."

Xi extended his hand with the box lying in his palm. Daniel took the container and opened it. Inside was a diamond-cut gold chain with a triangle gold piece attached to the chain. Xi reached for the beautiful item, removed it from the box and held it in front of Daniel's face for him to see. Daniel smiled.

Daniel opened his hand and Xi put the object in Daniel's palm. It was a one of a kind piece of jewelry. Each side of the triangle was twisted 90 degrees, giving off a unique reflection of light.

"When Xi shot in St. Louis, I give you bullet that Xi makes come out of body so Daniel protects from losing. Then Daniel give back after Xi out of hospital. This the bullet and Xi make into triangle. Then have covered with 24-karat gold in Denver. Jeweler say pretty but not know nothing else.

Triangle will alway remind Master Daniel White that you have special power that many want, but not know how to use right. Never take off. Whenever Daniel think or confused put triangle in hand and squeeze or push against chest.

Three points on triangle are three paths Master Daniel travel and learn to be Master. Each side mean … body … mind … and soul. Daniel have learn to master each to high level. Higher than most people here in our world. Turn and twist on each path mean many different challenge to reach Master. Not journey that easy and straight. You will never forget your journey.

Inside triangle space is peace, protected by strong mind, body and soul. Daniel now have inner peace."

Daniel stared at his dear friend and didn't say a word. Tears rolled down Daniel's face.

"Thank you, my friend, for your patience and teaching me the ways of the Master."

"Welcome, Master."

Xi put the chain necklace holding the beautiful and unique triangle over Daniel's head. He then bowed to his fellow master that had earned the special gift. Daniel bowed back.

"You put on shirt now. Work must be done about terrorist," Xi said.

Daniel put his hand on the gold triangle and held the suspended precious item in his hand. Then he closed his massive hand around the three pointed icon. He felt his hand begin to heat up and the warmth traveled throughout his body.

"You feel power, Daniel?" Xi asked with a smile on his face.

Daniel smiled back. "Yes, I feel it."

"It be with you forever. Now, better dress. Work to do."

"One more thing, Xi," Daniel said as he was putting on his shirt. "When I was at the airport ready to put Susan and the kids on the plane, I got a thought that something was wrong. Is that what was happening? Intuition?"

"Xi send Daniel message. Have dream that bad danger to happen to family. You can do same now. You not understand before but now do. No such thing as intuition or co … coinci …"

"Coincidence?" Daniel said trying to help Xi.

"Yes. Everything happen for reason. We not talk about this now, but soon Daniel go to far away place. Be ready to go."

"Where?" Daniel asked.

"Xi say we not talk now about journey. Just be ready."

"Okay. So when did you have this dream?"

"Today when you leave here to get family and take to airport. Xi say dream but maybe better say have special thought that power bring. You will get special thought …dream. You see soon. Not dream but thought and thought never wrong. Always obey thought. Understand? After thought, Xi know time for you to be Master. You prove to Xi many time and pass many test that Daniel ready."

"Yes, I understand Xi. Thanks for sending me the warning. I better get dressed. Thank you, Master."

"Welcome Master Daniel White. Only call other Master when in private. Many other not understand. Welcome to Master world."

Chapter X

Signs

Late that evening, Susan's family arrived at the Naval Observatory under close security with Merlin in charge. Daniel and Susan greeted them at the door and after entering, Susan showed her exhausted family to their rooms. Daniel and Merlin discussed what was happening in Milwaukee.

"I'm going to be busy first thing tomorrow. I've got a briefing with the president and the intelligence agency's heads at the White House. I want you to check with our investigating team handling the airport bombing and when I get back, which should be about 9:00 a.m., let me know what's happened."

"Done. I'll have a complete report ready," Merlin answered.

"One more thing. I got an envelope at the office today," Daniel said and explained what the contents were.

"That bastard. You should have blown his brains out. Do you think it really was from him?" Merlin asked.

"I'm not sure. On the table in front of where he was standing was a copy of the European edition of the Washington Post. I recognized it because there was a picture of the president on the front page. I examined it closely and saw the by-lines. I read that edition.

It's at the CIA now for analysis and Bill Angus said we will have a report and results from forensics tomorrow sometime."

"Damn … al Qaeda … bin Laden. This shit has got to stop," the Wizard said quietly.

"They almost got my family, Merlin," Daniel said with all sincerity.

"I don't know what to say Daniel, other than I'm sorry. How's Susan handling it?"

"She doesn't know all the facts and thinks that the jet had some type of malfunction."

"Are you going to let her know everything?"

"Always do."

"Well, I better get going. We've got a busy day ahead. I'll see you tomorrow," the Wizard said as he headed to the door.

Daniel and Susan were in their bedroom getting ready for bed.

"Everyone settled down?" Daniel asked Susan who was lying in bed.

"Yes. Dad was really beat and curious about what exactly is happening. What is happening Daniel?"

Daniel was only in his under shorts and got in bed.

"I'm not sure yet. It could have been an attack by al Qaeda or just something wrong with the jet."

"I'm not buying the "something wrong with the jet" theory, Daniel. You acted real strange at the airport. What happened to you there?"

Susan noticed the gold triangle hanging from a chain around Daniel's neck. Before Daniel could speak, she reached for the glistening triangle and asked, "I've never seen this before. Did you just get it? It's beautiful."

"Okay, lady. One question at a time," he said with a wide smile. "Xi gave it to me today as a present."

"Nice," Susan answered and looked into Daniel's cobalt blue eyes. "What happened at the airport?"

"I think someone planted a bomb on the jet. I had a weird feeling when we got there that something was wrong."

"Do you think it had anything to do with those two Arab looking men that were outside the security gate?"

Daniel looked at his lovely wife with surprise.

"You saw them?" he asked.

"Yes, I saw them and they looked really out of place and suspicious. And then when we were waiting in the car, I saw two of our guards go over where they were. Did they find them?"

"No. They were gone. Pretty observant of you, Mrs. White. I think they had something to do with it. I've got a team investigating and should have some information tomorrow."

"Why did you have my father and sisters flown here? And why was it Merlin that went to get them?"

"I wanted to make sure that they were alright and safe. It was a gut feeling … intuition or something," Daniel answered, knowing it was much more than that. He didn't want to get into an explanation of Xi's message and Daniel's master powers. He would wait for another time for that.

They continued talking for a few minutes and Susan then fell asleep in Daniel's arms. She was safe from the world for now. He remained awake for a long time, holding his wife and thinking about what was to come.

Daniel had finished his morning briefing and returned to Falcon's headquarters. The directors of the CIA, FBI, NSA, Secret Service and his top staff were waiting in the conference room when he arrived.

"Good morning, all," Daniel said smiling as he entered the room and made his way to his seat. The group all responded in a similar manner.

"I just finished briefing the president about what happened yesterday at the airport. He is not a happy camper this morning. So, let's get down to business.

Bill, what do you have?" Daniel asked the CIA director.

"I've got a lot of stuff to cover this morning. I'll start with what happened yesterday.

Item number one … the attack at Ronald Reagan airport was a bombing. The investigating team found pieces of a cell phone that was used as a detonator and the FAA investigators have pinpointed the point of the explosion.

The bomb, which consisted of a small amount of C-4, was placed behind a bulkhead in the tail section. It wasn't designed to blow the jet apart but to create enough damage to rip off the tail in flight. If it would have happened in the air, the crew and Daniel's family would have survived the blast and been alive until impact. I'm sorry to put it that way, Daniel, but it's the facts."

"No apology necessary, Bill," Daniel answered while thinking of what could have happened. The terror his wife and family almost experienced infuriated him.

"They're trying to track down the cell number. The theory we've come to is that the flight plan the pilots filed was for a departure time of 3:30 p.m. The bomb exploded at 3:44 p.m. Whoever called the cell phone at that time, probably wasn't in the airport vicinity and didn't know that the flight was aborted. It was a timed bombing.

We're looking for witnesses at Reagan who may have seen anyone suspicious around that time."

"What about the two guys I saw near the gate, Bill?" Daniel asked.

"We're looking for anyone who might have seen them and what they were driving. We're on that."

"They were part of it, Bill. Trust me on this. I'm 100 percent positive."

"The next thing we're looking into is how, where and who had access to place the bomb on the jet. We have a possible suspect who works for the charter company. He is maintenance ... a janitor who works at the center at night. Last night he didn't show up for work and we've checked where he lives. He's a bachelor, lives alone and has disappeared. Checking with neighbors, they said he would get visitors during the day and the males seem to be Middle Eastern.

We got a search warrant to his apartment and it's been cleaned out. They didn't find anything there. Right now, we've got an APB out on Hashim Al Ghafar. He's from Algeria and has been in the U.S. since 2000 on a student visa.

Al Ghafar has been attending a junior college here in DC and hasn't been seen there for two weeks. Right now the college is on semester break. His professors all state that Hashim is a good, conscientious student and noticed nothing out of the norm."

"How's the tow vehicle driver doing, Bill?" Daniel queried.

"He's doing fine. He received some second degree burns and was discharged from the hospital last night. One of our guys interviewed him while he was at the hospital. He knows nothing relevant to the situation," Bill answered.

"Now, item number two. Since yesterday, terrorist chatter has gone through the roof. Something is in the wind, people. The level is higher than pre-9-11. Anyone else getting reports like this?" Bill asked the group.

FBI Director John Lambert spoke up. "We've noticed excessive chatter also. I was going to mention that. My people are on high alert now. We've also seen a lot of activity within suspected cells here in the U.S.."

"Have you made any arrests, John?" Daniel asked

"No grounds to arrest them now. I've got search warrants on order but we're getting resistance from the judges who need to sign them," John answered.

"Wait a minute. We've got someone or a group who blew up a jet that the Director of Falcon Agency's family was supposed to be on. We also have a sniper killing senators … congressmen and civilian corporation executives … and judges won't sign a damn search warrant? What the hell is going on?" Merlin snapped angrily

"Let me make a phone call. How many warrants do you need, John?" Daniel asked.

"Seven, Daniel," Lambert answered.

"Get them ready … and John … I want you to personally deliver them to Chief Justice Baker. It will be a message of utmost importance if you deliver them John. Give me two hours after this meeting before you go to his office," Daniel ordered.

"And one more thing John, if your people get any, and I mean any little inkling of something out of the ordinary, make arrests on grounds of attempted terrorism against the United States. Those arrested, I want a level five interrogation on them."

"Level five, Daniel? That's usually reserved for interrogations overseas during war?"

"Isn't this war, John? Isn't what happened on September 11th war? Isn't bombing a jet in the United States war?

I want all the agencies to ramp everything up to the highest priority. It's time to turn up the heat to high. If anyone has questions about these orders, talk to the president. Anything else John?" Daniel was showing his authority with a sign of anger. There was no doubt who was in charge.

"Yes. We've been tailing an individual who has ties to Hamas and possibly al Qaeda," Director Lambert added.

"Where is he?" Daniel asked

"He's been hanging around Montreal."

"Montreal? What's he up to?"

"We think he's a contact to a terrorist cell or cells. He's good at what he does and is very deceptive, Daniel."

"How did he come under suspicion, John?" Merlin asked.

"He was crossing over the Canadian border at the Niagara Falls crossing and customs ran him through the computer system. His Canadian documents were in order and he came up clean in ours. But we have incorporated a new item in our database. If a name of a foreign national associated with countries in the world that support terrorism pops up, a warning flag is raised and a more intensive investigation happens. The ties with Hamas rose out of the ashes of intelligence. That's when we assigned an agency team to him."

"What was he doing in the U.S.," Raul asked.

"By the time the team picked up his trail, it might have been too late. It looked like he was just a regular vacationer at Niagara Falls. There was no unusual activity or contact," Director Lambert answered

"Can you bring him back into the U.S. and interrogate him?" Daniel asked with interest.

"Not without creating a scandal with Canada. We'd have to get their cooperation and let them know exactly why. It can't be on speculation. We have to have concrete evidence, not allegations."

"Does he have any associates that can tie him to terrorism?" Merlin asked.

"So far all we have is that he has a girl friend. There are no other contacts that we can identify. We've only been tailing him for a couple of weeks now and he is very cautious with his movements."

Daniel and Xi looked at each other at the same time.

"He … she," Daniel thought quietly remembering what Xi had said in a previous meeting.

"Who is this girlfriend, John? What's her background?" Daniel asked, looking back at Director Lambert.

"Her name is Monique Leclair and she's a Canadian citizen now. She immigrated from Pakistan nine years ago and doesn't have any known family. Got her college education at the University of Montreal, has a degree in Computer Science and works as a self-employed computer consultant. Never been married, no kids and doesn't seem to practice any religion. She is doing pretty well financially and lives in an affluent neighborhood."

"He …she," Daniel thought again, looking for a sign or an answer.

He had a feeling inside that touched a nerve. Daniel then reached to his chest and felt the triangle against his chest. Warmth around the gold triangle began to penetrate his chest and he felt it spread throughout his torso. Daniel looked back at Xi and smiled. Smiling back at his friend and fellow Master, Xi nodded his head in affirmation.

Then an unusual thing happened to Daniel. A vision appeared in his mind. Hidden behind a clump of tall bushes in front of a home is a person dressed all in black. It's early evening and the dark silhouette is hard to see. Over the person's head is a black ski hood and the person raises a rifle to their shoulder. To Daniel, the vision is as clear as could be and it seems to him that he is witnessing an actual event.

The sniper's hands have black gloves on and one finger on the right hand glove has been cut off. It's the assassin's trigger finger. Peering through a night scope, the sniper is taking aim at a man standing near his car in the driveway. The distance between the individuals is at least one-hundred yards. The man is getting something out of the back seat of the vehicle and is bent over.

The sniper is waiting for the man to stand up and Daniel sees the sniper's trigger finger inside the trigger guard beginning to press against the weapon's trigger. The unsuspecting victim stands up, holding a briefcase in his hand, and after a short moment, Daniel sees the sniper's finger tighten against the trigger. Daniel wants to shout a warning to the man holding the briefcase.

Without any sound being heard, Daniel sees a red dot appear on the man's forehead and the victim's head snaps backwards. The man drops his briefcase and, in slow motion, falls backward onto the lawn. The vision seemed to last forever but, in real time, it lasted no more than ten seconds.

"Daniel ... Daniel ... you okay, Daniel?" Kathy asked, snapping the vision out of Daniel's mind and bringing him back to reality.

Daniel paused for a moment and looked around the table. Everyone with the exception of Xi was staring at him.

"Sorry. I was in deep thought," he answered, with an embarrassed look on his face.

He removed his hand from his chest and felt the master triangle release its heat and return to its normal state. Daniel smiled and looked at Xi, who smiled back. Daniel had just used his master powers under a controlled state for the first time. It made him feel good.

Gathering his composure, he spoke to his associates.

"John, put a team on this Monique Leclair 24-7. I want to know of any unusual activity."

"Is there something I should know, Daniel?" Lambert asked, looking a little confused.

"For now, let's just say it's a gut feeling I have. Do you have anything else?"

"Yes, and what you just said might tie into the investigation into one of our agent's death. Remember I told you about Agent Kyle Peterson that was killed in Canada?"

"Yeah, what have you found out?" Daniel asked.

"Whenever an agent is wounded or killed, we have a procedure that immediately goes in place. All of their personal records, like bank accounts and investments, are scrutinized and that includes their homes. Their agent office files and records are quarantined and audited for any sign of problems or unauthorized contacts and intelligence information not revealed to higher-ups."

"You do this with all your agents?" Raul asked.

"Everyone, and that includes me. It's SOP (standard operating procedure) that I put in place when I took over as director," Bill answered with a smile.

"I like that. Maybe it is something that every agency should incorporate," Daniel answered. "Have you found anything yet?"

"We're going through his agency files now and yesterday we got a search warrant for his home. They'll be searching it today.

My point is, Daniel, that he was killed in Montreal and it is a suspicious coincidence, don't you agree?" Bill said, looking around the table for confirmation.

His peers were all shaking their heads in agreement.

"That's all I have for now. Thank you."

"Merlin, what do you have?" Daniel asked.

"Thanks, Daniel. Based on the information released here today, I have some requests. Bill, do your people have a dossier on this Kaleem and Monique Leclair?"

"I'm sure they do," Angus answered.

"I'd like a copy, please, and pictures of each. I want to see if we can get a match with the airline database we have now. Did they recover the bullet that killed Agent Kyle Peterson?"

"Yes, they did. You want that also or just the ballistics results?"

"Who did the ballistics test?" Merlin asked.

"Our lab did it."

"Then I'll just need the results."

"Are you looking for a match with the sniper shootings, Merlin?" Bill asked.

"Yes. Maybe we can get lucky. In fact, your lab did the entire sniper ballistics test. Would you have them see if there is a cross sectional match, Bill?"

"I'll have an answer for you tomorrow."

"Thanks, Bill. I appreciate it. That's all I've got for now, Daniel," Merlin said as he looked at the director.

"Thanks, Wiz. John, anything to add," Daniel asked John Ebersole, the head of NSA.

"Nothing that hasn't already been covered, Daniel. The chatter is unusually high in the Middle East. So, I agree with everyone here. Something is in the wind."

"I think we're all in agreement. Okay, anyone have anything to add?" Daniel asked the group.

Xi stood up. Looking at Daniel as if asking for permission, he spoke. "I speak to group please, Daniel?"

Everyone looked at Xi and it was totally out of respect. All present knew of Xi's background, achievements on the battlefield and in the private sector. Xi was never one to speak much and when he had something to add, it would have those present listening closely. This was the first time that he volunteered to say something.

"Xi, you may speak at anytime," Daniel answered.

"Thank you, Daniel and very important people. Xi not speak much and mostly listen all time. But, must make you be ready for danger to United States that not said yet." Xi had everyone's undivided attention as he spoke in his usual calm voice.

"Better check boat dock in Canada where big boat come to … boat that have French flag. Man … Kaleem man, be going to see other man on big boat … ship. He leave with case."

Merlin interrupted. "Excuse me, Xi, has he got the case now … has he been to the ship already?"

"Just know he have case in hand and leave ship with it. In case is same W.M.D. like happen in Louisiana. This Xi know."

"Biological weapons," Kathy whispered.

Everyone looked at her then back at Xi.

"Big danger to United State of America come soon. Big danger." Xi said in a firmer tone of voice as he emphasized the word danger.

"When did you find out about this, Xi?" Director Lambert asked.

"Few minute before Xi speak here. Have dream," Xi said almost embarrassed.

They all remained quiet, absorbing the news. They all knew Xi's dreams were always correct.

"That all Xi know now. If have more infom … in … for … ma … tion, Xi tell when get. Thank you." The master then quietly sat down and let the group contemplate.

After a few seconds, Daniel spoke.

"I believe what Xi says and it ties in with what we've been discussing. Gentlemen, turn up the heat and tighten your agent's procedure. We don't need another 9-11 or what happened in the Gulf of Mexico. Unless anyone has anything else, I suggest we get to work. The next 72 hours are crucial."

No one added anything else and all rose when Daniel did. There was no question that the United States was under the possibility of another attack by terrorists.

Chapter XI

New Attack

The meeting was over and Daniel was walking to his office with Xi at his side. Daniel was deeply worried about what happened the previous day and the meeting he just attended compounded his concerns.

"Xi, I had a vision during the meeting."

"Xi see Daniel having dream. That good."

"I saw the sniper, but he was … or maybe she, was dressed all in black. I couldn't identify whether it was a man or woman."

"Answer in dream, Daniel. Answer always in dream."

"Hmmm … so you're saying that in the vision there is a piece of evidence that will identify who the sniper is?" Daniel said as he stopped in the wide hall.

"Yes. Some part in dream you see, but not see. Daniel understand what Xi mean?"

"I understand what you mean."

"Let go for now. Later, you think what in dream again. Maybe you see. Must let go now. First dream as Master. Remember, when have, relax and look at everything. That is power of Master. Get easier when you have more. Then you see all. "

"Okay, these visions are good but confusing at times," Daniel answered as he and his friend continued walking to his office. He would let it go for now.

Three hours later, Daniel was in his office and about to take a break for lunch when he received a call from Bill Angus.

"Daniel White."

"Hi, Daniel. Bill Angus. Forensic matched the bullet that killed Agent Peterson with the one that killed Senator Johnson."

"What's the certainty on the match, Bill?"

"94.7 percent. It's a match for sure."

"Does Merlin know?"

"No. I called you as soon as I found out."

"Okay, I'll let him know. Do you have a team on Monique Leclair yet?"

"We activated one as soon as I got back to my office. I haven't received any reports as of yet. I'll let you know when I get word that they have her under surveillance."

"Thanks, Bill. Anything else?"

"I also have agents searching Canadian ports on the east coast and St. Lawrence Seaway for ships flying the French flag. Nothing yet on that either. I wish we knew what we're looking for."

"Me too," Daniel said quietly.

"I have one more piece of information. Forensic finished evaluating the picture of bin Laden."

"What did they find?"

"The first thing they checked for was authenticity of the photo. The newspaper on the table and the photo of bin Laden weren't taken at the same time. In other words, the newspaper was cut and pasted onto the picture and re-shot. The date was crossed out but we did find out that the paper was printed on September 27, 2001. Do you think he is alive or dead?"

"I'm not sure now if the son of a bitch is alive or dead," Daniel immediately answered. "I should have taken him out when I had the chance. Damn."

"You did what you thought was right at the time, Daniel."

"I just wanted him to suffer ... to slowly pay the price of 9-11 and all the suffering ... and pain he inflicted on innocent people."

The visualization of him and Usamah bin Laden alone in the cave appeared in his mind. If he had only killed him, maybe ... maybe the threat of al Qaeda terrorism would have slowed down. But, it was too late now and the current issues had to be met head on.

"They found an interesting thing though, concerning the writing on the back," Bill said. "It is Usamah's signature, but the message is not his handwriting. They reviewed and studied it over and over."

"Did forensics get a match on who wrote the message?"

"No, but they determined it was a female who wrote it."

"You've got to be kidding me, Bill. They can tell the difference between male and female handwriting?"

"Yes. Female writing usually has an easy flow to the style and these scientists have other factors they use in determining matches. It's over my head Daniel, but these people we have are the best."

"Any identifiable fingerprints?" Daniel asked.

"No. Both the envelope and picture were wiped clean. The package was mailed from Syracuse, New York, though. I've got our people on it and we're trying to find out if there are any females associated with cells in that area. So far we've hit a brick wall."

"Syracuse. Everything pertaining to what we are currently working on seems to target upstate New York and Canadian cities. What are your thoughts on this, Bill?"

"I've been thinking the same thing, Daniel, and I don't think it's just coincidence."

"My intuition tells me that Kaleem and his girlfriend are heavily involved in this," Daniel added.

"Your intuition?" Bill said laughing. "Daniel, you may call it intuition but the rest of us know it's more than that. There is something very powerful going on between you and Xi. You guys never miss. Spread some of it this way, please."

Daniel laughed also. "I'll try, Bill. Anyway, is that it?"

"Yes. I'll call you if anything else arises from this storm."

"Thanks. I'll talk to you later," Daniel said and hung up the phone.

Daniel leaned back in his chair and stared at the ceiling.

"What are we looking for," he said softly to himself while reaching for the triangle on his chest.

After a few minutes contemplating, Daniel went and got Merlin and together they went to the White House commissary for lunch. They discussed the situation briefly and then Merlin changed the subject.

"You're a changed man, Daniel," Wiz said with a serious look on his face.

"Is that good, Wiz?"

"I like what I see but don't understand it. You've always been a great person, but something is different about you now. Anything that I should know about?"

"What's changed about me?"

"I can't put my finger on it right now but you have a peaceful, almost holistic-like sense when you talk. I can also see it in your face. You give off a calm sense of tranquility."

"Well, I guess that is good. All I can say is I feel more spiritual than ever before and I love it."

"Well, whatever it is that has happened or come into your life, it's beautiful. When you're ready, share it with me sometime. I'd really like to know."

"I will, my friend … I will."

The thought came to Daniel that maybe Merlin, his long-time friend, may be ready to begin his Master's journey.

They returned to Falcon headquarters and when Daniel entered his office, the phone rang.

"Hi, Daniel White here."

"Daniel, Bill Angus. Any chance that we can have a meeting within the next two hours?"

"What's going on, Bill."

"We've found a file in Kyle Peterson's office and it's sitting here on my desk right now. I think you better read it. Peterson was on to something and it ties in to what is happening now with the sniper attacks and the two people up in Canada."

"Okay. Who do you want to be in this meeting?"

"Just Falcon people and myself for right now."

"Be here in an hour. Give me a hint what's in the file, Bill"

"Terrorist attack."

"See you in an hour." Daniel hung up the phone.

Daniel sat back in his chair, closed his eyes and reached for the triangle that was hanging from the diamond-cut chain around his neck. He felt his body totally relax and gradually he went into a deep trance.

Not knowing how long he had been under, he opened his eyes and sat quietly for a few minutes contemplating. He made two short phone calls and then called Kathy.

"Kathy, I want to have a special meeting in an hour. I want you, Xi, Wiz, Raul and two of our agents in this meeting. Bill Angus will be joining us also."

"Any two agents or do you have anyone special in mind?"

"Get Dan Aibaya (eye-bay-ah) and Pat Scott."

"They're both new to Falcon, Daniel. Are you sure?"

"They're new to Falcon but they've been in this business a long time. I'm the one who recruited both of them. They've got over forty-five years of experience between them. Yep, I want those two."

"Okay. I'll have everyone in the main board room at four."

"No, we'll meet in my office. I've got to run over to the White House for a few minutes. So you can set up my office."

"It'll be ready when you return."

"Thanks, Kathy. See you in a few." Daniel hung up the phone and left Falcon headquarters immediately, via the side exit. He needed to talk to the president.

Chapter XII

Scorpio File

*W*hen *Daniel returned from his visit with the president, he* walked directly to his office. Waiting for the Director of Falcon Agency were Merlin, Xi, Kathy, Raul, Bill Angus and the two Falcon agents Daniel had requested, Special Agents Pat Scott and Dan Aibaya.

Daniel had met the then, CIA Special Agent Pat Scott at Nellis Air Force Base in Nevada after Daniel's home in Colorado was assaulted almost a year ago. Daniel had been wounded and his fellow Falcon members transferred him to the infirmary at Nellis. The assault occurred as they were about to prepare and embark on the mission to Saudi Arabia to capture the false prophet, al Amin.

Bill Angus had assigned Scott as the Agent-in-Charge at Nellis after the Colorado attack and Pat had made a great impression on Daniel. Daniel made a mental note to try to recruit Scott into Falcon Agency. There were many agents in the FBI, CIA, NSA, Secret Service and other government agencies that wanted to join or transfer to the elite Falcon Agency. There was also an abundance of military intelligence individuals, including top ranking generals, trying to join. Rank didn't have its privileges in Daniel's eyes.

After being declined, one three-star general approached his good friend, the President of the United States, and asked if he would put in a good word for him. The president said he would but the agreement he had made with the Falcon Director was, Daniel had total control of all facets of the agency. The president didn't have any say-so when it came to the hiring practices of his top agency.

When the president did casually mention the general's name to Daniel, it was a death sentence to the general ever becoming part of Falcon. Daniel was determined not to be influenced by anyone when it came to the operation and employment at Falcon. He knew that many problems in other agencies resulted from the "cronyism" pressures other government officials were known for. It would not happen as long as Daniel was the director. He made sure that only the best of the best would become members, no matter what rank or who they were. For every one-thousand applicants, only two or three were selected for interviews and maybe only one of those applicants was appointed as a Falcon Agency Special Agent. It was the hardest United States intelligence branch to become a member of.

When Pat Scott submitted his resignation, CIA Director Bill Angus was not happy at losing a twenty-three year veteran, one of his best and trusted agents. But he did understand Daniel's motivation and didn't say anything to Daniel about his grand theft.

Falcon Special Agent Dan Aibaya had spent his entire career in the military intelligence arena of the Army. A Japanese-American by birth, he retired from the Army as a colonel and was one of the top, if not the best, intelligence officers in the entire military. An unimposing, softly spoken individual, Dan had met the Falcon director during one of Daniel's visits to Admiral Boryla's, Chairman of Joint Chiefs of Staff, pentagon office. As Daniel was leaving the admiral's office, he asked Aibaya, who was present at the meeting, to join him in the hallway. What was supposed to be a short conversation turned into an hour. They became impressed with each other's insight on intelligence. Dan let it slip that he was about to retire from the Army and Daniel extended an invitation for him to apply at Falcon.

When Daniel returned to his office, he had Kathy get everything she could on Dan. After reading the Colonel's profile, background and top secret accomplishments during his service to his country, Daniel knew that Dan Aibaya would be a valuable asset to Falcon.

Three days later, Daniel invited Dan to lunch and told him that if he wanted, he could become a Falcon Special Agent without going through the difficult interview process. Six weeks later, Colonel Daniel Aibaya (ret.) became Falcon Agency Covert Operations Special Agent Daniel Aibaya.

After Scott and Aibaya joined Falcon, Daniel saw that they were a natural fit. Each was extremely intelligent, had calming personalities and was humble and soft spoken. Merlin took both of them under his wing. When Xi met them, he too, told Daniel that they were an excellent fit. If Daniel had any doubts, Xi's statement removed them immediately.

The invited guests were seated at the conference table, waiting patiently for the Falcon director. He walked to his seat and sat down. In respect for Falcon's director, everyone remained quiet, waiting for Daniel to speak.

"Thanks for coming on such a short notice. Bill, I would like to introduce two of Falcon's agents that are here today. You know Pat Scott and I'm sure you're probably still pissed that I stole him from your agency."

That brought laughter from everyone.

"You got a good one there, Daniel. I should prosecute you for grand theft," Bill answered while still laughing.

"Please don't, Bill. I've got enough on my plate for now," Daniel answered raising his arms in the air as if surrendering.

Again, the group laughed.

"The other gentleman present is Daniel Aibaya. I'll let Dan give his background."

Agent Aibaya stood and presented his impressive resume in a soft spoken, humble manner.

"You have another good one, Daniel. I'm sure Admiral Boryla wasn't a happy camper either," Bill Angus said after Dan had finished

"I told him to get over it," Daniel said as they all laughed again.

"Okay ... Director Angus has an important update. Both Dan and Pat have been briefed on the problem we are facing, Bill. So, go ahead."

"Thanks, Daniel. I'm going to recap what has happened. An agent of the CIA, Kyle Peterson, was found murdered outside Montreal, Canada, recently. The CIA's policy, when something like this happens, is to quarantine the agent's office and files. We also search the agent's residence. A thorough investigation is conducted on every facet of the agent's activities and life.

A couple of days ago, during the search of Agent Peterson's office, a file was discovered taped under a desk drawer. This is very unusual because it is standard procedure that all files must be secured in a safe anytime an agent leaves their office.

The file was labeled "TOP SECRET" and titled "Scorpio". There is no record in our, nor any other agency's database, of any operation, mission or anything else named Scorpio. The file was turned over to me about two hours ago. After reading the contents, I called Daniel and asked for this meeting."

"Who else knows about this Scorpio file, Bill," Daniel asked.

"Just the agent-in-charge of Peterson's office search and myself ... and now you people," Angus answered.

"Good. Continue," Daniel answered softly.

"This is the original file found and I haven't made any copies, nor did the AIC (Agent-In-Charge).

During Agent Peterson's covert overseas assignment in Afghanistan, he uncovered a planned operation, better said as an al Qaeda terrorist attack, against the United States."

The group in the room all looked at each other. They all knew that something was in the works but this might give them assistance in thwarting the attack.

"Does this Scorpio file say when or where?" Merlin asked.

"No, it doesn't. Let me continue and you might get a better picture," Bill answered. "Kyle didn't discuss this with anyone in the agency, breaking the agency's rules and regulations regarding information of this caliber. He took it upon himself to conduct the investigation alone.

We all know that there are terrorist cells here in the U.S., but he discovered there is also an independent group operating outside of any known cells. Peterson ascertained that Monique Leclair and Kaleem Mushowui were two members of a special group. There is also a note stating he thinks that there are a total of six individuals in this pod."

"Any mentioning of how Peterson came to the conclusion that there are six, Bill?" Raul asked.

"No, there isn't any documentation on that. He had a list of six and Kaleem and Monique's names were on it. After Kaleem and Monique's names, were three question marks, followed by the name Scorpio. But he did write several notes saying the sniper shootings are a smoke screen being used to cover up the real objective of a biological attack. Peterson also noted that he received some information while in Afghanistan that this operation will be worse than 9-11 and what the St. Louis attack would have done. A target or targets weren't mentioned either.

Additional notes say that Iraqi scientists had developed a biological chemical compound that is more destructive than any known to man. This is the first I've heard about this chemical. It's called QD-9 and we've checked with all our agencies, the FBI, NSA, EPA ... everyone ... and no one has ever heard of this stuff.

Peterson's notes also stated that the informant said he'd seen it work in Afghanistan. This stuff is so deadly that when a small dose, two drops from an eye dropper, was released in a room 20 by 50 containing twenty Afghanis, they were all dead in less than three seconds.

A typical chemist test tube would be enough to kill everyone, in a capacity-filled professional basketball arena, in forty-five seconds or less. People, this is some powerful stuff."

There was a hush in the room for thirty seconds.

"Do you know what the symbol QD-9 stands for and what does this Scorpio have to do with this?" Daniel asked, breaking the silence.

"We have no idea yet what the symbol QD-9 means. Scorpio is the one who is going to release QD-9 somewhere," Bill answered.

"What's the connotation of the name Scorpio? I know it's a zodiac sign, but does anyone have any idea what else it could mean?" Daniel asked.

"Excuse me, sir. I studied astronomy and astrology in college and I can give a brief explanation," Pat Scott said.

"Go ahead, Pat," Daniel answered and sat down.

"Scorpio is the eighth sign of the zodiac and is symbolized by a scorpion. Scorpio's birthdays fall between

October 23 and November 21. Astrologers consider Scorpio perhaps the most extreme of all signs.

Scorpios are thought to be keen observers of people, potentially calculating and manipulative. They see more of people's deepest motivations than others do and have a tendency to be cynical. They're sensitive and never forget getting hurt by someone. Forgiveness is very difficult for the typical Scorpio and the intensity and focus of Scorpios gives them great ability to see a project through, despite all obstacles. They have strong leadership qualities, incisive analytic abilities, energy, and desire for financial security. They are motivated career people.

Scorpios are also renowned to flirt with danger and push themselves and those close to them to their limits. They like hidden causes and are like the volcano not far under the surface of a calm sea. They can erupt at a moment's notice.

Many are in the professions as forensics, law enforcement or detective work, the military, medicine, psychology and big business. That's a brief description from the astrological point of view, Daniel. And by the way, I'm a Scorpio," Pat said smiling and sat down.

"Can you write that down, Pat, and dissect it? There were a lot of keywords stated in that description that caught my attention. Words like extreme, calculating, manipulative, seeing a project through, despite all obstacles, and unforgiving. You might have described who we might be looking for. Put together everything you know about Scorpios," Daniel answered.

"Oh, one more thing, sir. The planet Pluto rules Scorpio, which is a water sign," Pat added.

"There are other keywords, rules and water. The other interesting part of Pat's excellent description were the dates, between October 23 and November 21. It's now October and maybe that is when this is supposed to happen. Let's get this info to our profiler also."

There was a knock on Daniel's office door. Kathy got up to answer it. She quietly talked to her assistant who handed her an envelope. Kathy closed the door and returned to the conference table to where Merlin was seated. She handed Wiz the sealed envelope and returned to her seat.

Everyone was looking at Merlin as he opened it. He read the message to himself in the quiet office. When he finished, the Wizard looked up at the group and then directly at Daniel.

"It's the report I've been waiting for. We've matched pictures of Monique Leclair with surveillance cameras in all the major airports where the sniper attacks happened. I'm talking, Seattle, Los Angeles, Kansas City, Detroit, Texas, Boston, Denver and five times in two months here at Ronald Regan airport.

The name, Monique Leclair, wasn't on any national or international airline manifests. So, she's using false passports and ID's," Merlin said while still looking directly at Daniel.

"Do your people still have her and Kaleem under surveillance, Bill?" Daniel queried.

"The last report I received was yesterday and they did have them both covered."

"Remember when Xi said he envisioned someone with a case leaving a French freighter in a Canadian port? This QD-9 might be what was in the case that came off the French ship," Raul added.

The room remained silent as each was thinking what the repercussions would be if this chemical were to be exposed to a large group of people.

"Kathy, would you make two copies of the file and give one to Merlin and the other to me after the meeting, please," Daniel requested.

"Yes," was her only response.

Daniel thought for a few seconds more before he spoke.

"Okay, I want Agent Aibaya to team up with Merlin and Agent Scott to team up with Raul. Merlin, you two are responsible for getting Monique Leclair. Raul and Pat, get Kaleem. Bill, make sure your people know that Wiz and Raul are in charge of those areas."

"No problem, Daniel," Bill said, answering Daniel's request.

"I want this to stay here. No other government entity or officials are to know about any of this. If word gets out to the public, we could have major hysteria. Bill, make sure the agent who found the file is told to keep quiet."

"I've already given him that order, Daniel," Bill answered quickly.

"Good. Wiz, find that case. We've got to get it fast. You've got full authority to use whatever means, and that includes using extreme prejudice if necessary, to get it."

Daniel paused for a moment.

"Wiz, I'm about to do something that's unfair to you but I have no choice. I'm going to be gone for a while and I'm putting you in complete charge of Falcon Agency. Before anyone says anything, hear me out."

Everyone had a combined shock and curious look on their faces with the unexpected news.

"Why would Daniel leave at such a critical time?" was on everyone's mind.

"I've informed the president about this decision on my part. Reluctantly, he agreed. Merlin, with the aid of everyone here in this room, you're fully capable of handling Falcon. I'm not going to tell you where I'm going. No one knows, not even my wife Susan."

"How long will you be gone?" Merlin asked with a deep concerned look.

"I have no idea … maybe a week … maybe a month or longer."

"You sure this is the right move, Daniel?" Merlin asked, still confused with the sudden turn of events.

"I'm positive," Daniel answered looking at Xi.

Xi sat quietly and nodded his head at Daniel.

"What if I need to get a hold of you?" Merlin asked.

"You won't be able to. I'll be incommunicado. If you think it's that urgent, tell Xi. He doesn't know where I'm going either, but he may be able to help you with your problem.

Understand this, people. You all know me very well and know I wouldn't leave, especially at a time like this, unless I was absolutely sure it was the right move. It is something that I have to do."

"When are you leaving, Daniel?" Kathy asked.

"After this meeting. I'll be taking Falcon I and flying out of Andrews in about two hours. The jet will return back here after it drops me off in Denver."

Daniel's close friends and associates had the initial feeling that he was deserting them but they did understand that whatever he had to do, it must be of vital importance and respectfully didn't question him anymore.

Daniel gave a few more minor instructions and the meeting adjourned. As everyone was filing out of his office, Daniel asked Xi to stay for a few minutes.

"You go on journey, like Xi say," Xi said after the office door was closed.

"I got the message after Bill called me with the news of the Scorpio file. You did tell me I was going to go. You understand why, don't you?"

"Xi understand and know Daniel must go."

"Any advice that may help me?"

"Be Master Daniel," was Xi's only response as both men looked into each other's eyes.

"I will, Xi ... I promise."

Chapter XIII

Montreal

*L*ate *the following morning, Merlin and Agent Dan Aibaya* flew to Montreal. Raul and Agent Pat Scott flew to Toronto. Their objective was to capture and arrest Monica Leclair, Kaleem Mushowui and find the case that may contain the chemical QD-9.

Merlin and Dan arrived at Pierre Elliott Trudeau International Airport around 2:00 p.m. in a small jet from the government aviation fleet. They were met at the VIP Corporate Center by Richard Harrison, the CIA Agent-in-Charge of Monique Leclair surveillance and left immediately for the hotel where they were based.

The drive to the hotel was unusually quiet for Merlin. He was always one to start up a conversation. But, he was busy thinking about everything involved with the current situation. As the Acting Director of Falcon Agency, he felt the pressure building.

They arrived at the hotel and Wiz asked Agent Harrison to meet in Merlin's room in five minutes. He wanted a complete briefing and also asked for everyone assigned to the surveillance team, with the exception of those presently on duty, to be there.

The group gathered in Merlin's large suite. Agent Harrison arrived with four other CIA agents assigned to the project.

"Is everyone here, Richard?" Merlin asked as an agent closed the door.

"With the exception of the two agents on duty right now, we're all here."

"Good."

Merlin introduced Dan Aibaya and himself to the group and they to him. After his brief reason for being there and reaffirming that he was now in charge of the operation, he asked Harrison to give his briefing.

"We've had the subject, Monique Leclair, under surveillance for two weeks now. We're using two men to cover her in eight-hour shifts and so she has been under a 24-7. Any movement from her residence has also been videotaped and we brought a tape along showing what we have so far.

The only visitor has been a man identified as Kaleem Mushowui. I'm sure you have the bio on him, sir. He has visited three times and the last visit was two days ago when he arrived by taxi. Since that time, Leclair has left the house only once and it was the same day that Mushowui was there. She drove to a grocery store with him and she returned alone.

Before coming here, I checked in with the team that is on surveillance now and no other developments to report, sir."

"Okay, Richard. Good job. We operate a little different at Falcon than at the CIA. My name is Merlin and some close friends call me Wizard. For the time being, please call me Merlin.

Tonight we're going to raid Monique Leclair's house. As I understand, the house is in an upscale neighborhood, so I want to do it under the cover of darkness. It will be a quiet operation. No lights or unnecessary noise. Let's just say it will be a typical undercover covert raid.

Attire will be black clothing and we'll scatter our vehicles around the neighborhood."

"I brought a schematic floor plan of the house sir, err... Merlin. We got them from the contractor who built the house," Harrison added.

"Good. Let's get down to business. First, we'll review the house blueprints and get familiar with the layout," Merlin said in a commanding voice.

For the next two hours, they formulated a detailed plan for the raid. Every facet was covered and reviewed twice. As far as Merlin was concerned, it should be a "no-brainer" as he described it.

"I want to look at the most recent tape of activity, Richard. It'll give us a chance to see what she looks like and a better perspective of the exterior of the house. Do you have it with you?" Merlin asked.

Richard looked at another one of his agents who produced the tape.

"Since there has been very little activity, everything from this morning back to when we were assigned this job is on this one. The team that is on duty now put a fresh tape in the camera this morning," Richard answered while handing Wiz the videotape.

"Okay, gentlemen. Let's watch a movie."

They all gathered around the television and watched the most boring hour and ten minute videotape they had ever watched. When it finished, Merlin partially rewound the tape and pressed the play button.

"Something isn't right. Watch this part real close," Wiz said staring at the screen.

The video showed a black and white taxi arriving at the Leclair residence and after paying the fare, Kaleem Mushowui got out of the cab carrying a large, black duffle bag. He walked to the front door and rang the doorbell. Monique answered the door and let Kaleem enter.

"Now, watch this part," Merlin advised.

The next scene showed the garage door opening and a Mercedes Benz backing out of the garage. As the vehicle cleared the door, Leclair could be seen reaching up to push the remote garage door opener in her car. Seated next to her was what appeared to be another individual wearing a black fedora. The person didn't move and seemed to be slouching down in the seat.

As the tape continued, there were no other frames of Monique or Kaleem in the car. There was a short stretch of her exiting the grocery store alone and then her entering the driveway back at her house. As she entered the drive, she reached up and pushed the remote garage door opener again and entered. Slowly the door closed.

"Merlin, did ..." Dan started to say when Merlin interrupted him.

"Hold on, Dan. Anyone notice anything peculiar?" Merlin asked the group.

"I was about to say that I noticed two things, Merlin," Dan answered.

"Oh ... sorry. Go ahead."

"Rewind the tape to where they were leaving the house."

Merlin tossed Dan the remote control and he reversed the videotape, stopping at the frame where the garage door was opening.

Dan began narrating. "We've got a white Mercedes Benz backing out of the garage."

When the Benz cleared the garage door, he paused the tape.

"In the stall next to where the Mercedes is parked is a black BMW SUV. Now watch this."

Dan fast forwarded to where Leclair was pulling into the driveway. As the door was opening, he spoke again.

"The Beemer is not there now and you can see a gray car in the third stall. Poof ... the Beemer is gone. Where did it disappear to?" Dan said with a smile. "And ... there is no way you can positively ID the passenger. All you see is a black fedora hat and the top of a suit coat that the passenger is wearing. There is no face recognition or shots in any frames," Dan said.

"Good job, Dan. How long was she away from the house, Richard?" Merlin asked immediately.

Harrison looked at his agents. "George, you were on that detail. How long was she gone from the house?"

"From the time she left and went to the store and returned, I would say not more than ten minutes ... fifteen at the most. The store is only about three blocks away," Agent George answered.

"George, did both vehicles tail her?" Merlin asked.

"Yes sir. It was the procedure used on this surveillance in case the suspect started acting weird. We could switch lead cars. When we saw that she was leaving the parking lot, car one went ahead and took up his position at the suspect's house while I tailed her." George answered.

"Did you get a positive ID on whether Kaleem was in the car on the way to the store?" Merlin inquired in a more stern tone of voice.

"We assumed it had to be him because no one else was seen entering Leclair's house. They were the only two in the house, sir." George was getting nervous.

"Hmm ... It could have been a mannequin in the front seat for all we know. Shit! Has anyone seen her for the past two days ... maybe walking by a window or getting the mail or anything?"

George and the rest of the agents looked at each other for an answer.

"I haven't, but at night, lights were turned on and off in different rooms," George answered and the others also echoed the same response.

"If you think back, they probably came on and shut off at the exact time. Timers, people … timers set for specific times. I'll bet my career that she's not there. Son of a bitch.

I still want to stay on our planned schedule. We hit the house at 2100 hours, under cover of darkness. In the meantime, let's get the license plate number of the BMW. Dan, take the rest of the team and all the vehicles and check out both international airports' parking lots. See if you can find the BMW there. She flies on commercial flights. While you're gone, I'll get Falcon in DC to check the airline flight schedules out of both airports. Which one is closest to her house, Richard?" Merlin asked.

"Trudeau International," Harrison answered.

"Hit those parking lots first. When you find the BMW, I want you to break into it and search for any clues as to where she might have flown."

"Do you think she really did fly to someplace, Merlin?" Harrison asked.

"No doubt about it. Now, you guys get going. Take all your gear you'll need for the raid tonight. You have a little over five hours and I want you to find the SUV. As of right now, Agent Aibaya is your Agent in Charge."

"But …," Harrison started to say when Merlin cut him off.

"If anyone has a problem with my orders, you're off the team. You have no idea what we're up against. So, do you have a problem with my orders, Agent Harrison?" Merlin asked in a commanding voice.

"No, sir," Harrison answered.

"Good. Anyone else?" Merlin asked looking directly at each CIA agent.

No one said a word, knowing full well who was in command of this operation.

"Okay, people. Hit the road. You have a lot of work to do," Wiz ordered.

As they were leaving, Merlin pulled Dan aside. "If any of them give you any shit, kick them off the team and call me."

"No problem, Merlin. I can handle it," Dan answered smiling.

"I have no doubt about it and if you want, you can call me Wiz, like my other friends do."

"Thanks. I better go. I'll call you with follow-ups, Wiz. Later." Aibaya said and left the room smiling. He knew that he now was an accepted member of the Wizard's inner circle and it made him feel great.

Two hours later, Monique Leclair's BMW was found in a long-term parking lot at Trudeau International Airport. The team broke into the vehicle and found a parking ticket with an entrance time stamped for two days prior. They also found a copy of an e-ticket receipt for a one-way flight to San Francisco. The name on the ticket was Monica Legros. Dan relayed Merlin with the information and had the BMW impounded. No other evidence was discovered in the SUV.

Upon hearing Dan's information, Merlin called Falcon headquarters and had Kathy get a west coast Falcon team to San Francisco International to review surveillance tapes and confirm exactly when Leclair had arrived. He also had Kathy get a copy of the flight's manifest and have the female names cross-checked with previous ones at airports where she was seen on surveillance security cameras. He was hoping to see if she was using the same ID's used previously. As luck would have it, the investigation proved positive. They now had solid proof that Monique Leclair and Monica Legros were one and the same.

Twenty minutes after Kathy had called Wiz, she called again. She just received information that California Senator Carlson had been killed outside his San Francisco office in broad daylight two hours prior. He was shot in the head. One shot-one kill. So far, there were no suspects.

"We know who did it, Kathy. Check all outgoing flight manifests at San Francisco airport for a Monica Legros or Monique Leclair. She's on the move and let's see if we can find out what her next stop is." Merlin said and hung up the phone.

"The bitch is on the move," Merlin said quietly to himself.

Twenty minutes later Kathy called Merlin again. "Merlin, she's on a non-stop flight to Oklahoma City under the name Monica Legros. I've got two agents based in Dallas on the way to the Oklahoma airport now."

"Good job, Kathy. Contact the agents and tell them to tail her from the airport and don't arrest her until she gets to a hotel. I want the rifle. Make sure they use extreme caution."

"Okay. One more thing. Kentucky Congressman Bob Fetterman was found dead outside his house this afternoon. He was shot in the head and preliminary information from the coroner's office says he was killed late last night by a single 7.62 mm bullet to the head."

"Leclair had to be in San Francisco last night. Check and see if there were any red-eye flights from Kentucky or Ohio to Frisco last night, Kathy." Merlin asked.

"Already did. There weren't any flights from Frankfort and that's where Fetterman was killed."

"We've got two snipers then. Have the security cameras been evaluated at the Kentucky airport?"

"I've got an agent on the way to Capital City Airport in Frankfort now. He should be there within the hour.'

"Damn. This is beginning to get messy. Have you heard from Daniel?" Merlin asked.

"Nothing so far and neither has Xi. Falcon I returned from Centennial Airport in Denver and that's all I know right now."

"Okay. I've got to go. Call me with anything new."

"Will do and good luck."

"Thanks. We need it."

Chapter XIV

Toronto

Raul and Agent Scott arrived at the Lester B. Pearson International Airport in Toronto and were greeted by the CIA-AIC for the Kaleem Mushowui surveillance. Raul was not in a happy mood. He and Pat were three hours late arriving because their jet had an in-flight mechanical problem and landed at Olmsted Airfield in Harrisburg, Pennsylvania. It took an hour and a half to get the part and repair the minor problem.

On the way to the CIA's Toronto-based headquarters' hotel, AIC Cliff Garrett briefed Raul and Pat on the situation. They had lost contact with him three days ago and finally made contact after 24 hours at the Toronto airport. The flight he arrived on originated in Montreal.

Mushowui was staying at a hotel close to the airport in Mississauga. He made two trips to a warehouse district two days ago in a rental cargo van. The building he went to houses a machine shop and Kaleem was observed loading six boxes into the van. He then drove to a FedEx terminal and unloaded the freight. As of right now, Mushowui was at the hotel.

"Cliff, did you check and see where the boxes were being shipped to?" Raul asked.

"We only had two cars on him and didn't want to lose him again. This guy is real slippery. He drove around downtown Toronto and ate at a ritzy restaurant and then returned to the hotel. Once we were sure that he was in his room, I sent one of my agents back to check. The boxes were already on a plane and the destinations were San Francisco,

Frankfort, Kentucky, Oklahoma City, Tampa, Cincinnati and Raleigh-Durham. All six boxes had different names on them and were shipped to hotels. Here are the names. Four of them were to women and the other two were to men."

"Did you call this in yet, Cliff?" Raul asked.

"Yes, and I was ordered not to do anything until you got here and turn the information over to you."

"Let's go to Mushowui's hotel now." Raul ordered with a frown on his face as he studied the list. "Have your agents meet us there."

Raul handed the list to Pat, who was sitting in the back seat. "Pat, call that information into Falcon headquarters and only talk to Kathy Starley about it. Tell her I'm calling Merlin now."

Raul called Merlin on his cell phone. Communication security wasn't an issue at this moment. Getting the information to Merlin was. When Merlin answered, Raul gave him all the details and also said that Pat was talking to Kathy at Falcon headquarters. Merlin gave Raul a briefing on the current situation and killings.

"I'm on my way to Oklahoma City. I want to get to Leclair. Looks like we got three snipers. Take Mushowui down now, Raul. Use whatever is necessary to do it. Do you understand what I'm saying?" Merlin said.

"Got it. I'll call when it's over."

"Let Pat handle the clean-up. I want you to go to Tampa. Have Kathy get what you need by the time you get there. You're going after the male sniper. Good luck," Merlin said.

"Thanks. You, too," Raul answered and disconnected the call.

The SUV sped up and headed to Mushowui's hotel. Agent Garret called ahead and advised his team on what was about to happen. They arrived at the rear of the six-story, red brick hotel and walked in via the service entrance. Waiting in the loading area were five more CIA agents. Raul took immediate control of the situation.

"I want one agent covering Mushowui's van; another one at the front and rear entrances. Cliff, put one man at each end of the hall Mushowui's room is on and one at the elevator. Agent Scott and I will take him down. What room is he in?"

"Sixth floor, room 632. Here is the keycard to Mushowui's room," Cliff answered.

"Questions?" Raul asked taking the plastic card.

There weren't any. "Okay, let's go," Raul ordered.

Three agents went to their ground floor positions while Raul, Scott, Cliff and two of his agents rode up the elevator to the sixth floor. On the way up, Raul and Pat discussed the raid plan. Pat would insert the card into the lock and slam the door open. Raul would enter, followed by Pat as backup. It was a simple operation and, with some luck, it would go down easy.

Agent Garret positioned his two agents at the end of the hall with orders to make sure no individuals entered the hallway. He took up the position at the elevator because it was close to room 632. Raul and Pat waited until everyone was in place and then walked four doors down the hall to Mushowui's room.

Pat got on the side of the door where the handle and security lock was and Raul was on the opposite side. Scott looked at his partner, waiting for the go-ahead. Raul nodded and Pat took the key card and began sliding it into the lock. When the card was all the way in, green LED lights flashed, indicating the handle could be turned. Pat reached for the handle and when his hand had it firmly grasped, he looked at Raul once more. Raul nodded his head. In one motion, Agent Scott pushed the handle down firmly and kicked the door open hard.

Mushowui was lying down on his bed, reading a pornographic magazine in just his underwear and black socks. On the night stand was a Smith & Weston SW9F 9mm pistol with the safety off. He hadn't heard from Monique and had the television on with the sound turned off. Kaleem was waiting for the news to come on and see if there was an announcement regarding any U.S. Senator or Congressman being killed.

He heard a slight sound from the doorway to his room. Curious, he started to rise from the bed and reached for his pistol. As soon as his hand touched the Smith & Weston, the door clicked and was slammed open. He turned with the pistol in his hand and aimed the weapon towards the open door.

Raul raced into the room with his 9 mm Berretta raised to the firing position. He immediately saw a man sitting on the bed, turning his body toward the door, with a pistol in his hand.

"Drop the fucking pistol, Kaleem. NOW!!" Raul yelled as he took aim at the man.

Mushowui didn't obey Raul's order and continued to turn his body toward the unexpected intruder. Kaleem's pistol barrel moved across the room toward the tall hispanic-looking man, who had a badge hanging from a shoestring tied around his neck.

Raul reacted. Mushowui didn't drop the 9mm and continued to move it toward him. Raul squeezed the trigger and a loud noise filled the room from a gunshot. Kaleem's arm holding the pistol continued to move toward the assailant, but the weapon would never be fired.

The 9mm round fired from Raul's Beretta streaked across the room at 260 feet per second and hit Kaleem Mushowui in the forehead, passed through his head and imbedded itself into the wall behind the bed. A blush of crimson red, skull and brain matter followed the projectile and splattered against the same wall. Mushowui was a dead man while still in his seated position.

Raul didn't have any choice. He had to fire in self defense. Mushowui slowly fell back to the bed, dropping his pistol to the floor. Still in his firing stance, Raul moved forward with his automatic pistol still aimed at the dead man.

Pat Scott was right behind his partner with his weapon raised. Both men moved in unison into the room and when Raul reached the side of the bed and saw the destruction the bullet had caused, he began to lower his pistol. He knew that the Algerian member of al Qaeda and Hamas was dead.

Scott reached down and picked up the pistol that Mushowui had dropped to the floor and flipped the safety on.

As Raul was putting his Beretta into his holster, he spoke. "Another asshole bites the dust. Fucking al Qaeda." He spat at the prone man with a round red dot on his forehead that was seeping blood.

Calmly, Raul turned as Agent Garret entered the room with his weapon raised.

"All secure, Cliff. We're okay," Raul said softly.

Garret lowered his pistol and placed it in his shoulder holster. He still hadn't said a word.

"I want the rooms cleared on this floor and locked down. Agent Scott is the AIC. He'll take care of everything. I've got to go to Tampa."

Pat Scott looked at Raul and smiled. "Damn, you blow away this clown and now it's time for a vacation? I'm ready for one, also."

Both men stared at each other and slowly they both smiled and then laughed.

"Sorry, Pat. It's not a Disneyland vacation," Raul said still laughing.

It was Pat's way of breaking the tension.

"We've got another sniper down there. Wrap up all the preliminary stuff and search the room. When you get done, let Cliff handle the rest.

I'll call Kathy and have her charter you a flight to Raleigh-Durham, North Carolina. Wizard is on his way to Oklahoma and Dan Aibaya will be heading to Cincinnati. We've got to get the other two snipers."

"Okay, my friend. Get out of here before I call the Mounted Police," Pat said with a grin.

Raul slapped his new friend on the back and left the room.

Chapter XV

Missing

*W*hen Merlin received the news of the sniper shooting from Falcon's Operation Coordinator, Kathy Starley, he knew he had to get to Oklahoma as fast as possible. He called Special Agent Dan Aibaya and told him of his decision as he was riding in a taxi to the airport.

"I don't feel that you're in a threatening situation, Dan. I want you to turn the house upside down. Look for any documents, bank statements, receipts, weapons and especially any evidence of QD-9. The case might be hidden somewhere in her house."

"If it's there, we'll find it, Wiz," Dan answered.

"I know. Is everyone cooperating with you?"

"Yeah. There's no problem here. In fact, they are bending over backwards to assist. Must have been something the Wizard said," Dan said laughing

"They pissed me off. If they would have done their job right, we might have been able to get her a couple of days ago or we would have at least known that she was on the move. We lost two days of contact and she's shot Senator Carlson in San Francisco."

Merlin gave Agent Aibaya a complete briefing of the current situation.

Two hours later, Dan and his team of CIA agents broke into Monique Leclair's house and began an intensive and detailed search. Two members were assigned a floor. Dan took the basement with another agent. There were some filing cabinets there and he had an instinct about the lower level.

After an hour of searching all the files, nothing was discovered. He began looking for a hidden safe and none was found. It didn't feel right. Something was missing. He walked around the large recreation room, moving furniture around. Then something caught his eye. The basement layout wasn't the same as the builder's blueprints. He recalled that the basement was a rectangle on the blueprints. What he was looking at were two rectangles, not one solid one. He went over to a wall that was covered with mahogany panels and started searching for anything unusual. At times he pounded and pushed against it, but to no avail. Searching as he went, Dan walked around the corner and didn't find any hidden switches or levers.

He began to get angry. Dan knew there was something wrong and in a weak moment, he punched the mahogany wall. It was a stupid thing to do and he realized it afterwards as he rubbed his sore knuckles. Then something registered. There was an echo when he hit the wall and an echo occurs only in a building if there is a chamber for the sound to bounce around in. There had to be a chamber behind the wall. Now he had to find out how to get in. He started in one corner and every few feet, he tapped the wall and listened to the sound. After finishing that wall, he continued around the corner and repeated the inspection.

Both walls gave out an echo. He then went to a wall on the opposite side of the room and tapped. There was a total difference. There was no echo. He returned to the walls that echoed and grabbed a metal ornament from an end table and started banging the wall real hard. Halfway down the wall, a mahogany panel broke loose. It was a door, and when he hit it hard, a hidden latch broke on the inside.

Dan pushed the door open and saw the broken latch on the floor. He pulled a flashlight out of his back pocket, turning it on and shining it into the black opening. The light's beam revealed an office. He walked into the room and shined the flashlight around, looking for a light switch. He saw one above where the broken latch had been attached to the wall. Aibaya flipped the switch and the room illuminated. Looking around he, found the missing part of the perfect rectangular basement.

In the hidden room were more filing cabinets and a large desk with a computer monitor on it. The walls were all paneled with similar mahogany panels as the exterior. Against the far wall was a large, black cabinet with double doors.

Dan started at the desk. He turned on the computer and while it was booting up, he began searching through the desk drawers. He looked at each piece of paper and when he determined that it didn't contain anything pertinent, he threw it on the floor. After ten minutes, the floor was covered with paper.

He didn't find anything of importance, got up to stretch his legs and gravitated to the black cabinet and opened the doors. On the top shelf was a row of videotapes. He pulled one down and looked at the label. In a flowery handwriting was an address. The last line of the address got Dan's attention: Washington, DC. He reached for more videos and they all had addresses on them.

Agent Aibaya looked for a container to put them in, and on the bottom shelf was a large duffel bag. He reached down, grabbed the handles and pulled it out. There was something in the bag and it seemed heavy. Dan set the satchel back on the floor and unzipped the long fastener.

Inside were a stainless steel briefcase and two rifles. He grabbed one rifle and removed it from the bag. The first thing Dan noticed was it didn't have a barrel and knowing weapons well, he recognized the rifle as being a Heckler & Koch HK

PSG1 rifle, with a permanently-mounted Hensoldt 6 x 42 with lighted ranging reticle. It was one of the best sniper rifles in the world.

In the bag he removed six rifle barrels and placed them on the floor. He had struck gold. Laying the rifle on the paper-strewn floor, he reached for the briefcase and carried it to the desk. "Will it open?" Dan thought to himself.

He reached for one latch and slid it sideways. The clasp snapped open. He repeated the movement with the second latch and it also snapped open. Taking a deep breath while placing his hands on each corner of the lid, he slowly raised the top while peeking inside. Dan was very cautious in case the container was booby-trapped. He didn't see any evidence of a trap and opened the top all the way.

The inside of the case was black rubber foam on the top and bottom sections. The only item in the padded container was a sealed pyrex glass test tube with a thick liquid in it. Next to the tube was a carved space where another tube of the same size could fit. The space was empty.

Dan realized that he may have found the briefcase that was carried off the French freighter and possibly the biological chemical QD-9. At that very moment, CIA Agent Richard Harrison walked into the hidden room.

"What have you got there, Dan?" Harrison asked.

Dan closed the case and looked up. "I'm not sure but there are a bunch of videotapes in that cabinet that have addresses on the labels. The addresses are different locations and I think they may be targets. I also found two HK PSG1 rifles and barrels."

Both men walked over to the cabinet and Dan showed him the material. Richard began to lean against the tall cabinet and when he did, it slightly moved.

"That's weird," Richard said and looked behind the cabinet.

"I think it's on wheels," he said and grabbed the side.

He then moved the metal storage facility easily away from the wall. As the black box moved further away from the wall, he saw a cable tied to the cabinet and as it tightened, a door that was completely hidden opened.

"I think I just found an escape passage," Harrison said.

Dan joined him and saw a wooden door partially open.

"It looks like it might lead outside. That's probably how she left undetected," Aibaya answered.

"Let me get one of my men to see where it leads."

The CIA agent quickly left the room and returned shortly with one of the other members of the team who disappeared into the dark tunnel shining a bright flashlight ahead of him.

"Richard. I've got to make a phone call and report what we have here. I'm sure I'm going to have to leave also. I'll need one of your guys to take me to the airport and you'll be in charge here. Have your men go through these file cabinets and see what you can find. I'll be right back," Aibaya said and left the room with the shiny steel case.

"Merlin, it's Dan Aibaya," Dan said into his cellphone from the living room upstairs.

He briefed Wiz on what he had found in the secret room below.

"I'm just about to land in Oklahoma city and one of our Dallas agents has Leclair under surveillance at her hotel. Get that package to the CIA lab in Washington now. If it is what we think it is, we need confirmation quickly. I'll call Bill Angus and let him know you are on your way and for him and an escort team to meet you at Andrews. Turn the case over to Bill only. He can handle it from there.

I then want you to fly to Cincinnati. We have three potential snipers right now and I have a feeling one of them is there. One of our Falcon agents is reviewing security surveillance tapes at the airport as we speak. He also has the hotel address where the suspect may be. I have another agent on the way to the hotel to confirm if the sniper has arrived.

One more thing. There was another killing in Raleigh-Durham a little while ago. It was Senior Congresswoman, Linda Wilson. One shot-one kill."

"A woman? Damn!" Aibaya answered.

At that moment, Agent Harrison walked into the living room holding some papers. He had a sense of urgency about him.

"Hold on, Wiz. I might have something else."

Harrison handed Dan the papers. "It's a hit list Dan. There are thirty-two names on it and look at the bottom, the handwriting," Richard said and pointing to what he was referring to.

On the bottom of the page were the capitalized words, Congress, Senate, President, VP, Department and the entire group of words were circled many times. Next to the circled group was the word, Scorpio.

"Thanks, Richard. Anything else?"

"Yeah. These pictures of Usamah bin Laden. They're autographed by the asshole.

The tunnel led to the outside and opened up in the flower garden. My guys are searching the cabinets, also. So far we found a bunch of wire transfer receipts from Swiss Banc."

"Okay. Keep looking and I do need a driver to take me to the airport now."

"I'll have one up here in a second and I'll call you with a detailed report after we finish here," the CIA agent answered in a respectful tone of voice and left the dark room.

Dan explained the pictures and what was on the hit list document to Merlin, and as he did, Merlin made notes. Aibaya continued talking on the phone as he and his driver left the house by the rear residence entrance. When he was outside, Merlin had been completely updated by Dan's detailed report.

"Has anyone heard from Daniel, Wiz?" Aibaya asked before the call was disconnected.

"No. Not one word," Merlin answered softly and disconnected the call.

Chapter XVI

Solitude

*A*fter *Daniel's meeting at Falcon headquarters when CIA* Director Bill Angus revealed the contents of the Scorpio file, Daniel went home and after packing, talked to his wife Susan. All he told her was he had to get away for a while and think. Susan knew there was more to what her husband said and questioned him.

"Daniel, are you alright? I've seen a change in you the past week and don't get me wrong, it is a pleasant change. You seem to be more at peace with yourself, calmer and quieter than usual."

"I'm fine, hon. I'll explain when I get back."

"Can you tell me where you are going?"

"Not right now, but I'm not going outside of the U.S.. It isn't like one of the missions overseas. I'll be alright. It has nothing to do with us. I love you dearly," he said and kissed her softly on her lips.

Still in Daniel's embrace, Susan whispered, "I love and trust you with all my heart. Come back when you are ready."

They hugged and kissed more passionately and then Susan walked Daniel out the door to his waiting security escort team. He put a large backpack into the suburban and returned to Susan. They said their final farewells and kissed again. Susan, Daniel's beautiful wife, watched as the three vehicles left the Naval Observatory compound.

"Come back soon, Daniel," Susan whispered and walked into the house.

Daniel had received the mental message that he needed to go into solitude that afternoon after Director Angus had called requesting a special meeting regarding the Scorpio file. He then made two phone calls. The first was to Susan telling her he would be going out of town for a while and the other was to his good friend, Armando, in Montana.

Armando was one of the original members of the Falcon Agency team. In Falcon's infancy, the secret team was called I.C.E., an acronym for International Covert Enforcement team. Later on, the name was changed to Falcon Agency to give it a better anonymous identity.

Armando had retired from the agency after getting wounded in Afghanistan. It had been the second time in as many missions that he had received wounds and decided it was time to get out of the business.

"I've become a bullet magnet and I better quit before it's too late," the tall, muscular hispanic had said when he informed the president that he was retiring.

He had met his wife, Sara, while he was recovering in a military hospital in Germany. Sara was the nurse who attended to Armando and they fell in love at first sight. Armando was also retired from his civilian business career. Born in the United States, his parents had immigrated from Mexico and he had joined the Navy after high school. As an excellent recruit, he was offered the opportunity to go to navy SEAL training where he met Merlin, Raul and Peter, now deceased. All four attended Northwestern University in Dekalb, Illinois, after leaving the Navy and it was there that they befriended Daniel White.

Armando, a computer technology genius with a degree in computer programming and technology, started a computer company in California. The company grew rapidly and eventually was bought out by a larger corporation. Armando received six-hundred million dollars for his share of ownership.

After retiring from Falcon, he and Sara purchased a large ranch in Montana, built a beautiful log house and some cabins along the shores of a lake, which also was part of the ranch. They rented out the cabins and just enjoyed their lives in the mountains. Sara was now pregnant with their first child. For the lovely pair, life was wonderful.

Armando received a call from his good friend and Daniel asked for a favor.

"How are you, my friend," Daniel asked.

"Great. Damn, what a pleasant surprise. It's good to hear from you, Daniel. What are you up to? Still the head-nuts of Falcon?"

Daniel laughed. "Yeah, still the director. Is this still a secure line?"

"Still is. The only calls I get on this phone are from you Falcon clowns."

Both men laughed.

"Listen, I need to keep this short. I need a favor."

"Anything, Daniel. Anything you want, my friend," Armando answered.

"I need to get away from Washington for a while. No one can know where I'm going and I need a place where I can be alone, completely alone. I figured your place might be the best location to go. No one would ever suspect me being there."

"Oh, Daniel. I've got the perfect place for you. I built a cabin deep in the mountains along a small river. There is no one around for miles. It's my place to get away when I want solitude. It's about an eight-mile hike and the cabin is fully stocked. In fact, I just made a helicopter trip up there two weeks ago and replenished the supplies. You are welcome to use it, Daniel. No problem at all."

"Thanks, Armando. It is imperative that no one knows I'm there."

"What about Sara? She'll know when you arrive," Armando asked, hearing the sense of secrecy in Daniel's voice.

"Just you two. If anyone calls or asks if you know where I am, you've got to deny it."

"Hell, Sara and I've never seen you. The last time we saw you was in Washington, DC when the president gave us the Medal of Freedom. Haven't seen you since then. How's that sound, buddy?"

"Great. It's going to take me until tomorrow morning to get there. I'll be flying out of Andrews on Falcon I in a few hours to Denver. From there I'll be doing some evasion stuff to make sure I'm not being tailed. I should arrive in Kalispell in the morning. I'll call you when I'm about an hour out. Is that enough time for you to pick me up?"

"Yeah. We're about an hour and ten minutes drive from the airport. I'll be there when you land. Look for a full-size, camouflaged HumVee and a big handsome mountain man."

Both laughed again.

"Thanks, Armando. I really appreciate it. I'll see you tomorrow," Daniel said.

"Look forward to seeing you, my friend. Later."

The phone line went dead.

Falcon I landed at Centennial Airport southeast of Denver. On board were the pilot, co-pilot and two Secret Service Agents assigned to Daniel. Daniel walked down the steps of the Gulfstream V jet and met with the two agents.

"I'm going on alone from here and it's an order. I want Falcon I refueled and to return back to Andrews with you men on board."

"But, sir ... we have direct orders from the president to always have a team with you when you leave your building and the observatory," an agent said.

"Don, listen closely to what I'm saying. I'm going on alone from here. The president knows what I'm up to and you will not be in any trouble. It's been cleared and it isn't your fault that you weren't informed because it was a short notice decision to leave on my part. So, have Falcon refueled and head back ASAP. Got it."

"Yes, sir," the agent answered as Daniel walked across the tarmac to the VIP lounge.

Daniel rented a car and drove north to Jefferson County Airport, located about eight miles north of Denver proper, where another private jet he had chartered was waiting for him. On the drive to Jefferson, he made deviations along his route, checking to see if he was being followed. After determining that he wasn't, he drove the last three miles directly to the airport. It was now late evening. He dropped off the rental car, boarded the jet and told the pilots to file a flight plan to Las Vegas.

The jet landed in Vegas at 0220 and after the sleek aircraft took off on its return flight back to Colorado, Daniel boarded another private aircraft he had chartered and at 0255 they departed Las Vegas. At 0445 Daniel called Armando's secured telephone and Sara answered. Sleepily, she informed Daniel that he had left approximately an hour ago for the airport. Armando wanted to make sure he was there as soon as Daniel arrived.

The jet landed at Glacier Park International Airport in Kalispell, Montana, at 0605. Daniel, dressed in insulated hiking boots, dark blue ski jacket and blue-jeans, deplaned the chartered jet with its turbine engines still running. It was cold out and as the sun was rising over the horizon, Daniel walked into the small terminal. As he entered the building, he was greeted by his tall muscular friend, Armando.

"Damn you look great," Armando said and both men hugged.

"You do, too," Daniel answered.

"Got any other luggage other than that backpack?"

"No. This is all I brought."

"Let's get out of here then," Armando said, grabbing Daniel's backpack.

They exited the deserted terminal and walked to the parking lot where Armando's HumVee was parked. As they walked to the vehicle, the corporate jet took off and was rising into the sky.

"Kind of fell in love with Hummers. Got three and I beat the hell out of 'em. Haven't broke one yet and I'm still trying," Armando said with a grin while throwing Daniel's backpack in the back seat.

They left the airport and began the journey to the "ranch" as Armando called it. On the way they discussed their families and then the topic switched to Falcon Agency. Armando still missed the action but was also very satisfied with his current life-style. He was still a member of the elite agency and, when he retired, he left the option open to be asked to help out at any time. It was totally his decision as to whether he wanted to or not. Armando's security clearance, equivalent to the top exec's of Falcon, was and would be in effect for life.

Daniel described the current situation with the Scorpio file but nothing about his reason and desire for solitude. Armando, knowing his friend well, didn't push the issue. If Daniel wanted to tell him, he would in good time. If not, it didn't matter to Armando. He respected his friend's wishes and privacy.

When they arrived at the large log house, Daniel was impressed. It was his first visit to the remote location. Based in a valley surrounded by the high, majestic Rocky Mountains, it was more scenic and beautiful than Daniel had envisioned. After enjoying the moment, the men entered the house and were greeted by Sara, a lovely blond lady dressed in a loose western blouse and blue-jeans. The pony-tailed beauty gave Daniel a hug and kissed his cheek.

"You look great, Daniel. We've missed you and glad you're here. I've got breakfast ready so come on into the kitchen."

Daniel could smell the mixed aroma of bacon, coffee and warm bread. His stomach growled.

"Boy, it smells great and I'm starving," Daniel said as they walked to the kitchen with his arm around Sara's waist.

They ate a big breakfast and then Armando and Daniel excused themselves and went to his office.

"I've got a good map ready for you. Let me show you how to get to the cabin. There are no trails up there and it gets a little tricky."

"How do you get up there. Didn't you say you took a helicopter up?" Daniel asked.

"I only use a chopper when I need to take up a big load of supplies. Otherwise, I hike. It really is a gorgeous trip up there. You'll enjoy it unless you want me to get a chopper for you."

"Hell no. I want to enjoy the journey," Daniel answered smiling.

"There is only one place to land a chopper and it is a tight squeeze. The pucker factor goes through the roof when the pilot hovers the egg-beater down into the small LZ next to the stream.

Let me show you the map. When are you planning to leave?"

"Right after you show me how to get up there," Daniel answered.

Armando showed Daniel the topographical map and the route he had laid out. It wouldn't be an easy hike through the mountains, but Daniel was eagerly looking forward to it.

"I built the cabin last year and had the chopper sling up the materials. I did something unique. I bought two large steel conex and had them slung up there with a chopper. Then I had a small tractor slung, too. The cabin is built into the side of a hill and hard to see from the front. I bermed up the sides with dirt and planted trees. They're pretty tall now.

I finished off the inside with rough wood. The conexes are side-by-side with a small hall between them. One I use as a kitchen and eating area. The other has two rooms for sleeping. I never know when I might take a guest up there and so far it has been only Sara and I that have stayed.

There is a high-frequency radio and generator in one of the rooms and about fifty gallons of gas in a bunker outside. There are also six kerosene cans for lanterns. I just stocked the larder with canned foods. Help yourself to whatever you want. The place is fully-furnished and really comfortable. There is also a bunch of fishing gear. The stream is great fishing.

In the rear bedroom, there is a hidden waterproof locker under the bed containing four rifles, two pistols and a shit-load of ammo. Knock yourself out if you want.

I've never seen anyone else up there but you never know. I call it a cabin but in all reality, it's a bunker. Now, there is a secret trick to getting into the cabin."

Armando explained the entrance process and then Daniel prepared to leave. Armando offered Daniel a pistol for the journey.

"Got two in my bag, buddy," Daniel said.

"Better get one out and put it on your hip. You're in mountain country," Armando answered with a wink. "There are grizzlies and mountain lions up there. I've never been bothered by any but you can never tell when one might get a hair across its ass and look at you as an easy meal."

Daniel thanked Sara for the great breakfast and said goodbye. He and Armando went outside.

"I'll give you a lift to the drop off point about a mile that way," he said pointing in the northwest direction.

They jumped into the hummer and drove to Daniel's launch point. They both got out and hugged each other.

"If you need anything or have a problem, use the HF radio like I said. Any idea when you'll be coming back, Daniel?"

"Not really. I'll call you and let you know when I'm on my way back."

"Ok, buddy. Be careful and have fun. See you later."

Daniel started walking away and, after a few moments, disappeared into the woods. His journey had begun.

Walking at a steady and even pace, he enjoyed the scenery and cool weather. The sun was shining but the warm rays didn't penetrate the tall pine trees. Occasionally, he stopped to read the map and take compass bearings. There were sightings of deer and elk on the journey and he thought he caught a glimpse of a bear in a small field, but it was too far away to know for sure.

Eight and a half hours later, Daniel arrived at the cabin location. He initially had a hard time locating it, because, as Armando had said, he had it well camouflaged. Finally, Daniel found it and smiled. No one would ever accidentally discover the secret place.

He found the door and there wasn't a lock visible. As per Armando's instructions, Daniel found the three hidden steel rods and removed them. The door then opened with ease. He walked inside and shining his flashlight around, spotted a kerosene lantern hanging from the ceiling. Below the lantern was a table with a box of matches. He lit a match and then the light. As the glow of the lantern increased, removing the blackness of the cabin, Daniel could see where he was. His new, temporary home was not as rustic as he expected. There were comfortable chairs, carpets on the rough wooden floor, a few pictures on the walls and in the corner a wood-burning stove with a tall stack of firewood along the wall. Daniel went over and started to make a fire. The inside of the cabin was very chilly.

After making the fire and feeling the warmth begin to replace the cold air, Daniel familiarized himself with the home. He loved it. Armando had outdone himself.

He then walked outside and noticed the sun had set. Nightfall was not far away. He went back inside, got an empty bucket and walked down to the stream. As he was filling the container with ice cold, clear mountain water, he saw a fourteen point buck with two doe and their fawn, across the stream getting a drink of water. Daniel stayed squatted down on his knees and just enjoyed the view. There were no sounds other than the stream's gurgling flow southward.

The buck saw Daniel. It didn't bolt, but calmly walked up the bank followed by his family and gradually disappeared into the mountain foliage. Daniel finished filling the bucket while smiling. He had found the perfect place to meditate and begin the next leg of his Master's continual training.

Back in the cabin kitchen, he checked out what Armando termed the "larder". It was fully stocked with every canned food item imaginable. He selected his evening meal of stew and ate. When finished, he cleaned up the area, then grabbed a lawn chair and sat outside. It was getting colder but the cool clean air was refreshing and it was quiet. Daniel sat down and looked up at the clear sky. Million of stars were twinkling above him. Slowly, he closed his eyes and began meditating.

An unusual feeling entered his body and Daniel raised his hand to the triangle resting on his chest. His body warmed, despite the cold air surrounding him. He felt himself slipping into deep thought and was totally focused on a vision that was beginning to appear. It was blurry at first and gradually became clearer.

It was Xi, sitting in his bedroom in the lotus position at Daniel's Washington, DC home. Xi had his eyes closed and Daniel could see him clearly as if he was actually in Xi's room.

"Maybe he was," Daniel thought.

"Greetings, Master Daniel, it Xi," were the words Daniel heard.

Daniel didn't answer..

"Greetings, Master Daniel, it Xi. It okay to greet me," the words repeated.

"Greetings, Master Xi. It's Daniel," Daniel answered not saying it verbally but mentally.

"You get rest now. Have busy day today. Long walk to Armando cabin. Get rest. All okay here."

"Thank you, Master Xi. I will get some rest."

Daniel opened his eyes and, while thinking about what had just occurred, smiled. He hadn't told Xi or anyone else back east where he was going, but Xi had said "long walk to Armando cabin". Xi didn't know about the cabin either.

Thinking that only a couple of minutes had passed, Daniel looked at his glowing watch dial. Forty-five minutes had elapsed since he walked outside of the cabin and sat down. He smiled again and rose from the chair, folded it up and walked inside the warm mountain retreat.

Closing the door and securing it for the night, he went to the fireplace, stoked the coals, added two more small logs and then went to bed. Laying on the comfortable down filled mattress covered with a thick quilt, he smiled again. The message he had received in Washington was true. He would find new powers in the far-away mountains and learn more about his mind, body and soul's unused powers. It was the next journey as a Master. He closed his eyes and fell into the deepest, most restful uninterrupted sleep.

Chapter XVII

The Message

*W*aking, *Daniel had no concept of where he was at first* because the inside of the cabin was in total darkness. The only light was from a lantern in another room, which gave him some indication where he was. He rose from the soft bed, stretched his muscles and walked toward the light in the adjoining room.

He was in the kitchen area and decided to make coffee first. While it was brewing, he got cleaned up and dressed. The aroma of fresh coffee filled the cabin. After pouring himself a large cup, he went to the door. After removing the security bars, Daniel opened the door and viewed a pleasant surprise. It was daylight. It had snowed that evening and there were two inches of fresh powder on the ground. Stepping outside, he smelled the clean, crisp air and inhaled a deep breath. The cold air filled his lungs as he looked at the glowing, picturesque scenery. The sun's warm rays were glistening against the white, pine tree branches that were covered with heavy snow and bending toward the ground under the weight.

Daniel unfolded the chair and sat down. He took a sip of hot coffee while absorbing the peace, quiet and tranquility of the hidden getaway. There were fresh tracks in the snow from deer and rabbits, but none were in sight. He leaned back in the chair and, while holding the warm cup in both his hands, closed his eyes.

A vision slowly appeared in his mind and he recognized it as one that he had seen before. Under the cover of darkness, a person dressed in black was hidden in a clump of bushes. When he had previously explained the vision to Xi, the Chinese Master had stated the answer was in the vision. Daniel was now intensely focused on who the person was.

A black hood was over the sniper's head, covering any sign of facial features. The rifle was raised to the shoulder, and the killer was taking careful aim at a target. Daniel saw the trigger hand that had a black glove on it. One finger of the leather glove, the trigger finger, had been cut off and was beginning to slide inside the trigger guard. As it was placed against the steel level, Daniel saw something that he hadn't observed in the previous vision. The fingernail was long, manicured and painted red. The revelation became clearer and focused clearly on the appendage as it slowly applied pressure to the curved metal. He saw that the finger was thin and feminine and was definitely one of a woman. It was a woman's finger, not a man's. As quickly as the vision appeared, it evaporated and was replaced by another.

The new one was of another person standing upright, dressed in similar fashion as the first, but was hiding behind a large oak tree. The visualization again repeated itself as a black-leather gloved hand with the killing finger of the glove cut off was inserted into the trigger guard. Experienced now, Daniel saw that the fingernail was also long and manicured with blue polish. It was also a woman's finger. As soon as he realized what he was seeing, the mental image evaporated and was replaced with another.

Lying down in a prone position was a silhouetted body in black attire. It was difficult to see against the dark ground as the sniper held a rifle to its shoulder. As in the previous visualizations, focus was on the trigger finger. The fingernail was cut short and the body of the finger was larger and thicker than the other two Daniel had seen. In this vision, it was obvious that the black gloved hand, with the killing finger exposed, was masculine. It also was pressing the curved metal and Daniel saw the muscles tighten as it increased pressure.

A shot rang out. Daniel jumped in his chair and opened his eyes. Looking around and listening closely, he saw and heard nothing. It all seemed too real but the loud repercussion of the sniper shooting was only in his dream.

He continued to monitor his surroundings, as his heart began to reduce its racing beat. Then he saw an antlered deer approaching from between the tall pines. The buck was not running but slowly walking and then two does appeared behind the massive male. Daniel didn't make a move as the majestic creature continued its path between the trees. Daniel realized that if there had been a shot, the animals would have been running in fear of their lives. It was a vision.

As the beautiful, majestic creatures made their way between the trees, a younger deer came bounding into view. Daniel saw that it was a yearling and couldn't determine the sex. It joined the others as they continued to walk closer to Daniel's position, when suddenly the buck stopped. It had picked up a strange scent and raised its head high with the nose raised higher while inhaling the strange odor. Turning its head toward Daniel, the colorblind buck lowered its head and stared at the black and white object sitting in front of a black hole, which was the cabin's door.

The antlered animal stared motionless, as did the other dark, tan family members. It was as if they realized that the silhouetted object was not a danger to them. Cautiously the buck, still looking at Daniel, started to move forward again. The other three animals trustingly followed their leader and guardian. When the buck was less than forty feet in front of Daniel's location, he stopped once again and stared at the black and white form. Daniel, not making a move, stared back into the large animal's charcoal eyes.

"You must stop the destruction. It is up to you. You have the power and knowledge," were the defining words that entered Daniel's mind.

The buck snorted twice and then nodded its antlered head. God's two creatures, one human and the other an animal, stared at each other for a few more seconds. The stately male deer then bowed its head again and began to walk, leading his followers off into the forest. Daniel's eyes followed the foursome as they gradually disappeared.

When the small herd was out of sight, Daniel took a sip of coffee. It was cold. He had no idea how much time had lapsed but new it was longer than he realized.

"Good morning, Master Daniel."

Daniel recognized the voice. He sat back in the chair and closed his eyes. The voice was not audible but in his head.

"Good morning, Master Xi," Daniel answered out loud.

"You slept well?"

"Yes, I did."

"And, you receive message?" Xi's voice asked.

"I received many messages, Master Xi ... all the messages that you sent."

"Ah, but Daniel ... I not send you messages. They come from Supreme Master."

"God? God sent me the messages?" Daniel asked out loud. "Are you sure?"

"You question Xi? Xi say from God, Supreme Master."

Daniel paused and thought he was hallucinating.

"You not having false thought. It true and all Masters know true. Part of being spiritual Master, Daniel. Understand?"

Daniel was still questioning whether he was mentally creating the visions and conversations.

"Not question, Daniel. Let doubt go and accept," Xi answered doubting mental question.

The doubt immediately left Daniel's mind and he smiled. He realized that the journey of a Master was difficult to accept because it was not following the normal pattern of what humans usually experience.

"That true. Sometime very hard. That difference between Master and other people," Xi answered Daniel's thought.

"You are on the journey of becoming a Master, Daniel. Believe it with all your mind, body and soul. It is my gift to you," another unrecognizable voice said.

It seemed that it was coming from the trees and Daniel looked at a tall, ponderosa pine tree whose branches were covered with snow in front of him. The voice wasn't Xi's but a soft whisper. Perched on a branch was a large bird, a falcon which was looking in Daniel's direction. It then screeched once and flew off between the pine trees, disappearing from Daniel's view.

"You see sign, Daniel? God give you sign," Xi's voice said, as if he was next to Daniel and witnessing everything.

"I saw it and believe with all my mind, body and soul, Xi."

"That good, Daniel. That very good you understand."

There was a moment of quiet and Daniel looked around. Everything was noiseless. Experiencing the moment, Daniel smiled. He broke the silence and spoke out loud to Xi.

"Xi, tell Merlin that there are two women snipers … two different women and a man who are the snipers. I had a vision and it was three different people who are doing the killing."

"I will tell. You see answer in dream. You do better now. Answer always in dream."

"Thank you. It was confirmed to me when I saw a buck and two does just a little while ago. There was a young deer with them also."

"You tell Xi male deer and two lady deer but you see four, right?" Xi asked.

"Yes, I saw a buck and two does and a yearling."

"Then there are four … a young one too," Xi said, guiding Daniel to a new assumption.

"Yes, there were four but the vision had only three snipers. I didn't see or have any image of anyone young."

"Believe in what you see. Not magic but true dream and when see deer with own eyes, that mean it truth. There are four."

Daniel thought for a moment before he answered. "Yes, there has to be four."

"Xi tell Wizard. You rest now." Xi's voice faded away leaving Daniel to contemplate what had just transpired.

Smiling, Daniel felt at ease with the experience. He rose from the chair, dumped the cold coffee onto the ground and went back into the warmth of the cabin.

Chapter XVIII

Deadly

*M*erlin *arrived in Oklahoma and immediately made contact* with the Dallas agent who had Monique under surveillance.

"Has she left her room yet," Merlin asked Agent Clayton.

"No. I've been watching closely. She's still inside."

"I'm in a cab now and should be there in about five minutes. If she decides to leave before I arrive, arrest her. Otherwise, keep a good watch. What room is she in?"

"311."

"Okay. I'll see you in a bit."

Merlin arrived at the hotel and called Agent Clayton from outside the building. The phone rang several times and he didn't answer. Sensing that something might be wrong, Merlin entered the hotel lobby and ran to the elevator. One was waiting with the doors open and he pushed the button for the third floor. The doors closed slowly and impatience entered the Wizard's body.

"Hurry ... Move," Merlin said out loud.

The elevator rose and, after what seemed to be eternity, the doors opened on the third floor. Merlin had his Beretta out and the safety off. He looked out the open doors, searching for the agent and signs of danger. Lying on the hallway floor was the body of a man. A pool of blood was around the body's head. Cautiously, Merlin moved forward with his pistol at the ready firing position, his eyes searching for movement. There wasn't anyone in sight. When the Wizard reached the body, he saw that the male figure had been shot in the head.

He checked for a pulse. As expected, there wasn't any. Merlin looked at the signs on the wall that indicated room locations. Room 311 was to his right and he moved in a crouched position toward it. It was two rooms down the hall when he saw the numbers 311 on the partially opened door. He stood upright and crashed into the room ready to shoot anything insight. The room was empty and he carefully made a thorough search, checking the closet, bath and under the bed. Satisfied that there weren't any occupants, he began looking for anything that might indicate what had happened.

The room was intact and the bed was in the same condition as when the maid had left the room. There wasn't any evidence that anyone other than Merlin had been in the room. He went to the phone and called the lobby desk.

"My name is Deputy Director Merlin Miles of Falcon Agency. Has anyone checked into room 311?"

"Just a minute, sir," a young female voice answered.

There was dead silence on the phone for a long time.

"Yes, sir. A Ms. Carol Hansen has."

"Get me the hotel manager," Merlin ordered.

"He's right here ... hold on."

"Hi, this is the manager,"

"This is Falcon Agency Deputy Director Merlin Miles. There has been a shooting on the third floor. I want it sealed off and for you to call the Oklahoma City FBI, now. Ask for the station chief and tell him that Director Bill Angus wants a team of agents here at the hotel. Also, tell him that there has been a killing. Do it now!" Merlin said and hung up the phone.

He then called headquarters and told Kathy what had happened. She had her assistant call CIA Director Bill Angus. Bill called FBI Director John Lambert, who in turn called the Oklahoma office.

"Merlin, Bill Angus. I got the news of the shooting. I called John Lambert and he is also making sure that there will be a team at the hotel."

"Thanks, Bill. I appreciate it."

"I also picked up the package from Agent Aibaya at Andrews and delivered it to our special lab in Maryland. It is top priority now and I should have an answer on the contents of the vial in short order. Agent Aibaya left after they refueled the jet for Cincinnati. Otherwise, that's it."

"That bitch Monique Leclair killed Agent Clayton in Oklahoma and I have no idea where she's heading. Kathy notified the airport personnel to be on the lookout. The car rental places are also being checked out.

I've got another problem. Two agents drove up from Dallas. One's dead and the other one is missing. I don't have a good feeling about this. I'm going to check out this floor. I'll be in touch."

"We'll get her. It is just a matter of time. Kathy sent over the hit-list that was found in Montreal. Everyone on it is now under close guard."

"Thanks. That it?"

"Yes."

"I've got to go. Talk to you later," Merlin answered and disconnected the call.

Immediately, his cell phone rang.

"Hello, this is Merlin."

"Merlin ... this Xi. You can talk now?"

"Yes, Xi, I can talk."

"Xi get message from Daniel. He say tell you there three sniper ... one man and two woman."

"You talked to Daniel, Xi? Where is he?"

Not wanting to get into how and when he and Daniel had communicated, Xi kept his reply short.

"He not say where at, but must get message to Wizard. Three sniper."

Merlin knew better than to question Xi. There was that special, mystical bond between those two friends and he trusted both with his life.

"Okay, Xi. Did he say anything else, like when he is coming back?"

"Not say. Sorry, Wizard."

"That's okay, my friend. We sure could use his help right now."

"Merlin ... Daniel help now. Just in special Daniel way," Xi explained.

"I believe you, Xi."

"Good. Xi go now. Talk to Wizard later," Xi said and hung up his phone.

Merlin thought for a few moments about Xi's and his brief conversation. "Daniel is helping now," Xi had said.

"Right now, we need all the help we can get," Merlin thought.

He began walking down the hallway with his pistol in hand. When he reached the emergency exit stairway, he cautiously opened the door. On the lower landing he saw the missing agent lying in a pool of blood. Merlin slowly descended the stairway with his Beretta at the firing ready position.

When he reached the agent, Wiz knelt and felt for a pulse. As he expected, there was none and he retreated back up to the hallway.

The hotel's security guards arrived. After Merlin identified himself, he took command of the situation. The third floor was cleared of guests and guards posted. An FBI team arrived at the scene within ten minutes of notification and took over the guard duties. Merlin introduced himself to the Agent-in-Charge. AIC Allen had already been informed who Merlin was and to abide by his orders. Merlin was very cordial to the AIC and provided him with all the details.

After the briefing, the local police authorities arrived and tried to take command. Merlin immediately stepped in.

"Excuse me, Captain … Mitchell," Merlin said looking at the captain's name tag. "I'm Merlin Miles, the Deputy Director of Falcon Agency. You are familiar with Falcon Agency captain, I'm sure. Well, I'm in charge here and, even though it is your jurisdiction, I'm overriding it."

"Sorry … Merlin, but you're in Oklahoma City and we don't give a shit who or what you are. I'm in charge here," the tall, burly captain said.

Merlin stared at the police officer and his blood began to boil. Calmly, Merlin walked closer to the heavyset cop.

In a soft voice Merlin spoke. "Well, Captain … err … Mitchell. I'm sorry you copped that attitude because you now have exactly fifteen seconds to get your fat ass off this fucking floor. If you don't leave, I'll have you arrested for obstruction of Federal justice. Now, do you understand what I'm saying or do I have to write you a fucking letter? Fourteen … thirteen … twelve…"

Merlin continued counting and the police captain saw other FBI agents approaching.

"We'll see about this. You haven't heard the last of me," the captain said, retreating to an elevator whose doors were open.

After the elevator doors closed and started to descend, Merlin turned to Agent Allen.

"What's your first name, Agent Allen?"

"James, sir."

"Well, James, it's a pleasure to meet you. Call me Merlin and you are now in charge of this investigation. Come with me for a minute," Merlin said walking away from the other agents. When they were out of ear shot of the others, Merlin stopped and spoke.

"James, we've got a delicate situation here and it has to do with terrorism against the United States. I can't give you all the details but I know who killed the agents. They were supposed to have her staked out. Evidently, they somehow got blindsided. Director Lambert knows what is going on."

"I know, Merlin. He called me personally on my way over here. The agents are ours and thank you for not embarrassing me in front of the other agents."

"I only embarrass assholes like that Captain Mitchell. Listen, I've got to head back to Washington. Here is a picture of who shot your agents. Keep this to yourself right now."

"I've got one. So do the agents at the airport, bus station and car rental places. All I need is a name."

"I can't give you a name because she is traveling under bogus ID's and it is a she. Her real name is Monique Leclair and she's a Canadian citizen. What name she traveled under doesn't matter because I'm sure she has a pocket full of passports. If your people see her, use caution. This isn't her first killing, James."

"Thanks. You want an escort to the airport?"

"No, thanks. Just a ride. I took a cab here," Merlin said.

"No problem and thanks again, Merlin."

Merlin left for the airport in an unmarked FBI car. After the agent escorted Falcon's Deputy Director into the Corporate Center, Merlin shook his hand and walked out to the waiting Falcon Agency jet. He needed to get back to headquarters.

On the flight he made a series of calls. The first one was to Kathy letting her know he was returning. He would need a ride from Andrews to headquarters. He then brought her up to date on what happened in Oklahoma City and of Xi's phone call.

"I know," Kathy answered after Merlin finished. "Xi told me that there are two women and a man."

"My guess is the person down in Florida is the guy. Have you heard from Raul?" Merlin asked.

"The last word I got, he was on a jet to Tampa," she answered.

"I'll call him and bring him up to date. Now where is everyone else?"

"Dan Aibaya dropped off the package at Andrews and should be landing soon in Cincinnati. Pat Scott is on his way to Raleigh-Durham. I've got backup waiting at both locations for them. Raul ordered his own."

"Okay. Anything else?"

"That's it."

"Good job as usual, Kathy. See you soon." Merlin disconnected the call and dialed Raul.

"This is Raul."

"Hey, it's Merlin. Where are you?"

"On my way to the hotel where this Jacque Cormier is supposed to be. Why?"

"You got backup or are you solo?"

"No. I've got a six man backup team with me."

"Okay, listen to what I've got."

Merlin brought Raul up to date and also about Xi's phone call.

"Daniel is helping from where, Wiz?" Raul asked.

"I don't know where but wherever he is, it's working," Merlin answered.

"Yep, I guess so. Listen, we just pulled into the hotel and I've got to go. I'll call when we're done here."

"Okay. Be careful and I'll talk to you later."

Merlin then called Pat Scott.

"Hi, Pat. Merlin here. Bring me up to date."

"Hey, Wiz. I'm in Cincinnati now and just finished reviewing the airport security tapes. Monique Leclair was here."

"No, she wasn't. It is virtually impossible to be in two places at the same time."

"I saw the pics, Wiz. It was her. I'm positive."

"There are two women snipers and one guy. The guy is in Tampa and Monique just knocked off two FBI agents in Oklahoma City. She flew there from San Francisco. So we have two look-a-likes."

"Twins maybe?" Pat asked.

"Possibly. I'm not sure."

"Well, whoever it is, that was in Cincinnati, rented a car and, right now, I've got a five-state APB out. I was hoping your call was that they found her."

"When you finish there, head back to DC." Merlin said.

"Got it. I should be leaving in about an hour."

"Okay. Later." Merlin disconnected the call and dialed Dan Aibaya's number.

"Agent Aibaya," Dan answered.

"Dan, Merlin."

"Hey, who the person was what's going on, Wiz?"

"Head back to DC. I've got a bad feeling and I need you in DC."

"On my way."

144

Chapter XIX

Transfiguration

*D*aniel *decided to take a walk along the river. The afternoon* temperature had dropped below freezing but he had the urge to get away from the cabin. He dressed in layers and, once ready, secured the door and began his hike. He let his instincts lead the way. As he walked, footsteps on his traveled path were imbedded in the snow behind him.

The forest was beautiful in its entire splendor. Tall ponderosa pine tree branches were bent from supporting their snow laden branches. A few birds chirped their warning signal off in the distance as Daniel meandered along side of the flowing stream. The untraveled direction that he chose was easy to walk, having no brush or rocks hindering the way. There was the mixture of scent from the pine trees and moisture in the chilled air. From the smell, Daniel knew that more snow was on the way. It was his inner sense that was working sharply and he knew that he better not stray too far from the hidden cabin. Montana's mountains were renowned for severe blizzards that occurred at a moment's notice. Many unfortunate victims had died in the back country because they hadn't been prepared or heeded the warning signs.

As he made his way through the powdery snow, Daniel had the feeling that someone or thing was either watching him or following. He stopped a couple of times, searching for any evidence, but there weren't any signs of an intruder and so he continued on.

Looking up through the trees, he saw the cloud cover getting darker. He estimated he had traveled about a mile in the mountainous terrain. Smelling the upcoming precipitation in the air, Daniel knew it was time to return to the safety of the retreat. He followed the path he had paved in the snow. A few minutes after beginning his return trip, it began to snow lightly. The sense of being watched was still with him but became stronger as he increased his stride.

Cautiously, he unsnapped the leather strap on the side holster that held the 9mm Beretta pistol. The skies darkened more and the snow began to intensify as he increased his pace. He could see his footprints in front of him and continued on that path.

Suddenly, his internal alarm sounded indicating that danger was stalking from behind. He reached his right hand to the pistol. While continuing to walk, he pulled the Beretta from the leather holster. In the same motion, he flipped the weapon's safety off, stopped in his tracks and spun around with the pistol raised in the firing position. His instincts proved correct but he was shocked at what he saw.

A large buck proudly displaying its wide and tall polished antlers was only twenty feet away. Seeing the human he was following stop and turn, the animal stopped also. Daniel was surprised and slowly lowered the weapon. As he did, the buck slightly raised his head, and then lowered it, as if acknowledging the human with a nod.

Daniel stared at the unmoving animal who just stared back at him. Daniel studied the beautiful deer and realized it was not the same one he had seen earlier near the cabin. This one was much larger than the previous visitor. He counted the points on the large rack and there were twenty. It was the biggest deer he'd ever seen and its size was close to the build of an elk. Both intruders to the forest continued to stare at each other for a few more moments.

The sudden increase in wind velocity snapped Daniel out of the moment. Snow that was resting on the ponderosa pine branches was released from the resting place by the wind and began plummeting down onto the two living creatures. The buck raised his head again and lowered it, signaling Daniel to continue on his way. Daniel smiled, as if understanding the message and while holstering the Beretta, turned and continued on.

After twenty steps or so, he looked back to see if the buck was still following him. Daniel stopped. The majestic creature was nowhere to be seen. It had simply vanished.

The wind and snowfall intensified and Daniel knew that it was now becoming a blizzard. The trees were swaying under the turbulent wind gusts and the new snow mixed with the falling snow from the pine trees began to cover Daniel's previous footsteps. He knew he had to hurry to the safety of the cabin and began to jog, carefully searching ahead for the trail he made. The previous markings were almost covered by the onslaught of the blizzard and visibility was drastically reduced. He reached up and pulled his down parka collar tighter against his head.

The trail markings disappeared and he was now in whiteout conditions. Daniel knew he was close to the cabin location now, but the weather conditions and Armando's constructing the hideaway almost to the point of invisibility on a clear day compounded the danger.

Daniel stopped and tried to get his bearings. All he could see were large pine tree trunks and white snow blowing between them. He didn't panic and knelt down on one knee. To his right was the stream, gurgling under the increase flow of the water. He looked to his left and heard a sound. It was the sound a deer makes ... snorting as the buck did back up the trail. Daniel rose from his knee and began walking toward the noise. As he walked in the blinding, whiteout blizzard, he heard the sound again and he increased his pace in that direction.

Appearing between two wide-dark tree trunks was the buck he'd seen on the trail. Daniel recognized where he was now. Five feet away from where the buck was standing was an embankment covered with deep snow. Deer tracks from where the buck was at that moment led to the building snowbank. Daniel walked toward the tracks and followed them to the embankment. The deep tracks ended at the door to the cabin. He pulled out the three hidden steel retaining bars to the cabin's door and struggled to remove the snow on the ground. Once he had the door pushed open sufficiently enough for him to enter, he turned toward the buck. It had disappeared again into the wall of pure white snow.

The vision of steam rising from the spout of a teapot entered Daniel's mind. As the stream of gray-white, hot steam rises, it slowly disappears into the air. The buck had disappeared with no trace of ever being there. Daniel searched for signs of the creature but there weren't any. He entered the warmth of the cabin, closed and secured the door against the howling blizzard outside.

Feeling the warmth of the fireplace, he began to remove the layers of clothing. When he got down to his flannel shirt, he untied his hiking boots and placed them close to the heat source to dry out. He sat down and took a deep breath. He knew that he had escaped danger, possible death, and reflected on what had occurred.

A few months ago, he would have been confused and thought he was hallucinating. But, after his recent Master mentoring by Xi, it was easy to understand. Daniel smiled and felt inner peace with his thoughts. He laid down on the sofa in front of the fireplace and closed his eyes. He wasn't tired and began to let his mind clear and slipped into deep meditation. The vision of his beautiful wife and two children, Allison and Lance, appeared. He smiled to himself. Ali and Lance were playing in the living room of their house at Grand Lake, Colorado. Susan was sitting and staring out the window that overlooked the lake. Daniel saw a sailboat gliding across the black-blue waters with its tall, white sail filled with invisible air. The vision slowly dissipated and was replaced by Xi sleeping in his room. All Daniel saw was Xi's face and his body was covered by a comforter quilt. That vision, too, slowly dissipated.

"Page 31," were the words Daniel heard clearly next.

There was no vision, dream or person seen.

"The answer is "page 31". There you will find Scorpio. "Page 31"," the verbal message repeated.

Daniel's eyes snapped open and he sat up looking around the room. The glow from the fireplace was all that illuminated the room. He stood up and went to the lantern hanging from a beam in the room. He lit a wooden match and ignited the lantern, turning the lever so the kerosene light glowed brightly. Searching, there wasn't anyone else in the cabin. He knew there wouldn't be and he heard the words again in the room.

"Find "page 31". There lies Scorpio."

Out loud, Daniel whispered, "I will but in what book?"

"Page 31," was the only reply.

Frustrated by not knowing to what book the "page 31" referred to, he asked again louder, "What book?"

""Page 31" lies Scorpio," was the only response.

Daniel returned to the sofa, confused, and sat down on the edge. He received a message and as Xi had explained, "the answer is always in the message. You have to look hard."

Daniel had just received the answer but not who, where or how to find the article, book or document that would reveal the final answer on "page 31".

"Am I delusional, God," Daniel asked out loud. "Am I? Answer me, please."

The only answer he heard was "Page 31".

He rose off the sofa, and added two more logs to the fire and then walked to the kitchen area. Filling the wash basin with the cool river water from the bucket, Daniel splashed it on his face using both hands. It felt good and invigorating as he splashed more, while rubbing his two-day old growth of beard stubble.

"Page 31," he heard again.

He knew he wasn't delusional and answered, "I understand the message. I will find Scorpio. I promise."

He splashed more cold water from the basin on his face and ran his strong fingers through his blond hair that was speckled with gray.

"I will find Scorpio."

He turned to return to the living room area and his heart skipped a beat. Sitting on the sofa in front of the fireplace was his close friend and mentor, Master Xi, who was staring into the fire.

Without turning his head, Xi spoke.

"Hello, Master Daniel. Come join me."

Daniel's heart began beating faster and he took two unsure steps toward Xi and stopped.

"Xi … Xi, how did you get here?"

"Come sit and Xi tell Master Daniel. Come … no afraid."

Daniel slowly walked forward until he was perpendicular to the sofa. He saw Xi turn his head toward Daniel and the kind Chinese man had a wide smile on his face.

"Sit, Daniel. Xi tell."

Daniel sat down at the opposite end of the sofa and the logs in the fireplace sparked cinders against the gold protection screen in front. He kept his eyes on his friend as their eyes connected. The fear and uncertainty evaporated from Daniel's soul and was replaced by inner peace.

"Xi, how did you get here?"

"Master have power to do many thing that other can, but not know how," Xi answered and then raised his hand in the air toward Daniel. "Daniel no talk and Xi tell."

Daniel started to answer and Xi kept his hand raised saying, "No talk."

Daniel quietly sat back on the sofa while focused on his friend.

"Thank you. Good to see you. Look good. Eyes clear and stress gone from face. Have good energy and peace. That good. Nice here at Armando cabin. Come close to Supreme Spirit. That why Master send you message to go from Washington, DC. Need purify mind, body and soul. You feel good now, Daniel?" Xi asked softly.

Daniel didn't answer.

"When Xi ask question, you can answer. No ask question until Xi say okay."

"I feel good Xi but a little confused on how you got here."

"That okay. Should be confused. Never see before," Xi answered smiling. "Remember Xi tell Daniel that Master have many levels. You on one and Xi on another. That because Xi Master long time and Daniel just become one.

Now you on another journey as Master and learn more how to use mind, body and soul. Xi job to help teach. Xi know that Daniel can learn and use power for best. Not show off special power and not let other know how until they ready. Daniel ready for more. Daniel, understand?"

"Yes. I understand," Daniel answered relaxing comfortably now on the sofa. He wasn't fearful of the unknown any more but welcomed it.

"Good. When Daniel go for walk and it snow, wind get strong, you begin come back here to cabin. You see deer behind you. That me. I watch over Daniel. Xi mission to teach and protect Daniel. Same for all Masters. Master teach and protect all.

If you see Xi as person, you run, but as big deer you not. Soul of all men and women is power because soul is Supreme Master inside. You can move soul from your body to other place.

Don't worry. Daniel look confused. Xi explain."

For the next hour Xi explained the spiritual process of transfiguration and transformation to Daniel. Xi never asked for a response from Daniel during the educational process.

Without pausing after his explanation, Xi said, "Daniel, you first learn about listening to message. Then learn about dream and answer always in dream. You see in dream sniper first time but second time see answer. Answer was in first dream but not see.

Now must understand, Daniel dream … or as you say vision … only for you. Xi not see Daniel vision and not have answer to Daniel dream. Daniel hear message, but Xi no hear. Only for Daniel.

Same when Xi have dream or message. Daniel not hear or know. Daniel understand now?"

For the first time in over an hour, Daniel spoke. "I understand, Master Xi."

"Good. So now Daniel know how Xi get here and now know how to send message using mind, body and soul. Xi know Daniel very good person and will use Master power to help other. That why Xi invite Daniel to be Master. Only good people become Master and only one who begin to know mind, body and soul. Must make commitment first. Daniel make commitment in Wisconsin long time ago."

"I remember it well, my friend, very well. I am so happy you came to me in Wisconsin."

"Ahhhhhh, Master Daniel, we come to each other. Nice magic, huh?" Xi asked with a big smile.

"Yes, nice magic, Xi," Daniel answered and closed his eyes for a moment appreciating the wonderful, spiritual enlightenment. As Xi had said, when Daniel was ready, he would be able to use his powers in the similar fashion as Xi, also. It was just a matter of time.

Daniel smiled at his new revelation and slowly opened his eyes. Xi was gone. Understanding what had occurred, he rose from the sofa and walked to the cabin's exterior door. With the locking bars removed, Daniel opened the thick wood door, revealing the raging blizzard outside. The snow was piling up and drifts were growing in size. He looked down at the entrance's threshold. There was no sign of footsteps.

"What were you thinking, Daniel?" he said out loud and laughed.

"I go now. Talk to Daniel soon," the answer came from nowhere.

It was Xi and he was laughing.

Daniel closed the door and after securing it, the message repeated itself.

"The answer is "page 31"."

Chapter XX

Tampa Sniper

*R*aul and his team comprised of Falcon, CIA and FBI agents gathered outside the twenty-story hotel in downtown Tampa. He had confirmation that a guest had registered under the name Jacque Cormier. Upon his arrival that morning, Cormier picked up a package from the front desk that had been air expressed from Toronto, Canada, and arrived the previous day.

Raul had the team stay at their location and entered the ornate hotel lobby alone. When he arrived at the registration desk, he asked the clerk to get the general manager.

"Just one minute, sir. I'll get her. Is there a problem that I may help with?" the young lady asked.

"No, there's no problem. I just need to talk to her. What's her name?" Raul asked.

"Ms. Garnet. May I ask your name?"

Raul handed the clerk a Falcon Agency business card.

"Just give this to Ms. Garnet and tell her I would like to meet her away from the lobby."

The clerk read the card. "Mr. Estavam … if you will go to the side door, I'll open it and take you to her office. I sense this is a matter of urgency."

"Very perceptive of you, miss. Thank you."

Raul went to the side office entrance door. The young clerk opened the locked door and led Raul to Ms. Garnet's office. Raul waited in the hall while the clerk announced the guest.

He didn't have to wait very long and the clerk ushered Raul into an average size office. She politely introduced Raul to Ms. Garnet and left the office.

Raul estimated Ms. Garnet to be in her early forties and was very attractive. She had black hair with deep green eyes. Dressed in a white pant suit, she presented a professional aura and it was obvious she took her position seriously. There was an air about her that was very pleasant. She didn't have the presence of having an over-inflated ego that many executives display.

"How may I help you, Mr. Estavam?"

"Well, the first thing is to please call me Raul. The next thing is we have a serious situation here at the hotel."

Raul explained the situation quickly, giving out only details that affected the hotel's safety.

"We're going to raid his room and it could be dangerous."

"I was at the front desk when Mr. Cormier registered. He looked very familiar. I've seen him here in Tampa before, but I don't recall where. I do know it wasn't here at this hotel, but I've met him before."

"Think about it. Anything will help. In the meantime, I would like your security force to make sure that no one goes to the fifteenth floor. I don't want anybody informed what is going on. We don't need a panic situation.

My men will secure the fifteenth floor and what I need right now is to know how many guests and what rooms they are in on that floor."

"I'm Pauline by the way," she answered as she turned to her desktop computer. She typed in a brief amount of words and the fifteenth floor guest list appeared on the screen.

"There are only two rooms that have registered guests. Room 1525 is a suite where Mr. Cormier is and, down at the other end of the floor, are Mr. and Mrs. Horning in room

1502. I know the Hornings are not in the room because our concierge booked a charter fishing trip for them. The boat left this morning and it's an all-day affair. They won't arrive back until eight o'clock."

"Would you double check. Can you call their room just to make sure?"

Pauline dialed room 1502 and let the phone ring.

"No answer."

"Okay. Please call the concierge and check with him."

She did as Raul asked and the concierge confirmed that Mr. and Mrs. Horning did leave for the fishing trip at 9 a.m.

"Thank you. I have six men outside and another one is seated in the lobby. We're going to take an elevator up and then shut it off. Once your security personnel see that we are on the fifteenth floor, would you please have them shut down the remaining elevators?"

"I'll personally handle the security team, Raul. I don't want any screw-ups."

"Thanks, Pauline. I really appreciate it. Okay, let's go. Oh, one more thing. I don't want the local authorities notified of what is happening here. This is a Federal matter. They'll only get in the way."

"That's no problem. I understand. My father retired from the FBI six years ago. He wanted me to go into that field. I like what I'm doing now but I do understand your procedures."

"Thanks, Pauline. We've got to go."

Both Raul and Pauline left her office and Raul went outside and briefed the team. He already knew what room Cormier was in when he talked to Pauline but didn't let her know. At this moment, two agents were in the stairway exits on the fifteenth floor. Raul called them on the secure two way radio and briefed them on what was about to happen..

After asking if there were any questions, they set out to capture the sniper, aka Jacque Cormier.

Raul and the remaining three members entered the lobby together. He stopped to give brief orders to the agent seated in the lobby and then continued to the elevators. Pauline was there waiting with a tall man dressed in a business suit and briefly acknowledged Raul as he walked by.

"Good," Raul said to himself. The security chief wasn't in a uniform. Uniformed people always made others nervous, especially in places like upscale hotel lobbies.

The four agents entered the elevator and removed their pistols from their holsters on the ride up. When the doors would open on the fifteenth floor, they would consider the area hostile territory, and wanted to be prepared to counter any surprise that may await them.

Raul watched as the floor indicator counted up. An agent opened the control panel and identified the shut-off switch. If they were to deactivate the elevator by pulling the emergency stop button, an alarm would sound. That was the last thing they needed to happen.

The elevator stopped at the fifteenth floor. As soon as the doors slid open, the agent turned off the elevator switch. The doors locked in the open position and Raul casually walked out as if he were a guest. As most guests do when they arrive at a strange place, he looked for signs indicating where his room was. At the same time he was really looking to see if anyone was in the hallway. There wasn't anyone.

Agents positioned at each exit stairway opened the doors, revealing themselves to Raul. Each gave the thumbs up sign, signifying all was in order. Raul then pointed his Beretta down the hall toward room 1525. He led the way with two agents following him two steps back and on each side of the AIC, Raul. The hallway was wide and carpeted with bright red, heavily padded carpeting. There were Victorian chairs with matching red velvet cloth padding on the seats, spaced evenly along the walls with pictures of castles hanging opposite of the chairs at eye level. The fourth agent remained at the elevators in case someone happened to be on an elevator that wasn't deactivated.

Room 1525 had a double door entry, typical of suites. When Raul passed Pauline in the elevator lobby, she had inconspicuously handed him the room key card as he passed by. Two agents positioned themselves on each side of the suite's door as Raul put his ear to the door, listening for any signs of sounds inside. He didn't hear anything but soft music.

Slowly, he inserted the card half-way into the key slot. He turned and looked at each agent, who nodded their heads in the affirmative. They were ready. Raul's left hand pushed the card all the way into the slot. With his right hand holding the Beretta on the L-shaped door handle, he pushed down and in on the handle when the two green LED indicator lights illuminated. There was no click when the lights lit up. When he pushed the handle down, the door opened easily. The soft music he heard through the door became louder, but the volume was low.

Raul stepped into the doorway with his Beretta in the firing position. His SEAL military training was still intact and all of his senses were at their peak. He took two more steps into the room on the heavily-padded, plush carpeting. There was no sound of activity and he continued down the short hallway. Reaching the corner of a spacious living room, decorated with expensive furniture and fixture amenities, he searched the room with his eyes. There wasn't anyone present and he briefly saw the view of the ocean out the window that stretched from floor to ceiling and wall to wall. This was definitely an expensive suite.

Off to his left Raul noticed a door that was half opened and assumed it must be the bedroom suite. There were no other door openings on the other walls. He moved stealth-like in the direction of the bedroom doorway, followed ten feet behind by the other two agents. Upon reaching the doorway, he stopped and put his back to the wall. The other two agents spread wider apart, with their revolvers at the firing ready position.

Raul took a deep breath and listened for any movement in the room. Not hearing a sound, he peaked his head into the door opening. Laying on the king-size bed was a man dressed with his shoes off. He was sleeping and Raul saw that there was a pistol on the end table. The sleeping man was in the middle of the bed. If he were to awake, he would have to scramble across the bed to get the weapon. It was to Raul's advantage. Before any unforeseen noise would wake up the sleeping man, Raul moved cautiously at first into the bedroom pointing his 9mm pistol at the reclined individual. One move on the man's part would force Raul to fire a warning shot.

Once Raul had disappeared into the bedroom, the other two agents moved to the doorway and covered Raul's back. One entered the bedroom while the other kept post outside. Raul quietly moved to the side of the bed where the pistol was, picked it up and stuck it into his pants waistband. Seeing that the agent had his pistol pointing at the sleeping sniper, Raul screamed at the sleeping man.

"WAKE UP, YOU ASSHOLE!"

Jacque Cormier jumped out of his deep sleep and sat up in the bed. He began to make a move toward the end table.

Raul yelled. "Make one more move and you'll have two bullets in your head."

Not saying a word, Cormier stopped moving immediately. There would be no sense to try to counterattack the intruders. It would mean certain death.

"Now raise your arms and put your hands on your head ... slowly!" Raul ordered and Cormier obeyed.

When the sniper's fingers were interlocked on his head, Raul ordered him to slide forward to the foot of the bed. Both Raul and the agent had their weapons trained on the sniper. When Cormier reached the foot of the bed and his legs were hanging over the side, Raul ordered him to lie face down on the floor, spread his legs wide and put his arms behind his back. Cormier followed the orders and, when he was in the ordered position, the agent cuffed both of Cormier's wrists and then both ankles. Once restrained, the agent pulled the sniper to his feet, dragged him to a chair and pushed him into the seat.

"Who the fuck are you?" Cormier asked in an accent.

Raul recognized it as Middle Eastern. "We're Federal agents and, as of right now, you are under arrest. Now, shut up and don't speak unless we ask you to. Understand?"

"Yes."

"That's the last word I want to hear out of you," Raul answered and walked out of the room to where the agent was in the living room.

"Let the others know it's secure. Then call down to the front desk and have the clerk let the General Manager Ms. Garnet know that Raul said everything is okay."

The agent left the suite and within seconds two more agents entered the room. One remained posted at the suite's entrance.

"Toss this room, but don't break anything. Look for all his personal belongings and weapons," Raul ordered and went to where Jacque Cormier was seated.

"You get his wallet?" Raul asked the agent standing guard over the sniper.

"It's on the bed with the rest of his stuff I found in his pockets. There were no other weapons."

Raul went over to the bed and began rifling through the wallet and other material found on Cormier, examining each piece carefully. As he was looking over the evidence, the other agents were going through the closets. Four Armani suits were thrown on the bed along with expensive, silk shirts and ties.

Another agent pulled two suitcases out of another closet and put them on the bed. He opened one and looked at Raul who was busy reviewing a set of documents.

"Raul. You better look at this," the agent said.

Raul walked around to the other side of the bed. Inside the suitcase was the body of a rifle and four rifle barrels. He recognized the rifle as being a Heckler & Koch HK PSG1 rifle with a permanently-mounted Hensoldt 6 x 42 scope.

"Houston, we have a winner," Raul said out loud. "The target range is now closed."

"Who are you fuckers? I want my lawyer! I'm a diplomat and I have credentials to prove it."

"I warned you not to talk. Gag the asshole," Raul ordered the agent guarding Cormier.

The agent ripped off a long strip of duct tape and wrapped it around the sniper's head, covering his mouth but not his nose.

"Try anything else and I'll have him cover your nose. Then you'll have to breathe out of your ass," Raul said with a mean look on his face.

Raul then stepped out into the living room and called Merlin.

"This is Merlin," the Wizard answered.

"Wiz, Raul. We got Cormier."

"Everyone okay?"

"It went down easy. No resistance. He was sound asleep in his suite. No shots fired."

"Damn. Good job, Raul."

"Thanks. We also got the body of a Heckler & Koch HK PSG1 rifle, four interchangeable rifle barrels and a bunch of firing pins and 7.62mm ammo. We hit the jackpot. Where are you now?"

"I just landed at Andrews and I'm on my way to the office. Have you gone through everything in the room yet? Any idea who Cormier really is?"

"Not yet. Listen. The general manager of the hotel was really cooperative and it's a ritzy place. I'm going to have the agents pack up everything and seal off the room. Finger printing is on its way here now. I'm going to take two agents and Cormier and fly back to DC. I'll bring everything we find here in his room with me. I'll go through everything on the flight back. Is that okay with you?"

"You're in charge of that end. Do whatever you think is right. Call me if you find anything leading to the other two snipers. They are still on the loose. We think that Monique Leclair might have a clone, look-a-alike or twin sister. We need anything that might lead us to where they might be."

"Okay. I figure we'll be leaving here within the hour. I'll call you from the plane."

"Good job, Raul. Awesome," Merlin answered.

"Thanks, Wiz. Has anyone heard from Daniel?"

"No. I'm sure we will soon. Got to go." The phone connection went dead.

Raul gave the orders to pack up everything and put the senior agent in charge.

"I'm going downstairs for a minute. You can reach me on my cell phone. I shouldn't be gone long."

Raul left the suite and rode the same elevator they took up to the fifteenth floor, down to the lobby.

He walked up to the reception desk and saw Pauline Garnet behind the counter. Seeing Raul, she pointed to the side entrance door and let him in.

"We better talk in my office," she said and led the way.

"I'll make this quick, Pauline. We have Jacque Cormier up in the room and we'll be leaving soon. I don't want to leave through the lobby. Will the service elevator take us to the rear of the building?"

"Yes. The dock is on the north side of the building. I'll have the security manager make sure the area is clear. Thanks for not raising a ruckus. Everything is normal in the hotel and no one suspects anything happened. I really appreciate it, Raul."

"You're welcome. We try to save all the dramatic cop stuff for the movies," Raul answered with a smile.

Pauline returned the smile. "I remembered where I've seen Jacque Cormier before. The hotel is a member of the Tampa area Chamber of Commerce and I've seen him there at meetings. I think he has some type of business here. I haven't had the chance to look through the membership log or call the Chamber yet."

"Would you recognize his real name or company if you saw it in the log?"

"I think so. I'm the VP of the Chamber and know most of the members. I haven't seen Cormier, or whatever his name is, at meetings the past two or three months. He just joined recently, like in the past six months. Hold on a minute. I've got a membership register in my desk."

Pauline went to her executive mahogany-stained desk and looked in a file drawer. She was excited to help.

"Here it is. Let's see now," she said while beginning to scan the multi-page roster. Her finger moved down the page and then she flipped to the next.

"Damn, I know it should be here," she said in a frustrated tone of voice.

The Chamber's roster was quite lengthy and Pauline continued running her finger down page after page.

"Here, wouldn't you know it. It's almost the last member. Here, look," she said to Raul who was beside her desk.

Raul moved behind Pauline and looked where her finger was pointed.

"This is the name of the company and the owner. Zuckowi International Consultants. President/Owner ... M. Said Zuckowi. This is the guy," Pauline said smiling while looking up at Raul.

Raul's heart skipped a beat. Not from the Zuckowi information, but the beautiful, radiant face that was looking up at him. Their eyes connected and held each other's gaze for a few seconds. He blushed and moved away.

"Can I have that book?" Raul asked, still looking at the beaming lady.

Pauline also had blushed and seemed embarrassed while she smiled. Her heart had also skipped a beat.

"Sure. Here take it with you," she answered, and stood up handing the book to the tall, handsome man.

Raul felt a little uncomfortable in the situation and knew it was time to go.

"Thanks a bunch, Pauline. We'll be down at the loading dock within fifteen minutes. I'm going to leave some men up in Zuckowi's or Cormier's suite. They need to fingerprint the area and do all that cop stuff.

I'll have the AIC ... err sorry ... the Agent in Charge stay in contact with you and keep you updated. There wasn't any damage done to the room and all you'll probably have to do is get housekeeping to clean up after they leave."

Raul was still uncomfortable and wanted to escape from Pauline's beauty.

"Okay, thanks. One more thing, Raul. Are you married or attached? I'm sorry to be so forward but I need to ask because I'm afraid that when you leave, I'll never see you again."

"Yes, I'm married and have been for nine years. I have a son also," Raul answered.

"Too bad. The good ones are always latched on to. It would have been nice to have met you ten years ago. Who knows?

Anyway, here's my card. If you ever get down this way, give me a call. I'm divorced and have no children other than this hotel," she said laughing.

"I'll do that. It was a pleasure and thanks again." Raul shook her hand and was tempted to kiss her, but didn't.

Pauline held onto Raul's hand with both of hers. Not speaking a word to each other, she led him to the lobby. As Raul was walking away, he glanced once more toward Pauline's direction. She was standing in the open doorway, smiled and waved goodbye. Raul waved back.

As he made his way to the elevators, he whispered to himself, "If only ..."

Pauline was one of two women that had ever affected him in that manner. The other was his beautiful spouse, Rebecca.

The team transferred Zuckowi to the airport along with all data and information gathered at the hotel room. Raul didn't let Zuckowi know that he knew his real identity. As the sniper was loaded onto the government jet, Raul walked away from the aircraft and called Merlin.

"Merlin here," the Wiz answered.

"Wiz, Raul. I think I've got Jacque Cormier's real name. You ready to write this down?"

"Yeah. Shoot," Merlin answered.

"His name is M. Said Zuckowi and he is the President/Owner of a company called Zuckowi International Consultants, based out of Tampa. Here is the address."

Merlin wrote everything down. "Good. I'll get our people on it. I'll have them run an international check also. It shouldn't take long to verify it. I'll call you when I have anything to report."

"That's okay. I'll be busy going through everything we are bringing back on the plane," Raul answered.

"Have you interrogated him yet?" Wiz asked.

"Not yet. I figured I'd wait until we get in DC. He has no idea that I know who he really is. I figure that gives us a big edge and we'll let him keep thinking differently."

"How did you find out his name?" Merlin asked.

"The general manager of the hotel recognized him. She's the VP of Tampa's Chamber of Commerce and remembered seeing him at meetings. I'll explain it all when I get back. Right now the pilots are starting the engines."

"Okay. Have a safe flight back. Have the pilots call Kathy and give her your ETA to Andrews. We'll have a team waiting to pick you up. I want him taken to a safe house in Maryland. You know where I'm talking about?"

"Yeah. I got it. Got to go. I'll call you later." Raul disconnected the call and boarded the jet.

On the trip to DC, Raul examined everything confiscated at the hotel, including Zuckowi's cell phone. There was only one number in the call log and it was from the hotel that Monique Leclair stayed at in San Francisco. He would have to obtain the call log from the cellular provider. There were no stored telephone numbers in the directory. He called Kathy at headquarters and left her the details regarding the cell phone. She would have the phone logs ready when Raul arrived.

On the plane, Raul and the other two agents created a detailed list of everything confiscated. Raul decided to re-examine Zuckowi's wallet. He removed all the receipts, credit cards, cash and business cards. The wallet was empty and he looked for any hidden compartments. Stuck behind a leather flap he found a piece of paper folded up. He removed it and unfolded the paper, laying it on the small table he was at. It was a telephone number beginning with the 202 area code, Washington, DC's area code. Raul called Merlin immediately. When Wiz answered, Raul asked him to trace the number.

"This might be the lead we needed, Raul. The arrangements for transportation to the safe- house are in place. When you land, you'll be taken there along with Zuckowi and the other two agents on board. I've called Xi in and we'll be there also, along with Pat Scott, Dan Aibaya and two other agents.

Xi and Dan are good with interrogations. I'll let them handle that end."

"Okay. Have you heard from Daniel yet?" Raul asked.

"Not a word," Merlin answered. "It's giving me an eerie feeling. It is so unlike Daniel."

"I feel the same way. It's a good thing we know him well. I trust whatever he's doing."

"I'm beginning to wonder how well we do know him. But, like you … I trust him and would never question his actions. I'm going to hang up now and track this telephone number down. I'll call you if I get an answer before you land at Andrews. Otherwise, I'll see you at the safe-house."

"Okay buddy. Later." Raul disconnected the call.

Chapter XXI

Danger in the East

*D*aniel *spent the rest of the day thinking about the "page 31"* message he'd received. Armando had a book shelf in the cabin stacked with various genre novels. He looked through the library and saw two Bibles, the Old and New Testaments. He removed both from the shelf and sat in front of the fireplace.

"Maybe, if it's spiritual, the answer might be in the Bible," he thought.

He started with the Old Testament and went to the obvious "page 31". It was the book of Genesis. He read page 30 through 32 and didn't find anything that would give a hint or meaning to the "page 31" message.

"Maybe it is passage 31," he whispered.

He read passage 31 and still didn't see any correlation. Daniel spent the next two hours looking for various angles of "page 31". He read passages, lines, page 31 in each section. Needing a break to clear his mind, he decided to make a great meal and relax.

Early in the morning he took out a frozen rib-eye steak to thaw out. He seasoned it and cooked it over the blazing fire in the living room. Daniel would have preferred fresh, but he prepared a couple of side dishes of canned vegetables and inhaled the meal. He realized it was now a little after nine in the evening as he finished cleaning up the dishes and kitchen. After adding a couple of big logs to the fire, he grabbed the New Testament Bible and went to the bedroom. Lying comfortably on the down-filled mattress and under the quilt, he began his search for the answer to "page 31". In less than a half-hour, Daniel slowly closed his cobalt blue eyes and fell into a deep comatose sleep. It had been a busy day with many thrilling experiences. Rest was a welcomed reward.

He awoke in the morning not knowing or caring what time it was. That was the advantage of being in solitude. Time was not a relevant factor at this moment. Daniel lay in bed on his back and stared up at the ceiling. He began to concentrate on relaxing each muscle in his body and clearing his mind of all thoughts. Within a few seconds, inner peace entered his soul and he slid into deep meditation.

"Good morning, Daniel," a voice he had never heard said.

Daniel answered mentally while smiling, "Good morning."

"You're not going to ask who this is?"

"Does it matter?" he asked, not answering the question. "You are my inner spirit, my soul and God within me speaking."

"Xi has educated you well, Daniel. You are correct in your answer. Now, please listen closely. There is danger near your home in Washington, DC. You must return soon. Others … those close to you … loved ones, need your guidance and help.

It will take the powers of both you and Xi to bring safety to all those around you. Many are in danger. Scorpio must be stopped. Otherwise, your world will be destroyed. Scorpio is planning to strike a vicious blow that, if successful, will kill more than those who perished on September 11th. The answer to your question is "page 31". You must go soon, Daniel."

In his deep mental regression, Daniel answered. "I will go now. In what book do I look for "page 31", Lord?"

"Seek and ye shall find. Now, prepare to return," the soft voice whispered.

Daniel didn't answer, knowing the message had ended. He opened his eyes and stared again at the beamed ceiling. He must return. Rising from the warmth of the bed, he got dressed and went to the living room area. The blazing fire from the previous evening in the fireplace had died down to smoldering cinders. He put a log on the cinders and stoked the hot charcoals. When he was satisfied that the log had caught fire, Daniel went to the kitchen and washed with the cold water from the bucket. The nectar from the river refreshed his facial nerve endings and he felt invigorated.

It dawned on him that there was a blizzard the previous day and evening. He walked to the cabin's door and removed the steel locking bars. As he opened the door, bright shards of sunlight entered the doorway. He pulled the door all the way open and looked outside. A three-foot white, powdery snowdrift had piled up in front of the exit and looking past it, Daniel saw more drifts as far as he could see. The bright sunlight reflecting off the snow created a blinding effect, forcing him to squint his eyes.

"This is going to be one hell of a hike back," he said out loud while he closed the door.

Returning to the kitchen, he prepared a hearty breakfast. It would be a long trip back and he knew he would need all the strength he could muster. As he was eating, he saw the HF radio on a small table in the corner of the eating area. It was his only means of communication with Armando.

Daniel picked up his plate and walked over to the radio, located the power switch and turned it on. A red light indicating the radio was receiving power, illuminated. Daniel smiled as he saw a list of radio frequencies taped to the wall above the receiver. He scanned down the list and saw the frequency for Armando's receiver and dialed it in.

"Armando, this is Daniel. Come in," he said into the microphone.

"Armando … Sara, this is Daniel. Do you read?"

The radio's speakers crackled with airwave static. Daniel waited a few seconds and repeated his call.

"Daniel, this is Armando. How do you read?"

"Hey, buddy. Got you five by five. How about me?"

Relieved with making contact with the outside world, Daniel responded. "Got you five by five also, Armando."

"We were worried about you, Daniel. You okay?" Armando inquired.

"I'm fine. There was one hell of a snowstorm up here yesterday and last night. Got about three feet of snow."

"Same down here. The drifts are about three to four feet deep."

"I've got to get back to Washington, Armando. I'm going to leave here in about an hour … around seven or so," Daniel said while looking at his watch.

"Daniel, it's going to be one hell of a trip … a lot more time than the hike up because of the drifts."

"I realize that. Is there anyway that you can get a chopper up here to pick me up?"

There was a long pause before Armando answered.

"Daniel … I can get a chopper with no problems but it won't be able to land near the cabin. The LZ is too dangerous even when the weather is good and no snow on the ground. There is too much of a chance of white-out conditions when the rotor wash kicks up the snow."

"Hmmm … How about that large clearing about two to three miles downstream of the cabin?"

"Hold on. Let me get a map," Armando answered.

There was nothing but quiet for about forty-five seconds and then Armando broke the silence.

"Okay, Daniel. Do you have the map I gave you?"

"I'm looking at it right now."

"Good. See where the river bends sharply to the east about two miles south of the cabin?" Armando asked.

Daniel followed his finger as it traced the river south and he saw where the blue line turned sharply east.

"I got it, Armando."

"Okay. There is a wide clearing there and the trees around it were burned in a forest fire a long time ago. You'll recognize it when you get there. That's the closest safe area for the chopper to land.

I figure it will take every bit of three hours for you to make it to that LZ. If you leave at seven, that will put you there between ten and ten-thirty. I'll have the chopper plan its ETA for that time slot."

"Sounds good, Armando. I also need to charter a jet out of Kalispell for the flight to DC. Can you make the arrangements?"

"No problem. What do you want?"

"The fastest SOB available," Daniel answered laughing.

"That would be the G-IV," Armando answered referring to an executive Gulfstream IV jet that was usually available for charter at Kalispell airport. Top end airspeed is 459 knots or 528 mph.

"That will work just fine. Sorry to put you through this," Daniel answered apologetically.

"Hey, partner, I know the drill and it's no problem. You better get going and I'll tell the chopper pilot to take you straight to the airport from the LZ.

A couple of other things, Daniel. In the storage area near the kitchen is a backpack with survival gear in it. There are a couple of two-way radios and there are fresh batteries in the right hand top drawer of the desk where you are sitting. Dial in channel eight on the hand-held radio. That will be the channel the chopper will be on. Channel 10 will get us here at the house, but I'll be monitoring both. Better pack a few goodies from the larder just in case. Damn, I sound like a mother hen," Armando said laughing.

Daniel laughed also. "I really appreciate it. I better get going. I'll call you when I get to the airport. Hey, don't let anyone know that I'm on my way back either. I'll have my accountant send you a check when I get back. I don't want the government to pick up this tab. It was my vacation."

"One hell of a vacation, partner. I'll talk to you later. Good luck on the hike and I'll be standing by on the radio."

"I'll call you when I'm leaving the cabin and thanks again, Armando. Daniel out."

"Base out," Armando responded.

Daniel left the radio on and went to pack and straighten out the cabin. He was ready to leave in twenty minutes and called Armando on the HF radio as he was about to leave. He took one more look around the precious retreat, smiled and opened the outside door. The temperature was in the low twenties, possibly the teens, but the sun was shining and there was no sign of foul weather in the skies.

"What a great day for a hike!" Daniel yelled, seeing his warm breath turn into vapor.

He secured the door and began heading south along the river's edge. Traveling along the river was easier than he had expected. The snow was only two feet deep. Occasionally he came upon a drift much deeper, but Daniel kept trudging along at an even pace.

A half mile down the river, he stopped to take a breather. As he was drinking from his water bottle, he saw a large buck and two does on the opposite embankment. He knew they were the same ones he had seen before. Both human and animals stared at each other for a few seconds. The large, brown buck raised its head in the air, sniffing for the human's scent. It must have picked it up and the buck tilted his head sideways and lowered his head as if bowing to the black and white human silhouette across the river.

Smiling, Daniel nodded toward the statuesque creature. Both continued looking at each other in respect, and then the male deer bowed his head once more, turned and walked away. The two does followed the male and Daniel then saw another white tail flash upward from behind a snow drift.

"It must be the yearling," Daniel thought.

"Page 31," were the next words he heard in his mind.

"Page 31," Daniel whispered.

He then rose and continued walking south toward the landing zone. His hearing sharpened as he walked along the flowing river. Small waves made splashing sounds as the flowing mountain waters rebounded off rocks on the river's bottom bed. He heard the sweet sounds of birds off in the distance, sending their songs through the crisp clean air and towering ponderosa pines. Daniel felt inner peace within himself and enjoyed God's gift.

He stopped once more and checked the map. If he had it figured correctly, the LZ was less than a quarter mile away. He looked down river and saw where the flowing waters began to turn toward the east. Then he heard the familiar sound of helicopter rotor blades beating the mountain air. Looking at his watch, he saw it was 10:05. Armando had figured it right. He folded up the map and began to walk briskly to the rendezvous site.

High in the sky, the chopper began its descent to the LZ. Daniel was standing near a tall, blackened pine tree that had been burnt during a forest fire. He looked up at the destroyed tree, seeing the charred branches that once held millions of pine needles that were now just burnt naked appendages.

The chopper was on final descent and its rotor wash began to hit the pure white layer of snow covering the landing zone. Fine particles of snow began to swirl and rise around the aircraft as it lowered closer to the landing area. The chopper continued down to meet the surface and then it disappeared into the rising swirl of white powder. Daniel knew the pilots were now in the dangerous whiteout situation.

As if witnessing a spiritual visual revelation, the helicopter began to reappear through the cloud of snow that began to dissipate. It was the sign that the aircraft had landed and Daniel began to walk toward his rescuer.

He boarded the chopper through the side door and was met by a smiling crew member of the large Bell 214-ST transport. He put his backpacks on the floor and strapped himself in a seat near the doorway. Giving the thumbs-up sign to the crew member, who had closed the sliding door, the helicopter began to rise, sending another whiteout cloud up into the air. Daniel looked out the window and all he saw was a solid wall of pure white. It looked as if he was in a cloud.

Gradually, the cloud got thinner as the aircraft rose higher and then the Montana mountain landscape appeared. Lush, deep-green pine trees were below him and he saw the narrow black river, speckled with white waves snaking through the forest. As the aircraft began to turn toward the airport, he closed his eyes and listened to the humming of the turbine engines.

"Page 31," were the words he heard above the whining sounds of the jet's turbine engines.

Daniel called Armando from the chopper via the two-way survival radio to let him know he was on his way to Glacier

Park International Airport in Kalispell. He thanked his friend again. When the helicopter landed, the corporate Gulfstream IV was standing by on the tarmac, waiting for the unnamed VIP passenger.

Daniel walked to the large white jet and was greeted by the captain.

"Good morning, sir. I'm Captain Walker T. Williams."

"Good morning, Walker. I'm Daniel. Please file your flight plan to Andrews Air Force Base in Washington, DC."

"Ah … sir, that is a restricted airport and …"

"I'm very familiar with what you are saying, Walker. You will have clearance to land at Andrews. Use the call sign, Falcon Zero Four. Everything will be all right and you'll receive clearance to land. Once we're on the ground, keep the engines running and take off immediately after I get off. Are the fuel tanks topped off?"

"Yes, sir."

"Good. The G-IV's range is 4,900 statue miles so you will have enough to make it to Andrews and reserve to fly wherever you want to refuel for your return trip. Let's get going, Captain Walker T. Williams. And one more thing, call me Daniel, not sir," Daniel said with a wide grin.

The captain knew he didn't just meet a typical VIP. This Daniel knew what he was talking about. They boarded the jet and took off on the flight to the east coast.

After the jet was airborne, Daniel removed a file from his backpack. Stamped on the cover in capitalized, bold red letters were the words TOP SECRET. Underneath those words were "Scorpio File". Daniel opened the folder and began to read the contents of what the now dead CIA agent Kyle Peterson had compiled. The papers were in random order and he first looked to see if any pages were marked with the number "31". There weren't any and he then began reading each page slowly, searching for any clues or information that might disclose the identity of Scorpio.

For the next three hours and ten minutes, he studied the file's contents. Engrossed and totally focused, he was disturbed by the co-pilot.

"Excuse me, Daniel. We're on final approach to Andrews Air Force base. We'll be on the ground in about four minutes."

"Oh … thanks," Daniel answered and put the classified file away. He smiled to himself as he looked out the jet's window and smiled again when he saw Washington, DC's, skyline. The smile wasn't only from knowing that he was almost home, but he had discovered a pertinent piece to the Scorpio puzzle.

The jet landed and was met by a security truck on the taxi-way. The "Follow-Me" vehicle led the sleek aircraft to the VIP terminal and stopped directly in front of the facilities. The co-pilot opened the door and Daniel thanked the crew and exited the jet, whose engines were still running. As soon as Daniel stepped off the stairway, the co-pilot closed the door. Daniel entered the VIP lounge area and glanced over his shoulder when he heard the G-IV's engines throttle up. It was taxiing for take-off.

"Page 31," the bearded handsome man, dressed in blue-jeans and hiking boots, said to himself as he walked toward the VIP counter.

"I'm Daniel White, the Director of Falcon Agency. I need a ride to my office please," Daniel said to the uniformed Air Force officer.

"I almost didn't recognize you, sir. Looks like you been on a camping trip. I hope you enjoyed yourself, sir," the Lieutenant said smiling.

"I had a great time, Lieutenant … a great spiritual time," Daniel answered with a wide grin.

Chapter XXII

Director Returns

It was mid-afternoon when Daniel walked into Falcon's headquarters. He was still dressed in his Montana attire and hadn't shaved in four days. He was rough-looking, but in a handsome way. The Secret Service guards at the entrance recognized the director and were a little shocked at his appearance. Daniel acknowledged them as he presented his credentials with a big smile.

As he always did, instead of taking the elevator up to the executive office second floor, he walked up the stairs. Entering the reception area, Daniel noticed that it was quiet as usual. Used to seeing well-dressed individuals enter the area, the receptionist looked up and saw a rough-looking mountain man walking toward her. She wasn't sure at first who it was and then realized it was the Falcon Agency Director.

"Good afternoon, Sheila. How are you?" Daniel asked.

"Good ... good afternoon, Daniel," she answered in a shaky voice and smiling.

"Where is everybody?"

"They're in the large conference room right now. Merlin is having a meeting with Raul, Xi, two of our agents, Dan Aibaya and Pat Scott, Kathy, Director Angus, Director Lambert and the directors of Homeland Security and the Secret Service."

"If I walk in, do you think I'll scare the hell out of them?" Daniel asked laughing.

"I think they will be very happy to see you, Daniel. We've missed you," Sheila answered blushing.

"Well, I guess I'll go spook the spooks."

He walked down the hall to the large conference room whose door was closed. Without knocking, Daniel opened the door. Everyone turned their heads toward the doorway and saw Daniel with a backpack slung over his shoulder.

"Holy shit," Merlin said first. "Heeee's back."

Everyone stood up to welcome their friend and director's return.

"Damn, Daniel. You look like Grizzly Adams," Merlin laughed as he shook Daniel's hand and then gave him a big strong hug.

Everyone had smiles on their faces. Daniel greeted, shook hands and hugged everyone. He too, had missed them. Xi, as usual, was the last to greet his spiritual friend.

As they hugged, Xi whispered to Daniel, "Welcome back, Master Daniel."

Daniel whispered back, "Thank you, Master Xi."

No one else heard the exchange of special words.

"I'm NOT sorry I interrupted … gang. I'm not going to say anything about where I was … so please, don't ask. We've got a lot to do. How about everyone having a seat and bring me up to date on what's happened while I was gone," Daniel said, knowing they had to get down to business.

Everyone took their seats and Merlin, still with a big smile on his face, began the briefing.

"Raul got one of the snipers who was down in Tampa. I think he should start," Merlin said and nodded toward Raul.

The tall, handsome hispanic man, Deputy Director of Legal Affairs, Raul Estavam stood up and explained the capture of M. Said Zuckowi, aka Jacque Cormier.

After explaining the capture, Daniel asked where Zuckowi was.

"Right now, we've got him at the Maryland safe-house. Bill has some of his agents interrogating him. I already interrogated him after we brought him there.

We got the international intelligence report already. He was born in Jeddah, Saudi Arabia, and, low and behold, he was friends of guess who as a kid? Usamah bin Laden. They grew up together and Zuckowi also comes from a wealthy family. We traced him to Pakistan and he fought for the Mujahideen in Afghanistan against the Soviet Union's campaign. There is a space gap of five years where we don't know what he did.

In 1994 his wife and a son were killed in a shoot-out with American forces in Somalia. He and his two daughters escaped Somalia and went to France for two months. Then, they immigrated to Canada in late 1994.

The two daughters were married to Saudis and their husbands went to Afghanistan. We do know that they were being trained in one of bin Laden's training camps. After 9-11, when the United States attacked Afghanistan, both husbands were killed by our ground troops. Positive ID was made on both of them by military intelligence.

Funny thing on this matter. Both were killed in a cave complex in the Tora Bora Mountains. It seems that it was the same complex Falcon attacked on our last mission there. As Daniel would say, "What a co-wink-a-dink"."

Everyone laughed.

"As far as the two daughters are concerned, the last place they were known to be was in Montreal, Canada."

"Do you have their names?" Daniel asked.

"Only their Arabic names. One is Azzah, which means young female gazelle in English and the other is Atiya which means gift. Both had the last name Zuckowi."

"What about the sister, Raul?" Daniel asked.

"We don't have anything else on her. I would imagine she changed her name also. We've checked and nothing has come up."

"Does Zuckowi know that we know he has two daughters?" Daniel queried.

"We didn't say a word about them. It gives him a false sense of security that he has a secret that we don't know. Kind of sets him up for later," Raul answered.

"You said that both sisters were married. Any kids?" Daniel asked.

"None that we know of."

"Okay, what else do you have?"

Raul nodded to Merlin, which was his way of indicating he was done speaking and turning the floor over to the Wiz.

"I traced a phone number that Raul found in Zuckowi's wallet. The number is registered to Senator Nigel Mason from Indiana and the residence is an expensive townhouse in Georgetown," Merlin said.

"Wait a minute, Wiz," Daniel interrupted. "The Georgetown, Maryland?"

"Yep, the one right up the road."

"Sorry, continue."

"I sent a team up there to check it out. It's a small community and the Senator does live there. It's one of the homes he owns. He has one here in the DC area plus one in Indianapolis.

I also got a bio on him. He's been married for nineteen years, three kids and seems clean. No record other than minor traffic tickets. This is his second term as a senator. He also had three previous terms as a congressman. I don't see anything unusual."

"He actually lives … stays in this place?" Daniel asked.

"When he's here in DC, he does. He's here in town. You want us to pick him up?" Merlin asked.

"Shit no. Knowing these senators and congressmen, you pick them up and the news media starts going bonkers. We don't need that right now. Why would a sniper have a seasoned senator's telephone number? Put a tail on him and his house 24-7. Let's see if there is any unusual activity."

"Dan. You handle that please," Merlin said to Agent Aibaya.

"Done deal, Wiz," Aibaya answered.

Hearing Dan's response made Daniel smile. It was obvious that while he was away, Merlin and Dan had bonded. The Wizard let's only close friends call him Wiz or Wizard.

The rest of those present each took their turn explaining what they knew, with the exception of Xi. When it was Xi's turn to speak, he passed.

"Well, looks like we have our hands full," Daniel said as he stood up and took control of the meeting.

"While I was away, I kept getting the message that the answer is on "page 31". Now, I have no idea in what book, magazine, newspaper or whatever this "page 31" pertains. I started to search in the Old Testament of the Bible, but I didn't finish. There wasn't anything on "page 31".

The next thing I need done is to have a combination effort, from all agencies, to find out where this "page 31" is. It sounds like a bitch of a job, but the answer lies there. Kathy, will you coordinate that?" Daniel asked his operations coordinator.

"Sure. I'll assign different agencies to different media areas so they're not overlapping," she answered.

"There haven't been anymore shootings since a day ago. We have one sniper and the other two are dug in or maybe it's three dug in. I don't feel that Scorpio is a sniper. I think

Scorpio has another mission and doesn't want to jeopardize being caught. It has to do with QD-9 and I think Scorpio is the one who will actually use the chemical in a suicide attack.

Now with the new turn of events of the senator's telephone number, the attack may happen here in DC. I said may. So let's not just focus on DC.

Okay, good job people. If no one else has anything to add, I'm going to head home and scare the hell out of my wife and kids," Daniel said smiling.

Everyone stood up and Daniel added one more thing. "Kathy, Raul Wiz and Xi, please stick around."

It was Daniel's way of telling the others to leave quickly. Welcome back gestures were given to Daniel as the others left the conference room. When all but the invited were remaining in the room, Daniel closed the door.

"Please sit down for a minute. Thanks and good job. This place operates great without me. I should take more vacations," he said laughing.

"Bull shit. It runs better when you're here," the Wiz answered also laughing.

"Thanks. I noticed that Dan calls you the Wiz now. You've let him enter your inner sanctum I see."

"The guy is very good, Daniel. We need another twenty like him," Merlin answered.

"How was Dan, Raul?"

"He was awesome also, Daniel. So we only need nineteen more," Raul answered which brought more laughter.

"Glad to hear that. Now let's get serious. Kathy, get the research project going and it is your number one priority. If you need any help, grab whoever you want. The answer to this whole puzzle is somewhere on "page 31". If you have any problems, let me know. You can get started now and thanks, Kathy."

The Operations Coordinator left the room and it was the four combat veterans of Falcon Agency remaining.

"Well, guys, I wanted to explain my absence to you. I had to get away and meditate and get in touch with my mind, body and soul. The timing was good and I learned a lot.

On my way back here I read the Scorpio file and found two links that we may have overlooked. The first one is, I think Peterson knew that the two sniper women were sisters and possibly twins. Twice in the file the word Gemini was written in the margins. Gemini ... twins. It's kind of funny how this is turning into a zodiac puzzle.

The next thing is this. I believe Scorpio is young. I have no idea whether it's a he or she but I'm convinced that whoever it is ... is young, like twenties or early thirties."

"What makes you think that?" Raul asked.

"It falls into a pattern I saw while I was away. A couple of times I saw a large buck and two does in the mountains where I was. I saw them three times. They weren't scared of me either. It seemed like the buck was sending me a message and I've interpreted it to be the three snipers, one male and two females."

Daniel had their undivided attention. They knew Daniel and Xi's spiritual guidance and visions were very important.

"The unusual thing about this happening is each time the deer appeared, there was always a yearling hiding close by and I would see it for only a fleeting moment when the buck and does walked away.

I now know it was another message. We know who the snipers are and the yearling is Scorpio. I never could see the yearling good enough to determine its sex. It was always just a brief glance.

That told me another thing. Scorpio is skittish, maybe unsure due to its age and immaturity and stays close to the snipers, the female snipers."

"That's why you asked if either woman had kids," Merlin said.

"That's right. There is a tie-in between one of the women and a young person. Now, I'm not sure how Senator Nigel Mason fits into the picture. Anyone have any ideas?" Daniel asked the group of close friends.

The room remained quiet while everyone searched for the answer. After a long period of silence, Xi spoke softly.

"Maybe senator not part of picture. Only thing is telephone number. Maybe telephone number code for other number. Maybe accident that code is same as senator number."

Everyone seriously thought about Xi's statement.

"Well, let's think about it tonight. I want to go home and see the family," Daniel said. "Do you want a ride to the house, Xi?"

"Okay. I go home with you, Daniel."

The men all shook hands and left the room. In the lobby Daniel's personal security team was waiting for him. Sheila had notified them that their boss was back in town. One agent took Daniel's backpack and they all left the building.

On the drive to the Naval Observatory, Daniel and Xi were alone in the back seat of the limousine.

"It was quite the trip to Montana, Xi."

"It good you go. Need more teaching on Master. You do very good, Daniel. You think better now."

"I know and it feels great," Daniel answered, leaning back into the seat.

"You need family now. Most important. Bring balance to Daniel," Xi whispered.

"I know that also. I'm a little out of whack now … out of balance. Yes, I do need my family, Xi."

"That good. Xi need balance soon. Must get home to Colorado see family. Also need mountain energy. Soon Xi go home, Daniel." Xi said in a soft spiritual voice.

"I understand, my friend," his close friend answered, knowing the feeling well.

They arrived at the compound and Xi stayed back and let Daniel enter the house alone. He didn't want to spoil or interfere with Daniel's surprise. Daniel entered the foyer and heard Susan talking to the children in another room. He didn't announce his arrival. After putting his backpack down, he walked quietly in the direction of the conversation.

Susan, Lance and Allison were seated in the family room with their backs to the door where Daniel was standing. He stood there leaning against the door jam, admiring and listening to the conversation. Susan was reading a book to them about different types of dogs.

"By the sound of this conversation, it seems like we might be getting a new member to the family," Daniel said, startling them.

All three turned to see who it was and seeing a tall, bearded man with a plaid wool shirt and dark blue, down-filled vest leaning against the doorway with his arms folded, they all jumped up. Even in his unusual rough appearance, they recognized their guardian and ran to him.

Ali's eyes were wide open, filled with joy and excitement.

"Daddy's home," the young lass yelled as she ran to her father.

Daniel scooped up Ali in one arm and Lance in the other. The children hugged and kissed their dad. Daniel felt their sincere love and Susan, watching the children express their affection and devotion to Daniel, smiled as a warm sensation entered her soul. She stayed back a few steps and enjoyed the precious moment.

Daniel lowered the children as they chattered how much they had missed him and battered him with questions.

"My turn," Susan said and walked into Daniel's strong arms.

She pressed her svelte body and firm breasts hard against Daniel's strong torso, wrapping her arms around his neck tightly as he encircled Susan's thin body with his powerful arms. They kissed each other in a tender way and stayed joined in their embrace for what may have seemed like an eternity to the children. Both Ali and Lance stared up at their loving parents, knowing that they loved one another with undying devotion.

Susan unlocked her arms from around Daniel's neck and cupped her husband's bearded face with her hands.

"I love you," she said and kissed him again on the lips

Holding each other with arms around their waists, Daniel and Susan walked to the seating area and they all sat down.

"So, what kind of dog are we getting?" Daniel asked his excited children.

"Mommy, show daddy the picture," Ali said.

Susan got the book and gave it to Allison, who put the opened book in her lap.

"This one, daddy. Isn't it neat?" Ali said pointing to a picture of yellow Labrador Retriever.

"Dad, read what it says about them," Lance said.

Daniel read out loud the detailed, descriptive traits of the animal. The children sat back and envisioned the dog. Susan stared at the scene as Daniel read in a quiet voice and smiled.

When Daniel finished, he said, "It seems like this dog is really nice. Maybe we should see if we can find one. But I wonder … who will take care of it?" he asked, teasing the children.

Both answered in unison, "I will!"

"Can both of you take care of it? That's a lot of work, you know."

"I'm sure Allison and I can take care of Charlie," Lance said.

"Charlie? You already have him named? What if we get a girl dog?"

"We call her Charlie, dad. You're so silly," Ali added.

Daniel laughed. "Looks like I walked into that trap," he said looking at Susan.

"That will teach you not to go away for long periods of time. We plot against you when you're gone," she said laughing.

"Okay. Then I guess we better find Charlie and bring him … or her home. How about we look on Saturday."

"Oh, this is so neat," Lance said as Ali clapped her hands with joy.

They talked a few minutes longer and then Daniel went upstairs, showered and shaved. It was good to be home. He felt balance and inner peace begin to return to his mind, body and soul.

Chapter XXIII

Merlin's Message

The following morning, Daniel arrived at Falcon headquarters early. He needed to catch up on some paper work. After an hour at work, Kathy knocked on his office door.

"Good morning, Daniel. Coffee?" she asked, holding a large cup of steaming brew.

"Good morning. Coffee sounds great. How are you?"

"Very well," OPS answered. "I've got the "page 31" project in motion with all the agencies. No results yet. It's too soon."

"You know, after thinking about it last night, I'm not sure we'll ever be able to find what it's about. "Page 31" covers so many darn things ... books and whatever. I want to keep the project moving though."

"If it's meant to be, it's meant to be, Daniel," Kathy said.

"I know. What's today's date?"

"Thursday, October 21st."

"We're about to enter Scorpio, October 23 to November 21, as I recall. Can you get one of our people to research what major activities or events that are scheduled starting on the twenty-third through the twenty-first of November? Let's look at both public and government functions."

"That shouldn't take too long. I'll get on it right now."

"You have your plate full, dear. Have one of the agents do it."

"Oh, sorry. That's what I meant."

"Okay. Let me know as soon as you can."

"I'm on it, Daniel."

"And let's schedule a meeting after lunch with everyone that was present at yesterday's meeting."

"Two o'clock, okay?"

"Perfect. By the way, have I told you lately what a great job you do?" he asked, smiling.

"You do all the time and thanks again. I'm out of here before you make me cry," Kathy said laughing, as she walked out of the office.

Daniel continued working for another two hours in his quiet office when Merlin walked in.

"Good morning, partner."

Daniel looked up, "Hey, Wiz. Good morning."

"Got a minute?"

"For you, an hour. What's up?"

"I've been thinking about the Scorpio thing. All the past terrorist attacks by bin Laden and al Qaeda have escalated in damage with each new attack. They seem to want to increase the damage and death each time

The first attack on the World Trade Center in 1993 killed 6 people but was intended to kill thousands. Next, there were the bombings in Lebanon where almost three hundred died. That was Hamas but it showed al Qaeda that mass numbers could be killed.

Over the years with the suicide bombings of embassies, the death count was high in each one. But it wasn't their goal and neither was 9-11. They want hundreds of thousands like they were trying to do with the last attempt in St. Louis. That one would have been catastrophic if we hadn't stopped it.

Now we're facing something worse than all of them combined. I feel that the attack is pointed at a specific focal point that we never imagined could happen."

"Any ideas what or where it is?" Daniel asked.

"Not now. But when you think about it, Daniel, no one expected airliners to crash into the trade center or the pentagon. There was intelligence evidence that it could happen and we even warned them with the data and pictures we found.

With this QD-9 chemical and its potential for a massive death toll, I think we should look at some place big, where a lot of people are gathered. Some place where the news media will be swarming like flies. And I also feel that it will be an attack that will cripple the U.S. so bad if it is successful; we might even be reduced to a third world country."

Daniel sat back in his chair and unconsciously reached for the triangle pendent on his chest. He felt the warmth of the triangle against his body.

"I asked Kathy to make a list of all major functions that are scheduled beginning on October 23rd to November 21st. That's the time period of Scorpio. She should have it ready for the meeting at two o'clock. Check with her when you leave and see how it's coming along.

I agree with you Merlin. I wish we could find out what this "page 31" is."

"Sometimes, we look so hard and far away, and the answer is at our feet. Maybe this is one of those situations."

"Are you thinking that is might happen here in DC?"

"It could or New York or some place like Boston. If it happened on Wall Street, our economy would be brought to a screeching halt. I do feel that it will happen here on the East Coast though."

"Why's that?"

"Remember when Pat Scott explained Scorpio? One thing he said at the end was, "the planet Pluto rules Scorpio, which is a water sign." That is what he said, verbatim. Scorpio and water. I think the attack will be close to water. So, that rules out the Mid-West. There is nothing strategic along the Gulf Coast of Mexico that would cause a major effects. There are no major cities.

The West Coast has LA, Frisco and Seattle. Lots of people and industry, but nothing important enough to could close down or really affect America's power.

Wall Street and Washington, DC are the most powerful locations in the U.S. ... and they are close to water."

"Here is another thing. This is an election year and both the democratic and republican conventions are over. They had a great opportunity to strike and kill a lot of people at those places, Boston and New York," Daniel added.

"We had those covered like a blanket and it would have been too obvious. They want total surprise and are looking to make a bigger and more emphatic impact, Daniel."

"Damn, Wiz, you're on it ... and you said Falcon runs better when I'm here. You're full of shit," Daniel said, breaking into laughter.

Merlin smiled and then laughed in embarrassment.

"It all came to me last night, buddy. Your return got my juices flowing. So nice try," Merlin answered.

"You know, thinking about what you just said, Wiz. You are right. What better targets than those you've already attacked and didn't destroy, DC and New York. Both are international cities of power."

"They are ... THE ... biggest cities of power in the world, Daniel."

"When you check with Kathy, tell her to have whoever is searching for the major functions that are scheduled during that time frame, to focus first on New York City and here in Washington."

"Done deal, my friend. I better get going. I've got a lot to do before this afternoon's meeting."

"Wiz, this will be the first item on the agenda at the meeting. I want you to explain everything you just told me. Wiz ... thanks. You're one hell of a guy," Daniel said, standing and extending his hand to his great friend.

Merlin shook Daniel's hand with both of his as each looked each other in the eyes.

"I could never have done it without you, Daniel. Now I'm out of here," Merlin answered sincerely and without another word being said between them, left Daniel's office.

Daniel closed his eyes and thought. "God, I need help. Where is "page 31"? Where is it? What's on this "page 31"? Is the identity of Scorpio on "page 31"? God, I need an answer."

The only mental response he received was, "It's "page 31"."

At 1:55 p.m., Daniel left his office and went to the large conference room. Thinking he was early, he walked into the room and everyone was there.

"Afternoon, all. Looks like everyone is eager to get started."

He took his seat and continued. "Earlier today, one of my illustrious deputy directors walked into my office and said some great things. After listening to Merlin, I agreed with his concept whole heartedly. I won't say any more and let him explain his theory. Wiz, the floor is yours."

"Thanks, Daniel," Merlin answered and stood up.

In ten minutes the Wizard explained everything he had expressed to Daniel earlier that day. Everyone present gave him their undivided attention and he was never interrupted. When he finished, no one spoke for an uncomfortable period of time.

Both Merlin and Daniel looked at each individual and saw that they were formulating in their own minds where the attack could take place.

Kathy Starley spoke next. "I've got a list of all functions, large and small that are scheduled between October 23rd and November 21st in New York, here in DC, Boston and Philadelphia. On the list are sporting events, private conventions, award ceremonies, reunions, concerts and political rallies. I had copies made for everyone, so here we go."

She went to the back of the room and picked up a box filled with papers. After handing Daniel the first one, everyone saw that the stapled stack of papers was at least one inch thick.

"How many pages are in this, Kathy?" Daniel asked.

"Ninety-eight. They are still researching other cities but the ones in these booklets cover everything happening or scheduled in those cities," she answered, as she continued passing them out around the table.

Daniel opened his and fanned the pages. The lists were single-spaced and in 10 font. Looking down on the bottom of a random page he saw that it was numbered. He immediately turned to "page 31". The list was in alphabetical order with functions beginning with the letter V. In the header margin, the city of New York was printed. Each column had a header. Looking, he saw: Function, Event Center, Participants and the last one was labeled Date. Daniel scanned slowly down the four column page focusing on the Participants column first. The highest number was 7,500 and the lowest 400.

Looking at who and what function expected 7,500 participants; he read "Veterans of Foreign Wars", then the name of the hotel where the event was to take place and the date. He then started at the top of the list and continued down to the bottom, hoping to find a connection to the message "page 31". It wasn't there or, if it was, he didn't recognize it.

He looked up and saw that everyone but Xi was scanning the booklet silently. Xi had his eyes closed and Daniel knew he was meditating. Maybe Xi was spiritually searching for the answer or a message, Daniel thought. He let everyone look through the booklet for another few minutes. Some were making notes in the margins and others were scanning each item. When Daniel figured they had spent enough time looking he broke the silence.

"Okay, people. These books are TOP SECRET and are to be treated that way. No copies are to be made without my authorization. Any questions about that?"

There weren't any.

"Good. Now let's start with Senator Nigel Mason. Dan, you were assigned that detail. What do you have?"

Falcon Agency's Agent Dan Aibaya stood up.

"He's under a 24-7 surveillance with three teams of two agents working eight-hour shifts. The teams are made up of CIA, FBI and two of our people. They have video cameras and are filming every move the senator makes.

We've been in his townhouse and searched around and found nothing unusual. No weapons were found either. I was there when the search was going on and accidentally lost four bugs in the house." Dan looked around the room and smiled.

"Lost, huh?" Merlin asked.

"Ah … lost, Wiz. I didn't think a judge would give us a court order to bug a senator's residence without any reason other than suspicion."

"Hell of a place to lose bugs," Merlin answered and there was laughter in the room.

Smiling, Dan continued. "Anyway, phone records have been evaluated and numbers called and received were cross checked. Nothing unusual was found. We also checked his cell number records and again, nothing.

We've checked out laundry companies, maid, swimming pool and lawn service companies. Nothing. The security company and employees have been checked out. Nothing unusual there either. He has no known mistresses, girlfriends and we even checked for boy friends just to make sure. There are no bad rumors about this guy other than he is one hell of a good senator who is ethical, conscientious, has excellent moral values and a great voting record.

People, Senator Nigel Mason is clean."

"Thanks, Dan and good job. Stay on him for now," Daniel answered.

"Next, Bill what do you have?"

CIA Director Bill Angus stood up.

"So far not very much. The HK barrels found in Zuckowi's hotel matched the sniper killings in Raleigh-Durham, Colorado and Jonathan Gray in Dallas. The bullets that killed those people were fired from those different barrels and we were able to match the firing pins used. His prints were all over the body of the HK also.

His house was pretty clean and he officed from there. No other business office has been located. Checking with neighbors, they said he worked out of his home. They also said that he rarely had visitors and was somewhat of a recluse.

We didn't find any fingerprints other than his and those of a maid who comes in twice a week. There were no pictures of people, papers, files, notes, address books. Nothing was found as far as data is concerned.

Two black, one-piece jump suits were hanging in the closet. We're trying to match the dirt particles imbedded in two pair of shoes and on the jump suits with soil from the assassination sites. I should have an answer in another day or so on that. What it looks like is, his main job was a sniper, and, the consultant business was just a front.

He has a total of $785,957 in four bank accounts. They have been frozen and can't be touched by anyone other than the U.S. government. Deposits were made via wire transfers from the Swiss Bank in Zurich. We traced those back but, you know the Swiss banking system, they won't release who the sender was.

He never remarried and so far we haven't been able to find any girlfriends. Like Dan did, we even checked for boyfriends. We didn't want to be out done by Falcon," Bill said grinning.

That remark brought laughter in the room.

"He did say during our interrogation that he doesn't have any children, grandchildren or relatives here in the U.S. or Canada. We all know that is a lie because he does have those two daughters and one does or did live in Canada.

We've got positive ID's on Monique Leclair from the surveillance tapes at the airports and I've already gave that info to you. All the airline manifests, both national and international, have been checked. We know she didn't fly under the name Monique Leclair. All that info has also been turned over to you.

The findings from our biological weapons lab is also in. This QD-9 is the worst chemical ever made. It is ... let me quote what the senior scientist said.

"Bill, I don't know where you got this shit but it is the worst fucking stuff ever invented. It will kill a person in less than two seconds and spreads faster than diarrhea shit from a cow flying at Mach-5."

That cracked everyone up and they were all laughing at Bill's Texas drawl impression of the scientist, even though the topic was serious.

"This guy, Joe William Anderson, is one hell of a character and the best biological chemist in the world. He's breaking down QD-9 to see exactly what the components are. That will take a lot more time and I can't push him on that. The more I push, the slower he gets.

The last thing I have is that the terrorist chatter the past few weeks has been unusual. When something is brewing, chatter rises. The past few weeks it has been erratic … through the roof one day and then dead quiet the next few days. There is no consistency. We haven't got a grip on it right now."

"How's it been since we got Zuckowi?" Daniel asked.

"Normal. No rise or decline."

"Thanks, Bill. John, you're next," Daniel said to the FBI Director.

'Thank you, Daniel. Well, we have two of our agents dead in Oklahoma. They both were shot with a 9mm pistol and we're pretty sure it was a German-made Walther P5 because that pistol has a strange system of ejecting cases. The ejection port is on the left side, and empty cases are ejected in that direction, whereas almost every other pistol ejects from the right side. We recovered one casing and ballistics was able to find the ejecting marks on it. They said it is a 93.7 percent probability that it was a Walther P5 9mm.

It was adapted with a silencer also. Both agents were shot at short range and the one in the stairwell was shot twice. There was a limited trace of gunpowder which indicates a silencer, along with striation marks on the bullet where it passed through the silencer.

The reason I'm telling you this is one of the female snipers has a pistol with a silencer and we have to keep that in mind when we find her or them.

Now this ties in with the bombing of the jet that was blown up at Dulles, Daniel."

Daniel flashed back to the situation where his family was almost killed.

"The janitor at the jet center, Hashim Al Ghafar from Algeria, was found dead yesterday morning down on the southern tip of Eastern Maryland. A fisherman found him in a marsh area off of Highway 5, near the little settlement of Ridge.

We got involved when the local sheriff found an Algerian passport in the marsh close to where the body was found. Ballistics report found that he was killed with a 9mm Walther pistol and the bullet matched the ones that killed our agents in Oklahoma.

That tells us that Azzah or Atiya Zuckowi, which ever one is Monique Leclair, was here on the East coast and possibly in the DC area. We've emailed and faxed pictures of her to all the local authorities in Virginia, Maryland, West Virginia and Pennsylvania."

"Better expand that to every state on the East coast, John. She might be traveling north or south or maybe in this area. Let's not take any chances," Daniel suggested.

"They'll be out right after this meeting. That's all I have right now." Lambert answered.

"I have another idea and, John," Daniel said. "I want the FBI to handle it because of its contacts with the media. Let's get Leclair's picture to the television stations and hit the airwaves with it. She's wanted and under suspicion for the murder of Hashim Al Ghafar ... is armed and to be considered extremely dangerous. If she and her sister have split up, we might get lucky and get leads on both of them. They're twins ... look-alikes.

Don't mention anything ... and I mean nothing about any sniper killings or the QD-9 threat. Just the killing of Hashim Al Ghafar. Emphasize to the stations that this is a serious situation and urge them to continue to blast the airwaves with it.

The sisters will do one of two things. Dig in deep or try to move out of the area. Either choice they make, works to our advantage.

One more thing. Focus heavily on the New York City area and here in Washington. I'm going with Merlin's theory."

They continued around the table and each person provided more information with the exception of Xi. He didn't say a word during the whole meeting. When they were done, Daniel asked Xi to join him in his office. He knew there was something going on with his close friend, the Master, and also got the message that he wanted to share it only with Daniel.

"You were real quiet during the whole meeting, Xi. What's going on, my friend?"

"Two thing, Daniel. Name where Scorpio attack not in book."

"You never looked in it."

"Not in book, Daniel," Xi repeated himself while looking at Daniel's eyes.

Daniel knew better than to challenge Xi and accepted what he said.

"Any idea where it will happen?" one master asked the other.

"No. But Xi get same answer Daniel get. "Page 31"."

"It has been driving me crazy, Xi. The answer is in the message, right?"

"Answer always in message. This toughest one ever for Xi. Confused like Daniel."

"Do you think it might be a derivative of "page 31"?"

"What derivative?"

"A different meaning. If you change the meaning to something else. I was thinking like ... 31 page instead of "page 31" or 13 instead of 31."

"I understand. Never work that way. Message never need change. Message "page 31". No change Daniel. Answer "page 31"," the Master answered.

Chapter XXIV

Gemini

*H*ighway *50-301 east-northeast out of Washington, DC, is* the link from the west shore of Maryland across the northern end of the Chesapeake Bay to the eastern Maryland shore. Once on the eastern shore, the highway leads to a small community of Queenstown where the highway splits and 301 continues northeast and Highway 50 turns southeast. A few miles from the highway divided intersection on Highway 50 is a narrow, crushed-seashell driveway leading to a rustic cottage hidden behind a hill.

Seated in a lounge chair on the rear porch, a petite lady in her early thirties was enjoying the peace and quiet. Dressed in blue jeans and a bulky, white turtle-neck wool sweater that accentuated her long, jet-black hair, she looked out over the sand hills through her dark lens, designer sunglasses. It was cool out, but the warm sun's rays removed some of the chill in the air. Occasionally, clouds would block out the sun, reminding her that it was still the fall season.

If anyone had approached the lady, they would have assumed that she was a corporate executive who was enjoying the solitude from her usual busy, weekly schedule. It would be a serious false impression. One of the deadliest snipers in the world was enjoying her rest period. Soon, she would be very active in a dangerous life-threatening combat situation with a group of killers from the country she despised. Americans had killed her lover, husband, and, supposed to be, life-long companion.

Revenge had begun and those she had killed, with no remorse, were only a small picture of what was to come. The United States would be brought to its knees, and with the death and destruction she would inflict, there would be no chance of America's rebounding for decades, possibly never. When the thought entered her mind, which it did many times during the day, she became even more determined to continue her mission of dominant devastation.

She had a concern now. There hadn't been any word from her father for two days. It was very unusual for him not to email her from the Tampa library. As an expert in the internet technology and computer field, she had trained him on how to set up untraceable internet accounts so they could communicate on a regular basis. Fifteen minutes ago, she had checked her email address in Paris and there was no message from him.

"Very unusual," she said to herself.

It didn't really matter. The mission was not dependent upon him. He was only a decoy to keep the American government and police distracted.

She was also somewhat unhappy that she would never be able to return to her lovely home in Montreal. She enjoyed the weather and community. But that was all she left behind. Kaleem Mushowui was disillusioned that he was going to be with her forever. She knew that he was in love with her, but the feeling wasn't mutual. Kaleem would never be able to enter that world. She planned to kill him.

Off in the distance, the female killer with red manicured fingernails saw the head of an individual who was walking in her direction, appear over a sand dune. The black hair, held back by a white headband, identified the intruder as her sister. The sister, her identical twin, was returning from her daily walk along the dunes to the Chesapeake Bay shore and, no matter what the weather was, she wore that identifiable headband.

As the lady reached the top of the last dune closest to her cottage, she saw a person sitting on the back porch. She stopped and her killer instincts went on edge. Then the trespasser waved as she rose from the lawn chair. The hiker recognized the lady as her twin sister, Azzah. Atiya moved quickly to greet her. It had been a month since she had last seen her and, even though Azzah was the first born and the dominating sibling, Atiya loved her with all her heart.

The Geminis met on the white sand near the porch and hugged each other tightly.

Speaking in Arabic, Atiya asked, "When did you get here?"

"About a half hour ago," Azzah answered in English. "How many times have I told you not to speak in Arabic? Use English only!"

Atiya was taken aback at the immediate reprimand.

"I'm sorry, Azzah. I'm just so happy to see you," Atiya responded in perfect English.

"Do not do that again. We are in a lot of danger right now and one mistake can jeopardize everything I have planned for a long time. The government people are looking everywhere for us now and talking in our native tongue will bring attention. Never do it again, not even in private." Azzah said, in a scolding tone of voice.

Always wanting to please her twin, Atiya was upset at herself for letting a moment of love weaken her mental preparation for their mission.

"I promise, Azzah, it will never happen again."

The sisters hugged one another.

"Very good," Azzah answered, looking directly into Atiya's eyes. It was her way of reinforcing her message.

"Now, let's go inside. We have much to do," Azzah ordered. "I put the teapot on and the water should be hot by now."

The Gemini sisters walked into the comfortable vacation home holding each others hands. After each making their own cup of gourmet tea, they sat down at the kitchen table. Azzah let her sister talk about general things and then Azzah became all business.

"I killed Hashim Al Ghafar yesterday. He screwed up the bombing of this Falcon Agency's family. I worked so hard planning that trap. All he had to do was wait. What a fool!" Azzah said angrily.

"What did you do with his body?"

"Dumped it in the ocean. By now, it has been eaten by the scavengers."

"What about the other two that helped Hashim?"

"They don't matter. They have no idea who really planned the bombing and Ghafar gave them each a thousand dollars just to be lookouts."

"Do you know who they are?"

"Of course. Don't be an idiot. They've already have flown back to France."

Atiya hated it when her sister talked down to her.

"I wish you wouldn't talk to me that way, Azzah. I don't speak to you that way."

"I'm sorry. You just act so immature sometimes and I feel you are challenging my intelligence."

"I never would do that. I just know you have worked very hard and I want us to succeed in this jihad."

"We will, Atiya. There is no doubt that we will. Now, where are the documents?"

"I'll get them," Atiya answered

She went to her bedroom, retrieved a stainless steel briefcase and returned to the kitchen, putting the case on the table in front of Azzah.

"Is everything inside?" Azzah asked.

"Everything is there. I checked the contents after I picked it up at the bus station."

Azzah unsnapped both locks and opened the metal case. Taking her time, she looked through every item carefully. There were three stacks of passports and there were no duplicate names on any of them. Along with the documents were matching driver's licenses from different states and the names and addresses matched. Two stacks were for females and each one had Azzah's and Atiya's picture on the identification. The hairstyles, color and makeup were different with each set of false documents. The third set was for their father, M. Said Zuckowi.

Looking up at Atiya, Azzah asked, "Have you heard from father?"

"Not since four days ago when he was going to North Carolina. Have you?

"No. I wonder how he did in Tampa. He should have called by now. I am beginning to think that something went wrong. It's not like him to not call and confirm the kill." Azzah said softly, thinking the worst.

Azzah snapped out of her thought and returned her focus on the case. She removed nine stacks of unmarked, well-circulated American currency that contained various denominations and laid them on the table.

"There is something missing. Did you take anything out of the case, Atiya?"

"No. I just opened the locks and checked to make sure that it was our case."

"You said you inventoried everything."

"I did not say that. What's the matter with you? You are getting angry at me for no fucking reason. I said I checked the contents. That's it," Atiya snapped angrily.

Azzah was taken aback. It wasn't often that her sister stood her ground against her. She looked up and smiled at the woman who was the mirror image of herself. Atiya had an angry look on her face

"That is good, Atiya. It is good that you can show some anger. I have always been worried about that trait in you. It is about time you stood up to me. That is why I talk to you the way I do."

Atiya didn't answer. She was still mad and walked out on the rear porch. Azzah let her be alone and continued looking through the case. Carefully, she removed the pad from the top lid. Hidden there was a sealed envelope with no markings on it. Carefully she opened it up, removed a piece of paper and unfolded it. Not looking up, she read the letter to herself and after reading the contents, returned it to the envelope.

Azzah smiled, sat back in her chair and looked out the rear window that exposed the porch. Atiya's back was to her and she was leaning on the railing with her head looking down toward the ground. Azzah knew she was still angry, but the envelope held the message that would change everything. She stood up and walked outside to her twin.

"Atiya, I'm sorry I treated you that way," Azzah said, as she approached Atiya. "I do have great news for you. I found the envelope that I was looking for in the case. It wasn't your fault that you didn't see it. I left instructions for the man in Europe to make sure it wouldn't be found easily if someone was to steal the case. That was my fault," she said, turning Atiya around and hugged the weeping sister.

They held each other for awhile, not saying a word. The sun had broken through the clouds and cast its rays down on them as they stood arm in arm on the porch.

"I guess the stress has caught up with me, Atiya. We are so close to finishing our objective. I'm sorry. I do love you so much and want nothing but the best for you," Azzah said, using words to comfort Atiya and mend the blood relationship.

They released their hold on each other as Azzah reached up and wiped away the tears from Atiya's eyes.

"I'm sorry, also. I guess everything has caught up with me and I forgot what my real purpose is. They think they have gotten away with killing our mother, brother and husbands. They will pay for it very soon," Atiya said, breaking into a smile.

"Yes, they will, my sister. When we get done with this, when Scorpio strikes, when America is brought to its knees, when the Satan's government cannot function and is in disarray, when their economy cannot function and terror is all over the United States, we will have our retribution," Azzah answered. "And when that happens, it will be only you, father and I who have done it."

"And Scorpio. You mustn't forget Scorpio," Atiya added.

"Yes ... and Scorpio. But Scorpio will be dead in body but will be a hero with our people. We will make sure that the rest of the world knows about Scorpio."

"What were you looking for in the case," Atiya asked, changing the subject.

"Here, look for yourself," Azzah answered, handing her sister the envelope.

Atiya removed the letter from the envelope and read the contents. She smiled when she finished reading it and looked at her sister.

"It is done. We now will spend the rest of our lives in comfort. Father will be so happy when we surprise him. He has no idea what this present is. I'm sure he'll be very proud of us. Do you think he will like it?" Atiya asked.

"He will love it. Who wouldn't? A luxury home on the ocean, at the gateway to the Mediterranean, is everyone's dream. He will love Tangier and we'll live like royalty. The Moroccan government will provide us safety and protection. That has been taken care of."

"So, the palace is now ours. We own it forever?"

"Yes, Atiya. It has been paid for and we own it."

"I am so happy. I can't wait until we see him in Mexico and tell him."

"We have only a few more days. Let's go back inside and finish what we have to do. I bought some more wigs for us that match the color of the old ones. But, we have new hair styles and they are different than the ones in the photos. It will make it easier when we go through customs. They are such idiots. We won't be challenged."

Both entered the cottage and continued with finishing their organization and plans for their final mission.

"Is the QD-9 still in the bank vault?" Atiya asked.

"No, Scorpio has it now. The QD-9 is in place."

"We are almost ready. I'm excited … really excited and ready for Tangier, Morocco."

"Me, too. I'm beginning to worry about father. I want to check to see if he has made contact," Azzah answered, feeling emotions of insecurity while walking to Atiya's computer.

After checking her email address in Europe, her concern increased.

"Where is he?" she asked out loud.

"Maybe he had trouble with the last killing," Atiya answered.

"Maybe."
"I have one more to eliminate. So let's get busy."

Chapter XXV

Birth of Scorpio

Lebanon, February 1983

*C*ivil war among the Christians, Muslims, and Palestinians in Lebanon began early in 1975 and lasted until late 1976. Syrian forces entered Lebanon in April, 1976, at the request of Lebanon's president, stopping Muslim and Palestinian advances. The war killed an estimated 50,000 Lebanese and twice that many suffered wounds. Civil war had devastated Lebanon's economy and tourism plummeted to a standstill. When a cease-fire was agreed on in October, 1976, both sides continually violated it and the war escalated again in 1977. The Palestine Liberation Organization (PLO) increased its attacks against the Israelis from the southern Lebanon and Israeli border. In March of 1978, the Israeli armed forces moved across the border in attempts to quash the attacks. They met heavy resistance and withdrew in June. A UN peacekeeping force of 6,000 military personnel was assigned to the southern Lebanon territory that the Israelis left behind and they, too, were unable to maintain control of Lebanese terrorists and military activity.

In 1981 Christian and Syrian forces were still at war with each other. Beirut was continually being attacked by Israeli air raids in retaliation for PLO attacks. These attacks weren't satisfactory enough for the Israelis and in June, 1982, Israeli forces again invaded Lebanon, with the mission focused toward eliminating Palestinian guerrilla bases. Approximately 7,000 Palestinians were forced to evacuate Lebanon. After the assassination of Lebanon's president, Christian forces entered

215

Palestinian refugee camps in the areas controlled by the Israelis and massacred over 1,000 civilians. The international community became enraged and outspoken, demanding a stop to the slaughter.

The assassinated president's brother was elected president a few days later and a military force, comprised of U.S. Marines, British, French, and Italian soldiers, entered Lebanon in an attempt to cease the killings and control the Lebanese militias. Peace treaty negotiations were in the making, which called for the removal of foreign troops. Syria, now with strong military presence in Lebanon, rejected the peace agreement and refused to leave the country. It had acquired extensive land positions and did not want to relinquish its holdings. The Israeli forces slowly retreated from Lebanon's southern area. At 1:00 p.m. Lebanon time, on the 18th of April 1983, a terrorist bomb destroyed the U.S. embassy in Beirut, killing more than 50 people. Then on October 23, 1983, a devastating terrorist bombing attack occurred and 260 U.S. Marines and 60 French soldiers were killed at their barracks by a truck bomb.

In early December of 1982, a twenty-six year old American diplomat was assigned foreign embassy duty to Lebanon and the man was excited to be on his first foreign assignment. He had earned his law degree at Cornell University and, after taking the summer off to relax and have fun, began his career in the diplomatic field that September. He had three months of initial training in Washington. Eager to put his career on the fast track, he volunteered for the first foreign assignment anywhere in the world. When he was accepted to the embassy in Lebanon, he had no idea what was in store for him. Lebanon's civil war was escalating and it was no longer the beautiful, safe resort area that the country had once been. He didn't care. Being young and eager, all he wanted was the experience to put on his resume to enhance his political ambitions.

For the first two months he adjusted to his position and the danger he faced in Beirut. Being a single man, he carefully sought out female companionship, but was warned by his supervisor to be very selective. There were spies lurking outside the embassy seeking to make contact with U.S. government employees. Aware of the dangers, he became close with a twenty-two year old Lebanese national, employed as a secretary by the embassy. Their relationship grew and, in March, they spent their first night together.

In early April, the diplomat's girlfriend announced to him that she was pregnant and was due in early November. It was not welcome news to him. He wasn't ready to get married and surely not prepared to be a parent of the child. And then there would be the stigma of a child out of wedlock that could hinder his political career. He didn't express his fears to the young Lebanese girl, fearing she would retaliate by telling his supervisor the predicament she was in.

Tensions were growing in the civil war, and terrorist activities by both sides escalated. It was now very apparent that leaving the grounds of the embassy was life threatening. On the 18th of April, a terrorist bomb destroyed the embassy, killing 63 people.

Both the young diplomat and the pregnant Lebanese girlfriend had just left the building for lunch and he was planning to tell her that he was not ready to be married. He was also going to suggest that the pregnant, Catholic woman have an abortion. It would be tough trying to convince her to do so, because of her religious beliefs.

They had just approached the rear gate sentry post when the bomb exploded at 1:00 p.m. Debris flew everywhere and they sought shelter in the guard shack. A van carrying a 2,000-

pound load of explosives was detonated by a suicide bomber and the bomb tore through the front portion of the seven story building. Most of the victims were at lunch in the cafeteria and were killed by the collapsing building. The devastation killed 63 occupants of the building, of which 17 were Americans. The young couple had escaped certain death by minutes.

They were taken to a U.S. military camp and, within two days, he was reassigned back to the United States. His pregnant, female friend was deserted by the American diplomat. Seven months later she gave birth to a child on October 29th, 1983, under the zodiac sign of Scorpio.

During the summer of 1983, Scorpio's mother's parents, a sister and two brothers were killed in another terrorist attack, leaving the single mother and child, along with another brother, struggling to survive. The threesome was forced to live in squalor. Neither one had any means of income. The embassy had shut down and the pregnant lady couldn't find a job. The brother also had worked for the embassy as a translator and was without employment.

Seven months after the Scorpio child was born, the mother was shot by American guards while she was trying to steal food from a military camp. The soldiers assumed that she was working for a terrorist organization and no mercy for suspected terrorists was ever given. The infant Scorpio's only means of survival was now dependent upon the only surviving relative, the uncle.

In 1984, the uncle made contact with an American military attaché friend, who had returned to Beirut, and the former Lebanese embassy employee explained his current situation. The attaché used his influence to obtain a visa for the uncle and child to immigrate to France and in December, 1984, they flew to France and were granted asylum.

For three years he worked waiting tables at a restaurant on the Champs-Elysees. After months of persistence, he was able to obtain a menial job at the U.S. Embassy in Paris as a low-level clerk. The uncle struggled to survive and take care of the young child.

In the spring of 1996, a member of al Qaeda, who was recruiting Arab males to join Usamah bin Laden's jihad, struck up a conversation with the uncle at a café across the street from the embassy. After discovering that the Lebanese man was employed by the American embassy, the recruiter befriended the uncle and over a three-week period, they met at the café twelve times. The recruiter conjured a plan to get the embassy employee to get him information.

Realizing what the recruiter was trying to do, the uncle broke off the friendship. This was a mistake on his part. He should have contacted the CIA staff that was officed at the Embassy, but he didn't because he was afraid he might lose credibility and his job.

On the other hand, the al Qaeda recruiter was worried that the Lebanese man would turn him into the CIA. Two days after the friendship was severed, Scorpio's uncle was found dead in an alley. He had been shot to death.

The young child, now twelve years old, was left to face the world alone. The apartment manager evicted Scorpio because of unpaid rent. Now the adolescent was destitute and out in the streets alone. To protect his job, the uncle had never told the embassy about the child, fearing that if his employer discovered that he had a dependent, they would terminate him. From the time he arrived in Paris, he lived a life of paranoia and uncertainty.

Now orphaned and with no known relatives, Scorpio never went back to school and joined a gang of gypsy street children. They trained the teenager in the art of shoplifting and pick pocketing. The turf the gang controlled was a tourist haven, the Notre Dame Cathedral grounds.

One day outside of the cathedral, Scorpio was able to steal a young lady's purse while the tourist was seated on a bench. The thief ran away as fast as possible to the other side of the cathedral and sat down on the manicured lawn. The teenager had scored and started rifling through the foreigner's belongings. As suspected, there was a large amount of French currency. Scorpio had stuck gold and would be able to eat well for a while, maybe even get a clean room and bed to sleep in.

The teenager made the mistake of not being aware of the surroundings and not getting far enough away from the crime scene. As the purse was being rifled through by the adolescent, a strong set of hands grabbed and pinned the thief to the ground. Scorpio couldn't move and was now trapped, with the evidence in hand.

The purse was stolen from a lady who was in her twenties. Unfortunately for Scorpio, the lady's father saw the whole event happen from a distance. M. Said Zuckowi followed the child and after the thief settled down on the lawn to search through the purse, pounced on the unsuspecting teenager.

Scorpio tried to yell but Zuckowi cupped his large hand over the thief's mouth. His twin daughters joined their father and after the teenager, who was pinned to the ground, realized that any effort to escape was futile, began to relax. The urchin was willing to accept the consequences. Zuckowi felt the child relax and then spoke, as he relaxed his grip.

"Do not try to run away and if you yell or scream, I will call the police. Do you understand? Shake your head yes, if you do," Said ordered in French.

The teenager nodded yes.

"I will not hurt you if you obey me. One wrong move and it is off to jail," Zuckowi said in a kind voice.

He partially removed his hand and was prepared to place it back on the child's mouth if the thief yelled. Realizing the man had the upper hand and total control, Scorpio didn't make a sound. Said then pulled the teenager up off the ground and held on to the child's arms. Azzah and Atiya looked at the crook and were shocked by what they saw. A skinny child, with black hair, deep blue eyes and only about five-feet two inches tall, stared at the ladies who looked identical.

"Why did you steal my purse? If you wanted money, I would have gladly given it to you," Azzah said, as she picked up her purse and contents off the ground.

"Here, take it," Azzah said, and stuffed franc notes into the child's pocket. "Where are your parents?"

"I don't have any," the beautiful child said softly. "They are dead."

"Where do you live, child?" Atiya asked.

"Anywhere and everywhere. I don't have a home," Scorpio answered.

"You live in the streets alone?" Said asked.

"Yes, but I have friends … many friends."

"Are they thieves like you?" Azzah asked gently.

"That is how we live. What are you going to do to me?" the teenager asked. "Don't call the police. They are not kind to people like me. They touch me all over when I'm in jail."

"They do? The police touch you all over? Even your private parts?" Azzah asked.

Embarrassed, Scorpio answered, "Yes."

"We will not turn you over to the police. Come child and sit down," Said Zuckowi said, while guiding the teenager to a wooden park bench where they all sat down.

Once seated between Azzah and Said with Atiya sitting on the ground in front of the street urchin, Azzah spoke first.

"Tell us about yourself. Where are you from? What happened to your parents?"

Still speaking in French, Scorpio calmly spoke for a good half hour and explained the tragic life of the refugee.

When the well-spoken teenager finished, all three kind tourists looked at each other in awe.

"Why are you so kind to me? I stole from you?" Scorpio asked.

"Because we also had tragedy in our lives," Said answered for his family. "We can help you and, if you want, we will help. Now, tell us what your uncle told you about your father."

Pulling two pieces of folded up paper from a pocket, Scorpio handed them to Azzah.

"My uncle told me that if I ever could get to America, this is who my father is. He tried to contact him in America. When he did talk to him, my father said that he never had a child in Lebanon and to never call again.

He is a very important man in the United States. He's with the government and is a powerful man. My uncle did a lot of research on him on the internet and told me he is very important."

Azzah unfolded the tattered papers as the teenager continued talking. She didn't recognize the name but knew it was the only lifeline the child had to the only surviving parent. The other paper was a Lebanese birth certificate. Azzah folded the important papers back up and handed them back to Scorpio.

"You will help me? You really will?" the blue-eyed child said, looking at each of the tourists.

"Yes, we will. This is no life for a child. How old are you?" Atiya answered.

"I'm thirteen years old."

"Do you only speak French?" Said asked.

"No. I also speak Arabic, English and German. My school and uncle made sure that I learned those languages."

"Such a talent for someone so young," Azzah whispered.

They continued talking and Scorpio's faith in the kind people began to grow. It was nice to be with people that could be trusted. Each member of the Zuckowi family took turns explaining their family background.

"We are now on our way to Canada to live," Atiya said.

"Is that a nice place?" the soft-spoken child asked.

"So we've heard," Said answered.

"If you want, you can come with us to the hotel and stay with us until we leave," Azzah said, as she looked at her twin sister and father for confirmation.

Both relatives shook their heads yes.

"But, what will I do when you leave for Canada?"

"Don't worry. I have a plan in mind," the father answered.

The foursome left for the hotel. For the first time, Scorpio felt safe, but remained a little guarded toward the kind people. At the hotel, Said ordered a fold-out bed to their room and let the child shower and get cleaned up. Azzah stayed behind and went shopping for new clothing for the ex-street child.

Prior to the Zuckowis leaving for Canada, Said made arrangements with an older couple, who lived in the outskirts of Paris, to care for the teenager after they left for Canada. He generously paid the kind couple four months in advance.

Prior to their departure to their new home in North America, the Zuckowi family promised that they would return to France in three months and take the teenager to Canada with them. There would be a lot of legal work to complete and documents to compile. Luckily, Scorpio had a birth certificate. They would be able to get a passport from the Lebanese embassy. But, as with most bureaucratic red tape in many foreign governments, it would take some time, effort and bribery.

Three months after the Zuckowi family left the child, they returned as promised and returned to Canada with the orphan. Scorpio was safe and had found a safe haven. But, the Zuckowi family never told the new member of their family what their real objective and plans were. They despised America and everything it stood for. It would take many years of secretly planning an attack against the United States, one that would create total chaos in the most powerful country in the world.

After two years in Canada, Atiya and her father moved to the United States and established careers as citizens from Canada. Said moved to Tampa, Florida. Atiya and the child born under the sign of Scorpio, moved to Washington, DC. Scorpio was happy to have a Canadian passport and legally assumed a new name. After the uncle and the child had visited the Louvre Museum in Paris, CJ became enthralled with Monet's paintings and studied the artist's works. Scorpio knew each painting created by the artist and, in most circles, would be considered an expert of his paintings.

After two years in DC and many attempts to contact CJ's father, Atiya finally talked to the Senator. He denied ever having an affair with the child's mother and threatened to have Atiya and CJ arrested and deported. Atiya explained to the young adult what the Senator had said. Anger built up in the teenager. Urged on by Atiya, Scorpio became convinced that what this trusted lady told her about Americans was true.

"We will take advantage of the United States' stupidity and arrogance. Some day soon, we will get our revenge for what they did to us," Atiya said.

"I want revenge for what my father did to my mother and me. I wish he were dead. I will never, ever refer to him as father again. He is like most Americans, selfish and a liar. I want him dead, Atiya." CJ answered with conviction.

"It will happen, child. Just be patient. Trust me, CJ, it will happen."

They lived a good life in Washington, keeping their anger for the country that provided them a safe haven, to themselves. CJ excelled in high school and graduated with honors. After graduating and wanting to continue living with Atiya, the young adult decided to attend college at John Hopkins University. Atiya and CJ had become close friends and confidants. They also had another thing in common. Both of them, along with Said and Azzah, were going to destroy the United States.

Chapter XXVI

Fire

Friday, October 22, 2004

*A*n *hour after the sun rose, Azzah woke up. She felt well* rested and laid in bed for a while thinking about what she had to do today. She would be leaving the cottage for the last time. In five more days, she, her sister and father would be in Tangier, Morocco. The thought of living anonymously in retirement, protected by a luxury home on the Straits of Gibraltar, made her smile.

She rose from the bed and walked to the kitchen, filled the tea kettle with fresh water and put it on the stove, turning up the burner to high. As the water was heating, she went to check her email account in Europe. Before she'd gone to bed, she had checked it and there still wasn't a message from her father. She and Atiya had searched all the news channels that evening, looking for any story that might give them an indication that their father was in trouble or may have been captured. There were none.

Azzah was very well aware that, even with the current uncertainty, they had to continue with the plan in place. It was a promise they had made to each other. If any one of them was captured or killed, the others were to maintain silent and continue on with the plan. Originally, they were going to release the QD-9 chemical at one of the political nomination conventions but they patiently waited for a better opportunity.

A week ago, CJ heard that a special meeting was scheduled in late October and they focused on the new opportunity. It would create more devastation and impact against the United States than any convention would.

The vial of QD-9 was in place. CJ had taken precautions that it was in the most unsuspecting location ever conceived. The United States government security agencies all thought that they were better prepared after the 9-11 attack in 2001. They did improve homeland security but had overlooked a major facet of the most vulnerable entity of the United States.

The teapot began to whistle and the sound stirred Atiya from her sound sleep. Azzah made herself a cup of tea and walked outside onto the rear porch. The cloudless sky's sun was shining and removing the evening chill from the air. Azzah sat down and enjoyed the quiet and peaceful scenery while sipping the hot tea.

"Good morning," Atiya said, as she joined her twin sister, disturbing Azzah's tranquil moment.

"Good morning, Atiya. Did you sleep well?"

"Yes. I slept through the night. I feel great," the sister answered, while holding a steaming cup of tea with both hands, and sat beside Azzah.

"There was no word from father. Something has gone wrong. I checked the contact site and there were no messages," Azzah informed Atiya.

"Do you think they may have captured him?" Atiya asked.

"I'm not sure but there is something very wrong. I am leaving this morning and won't be back. I'm going to take care of CJ's father in two days and, two days later, everything will be finished. I won't see you until we're in Mexico."

Still thinking about their father, Atiya asked, "Maybe we should try to call him?"

"No. What are you thinking? The agreement we made was never to use any means of contact other than the email box in France. Don't be stupid. We have too much to lose."

"Too much to lose? Azzah, we are about to lose CJ and maybe we lost father. All we really have is each other right now."

"The priority ... our priority is the mission ...to destroy the Satan United States. No matter who is left alive, it must be finished," Azzah said with a stern look.

Atiya looked back at her sister. "You're right."

They went into the cottage and Azzah began packing. She took her stack of false passports, ID's and one stack of currency, leaving the remaining packs for Atiya. She also checked the HK sniper rifle and two Walther pistols equipped with silencers. She put four extra clips loaded with 9mm ammunition for the pistols in her bag and one barrel and two 7.62mm bullets for the HK rifle. She wouldn't need any other ordinance for what she had to do.

After Azzah was packed and the bags were loaded into Atiya's SUV, they left the cottage. Azzah had parked her rental car in a restaurant parking lot near the small settlement of Queenstown and had walked the three miles to Atiya's cottage. Two vehicles at the cottage would create suspicion.

The sisters loaded Azzah's bags into her car and they hugged each other.

"I'll see you in Mexico and, hopefully, father will meet us there. I'll keep checking the email address. If he does contact us, I'll get word to you. Now be careful," Azzah said.

"I will. I hate to have to burn the cottage down. It has been a wonderful home," Atiya said.

"Yes, it is a nice place but just think of where we will be living soon. The house in Tangier makes this place look like a shack."

"Yes. Be safe, sister. I will see you soon," Atiya answered and they hugged for the final time.

Atiya watched as her twin drove off down the road toward the bridge that scanned the Chesapeake Bay and wondered if she would ever see her sister and father again. She had an uncomfortable feeling about the situation.

Atiya got into her SUV and drove to the small grocery store and gas station. It was time to make her final preparations for her departure. Atiya filled up her vehicle and two cans with gasoline and went inside to get a few items to tide her over for the next couple of days.

As she walked out of the building, she saw two pay phones at the end of the building.

"Maybe I should call father," she thought as she continued to walk to her vehicle.

She put the bags inside and then walked over to the pay phones. Knowing she was breaking the promise each had made to the other, Atiya started punching in numbers to her father's business phone in Tampa. She almost hung up the phone and then heard it ringing. Seven rings later, the answering machine responded. It was her father's voice on the message stating he was not able to come to the phone and to leave a message. Atiya hung up, not leaving any.

She went to the vehicle and returned to her home.

To close out the week on a positive note, Daniel scheduled a meeting with the team that was working on the Scorpio project, along with all the other agency heads. The meeting was to start at 2:00 p.m. in Falcon Agency's large conference room. The following day, Saturday, was the beginning of the eighth sign of the zodiac, Scorpio. He wanted to make sure everything was progressing at a fast pace.

As Daniel and Xi were leaving his office for lunch at the White House cafeteria, Merlin walked into his office with Raul. Seeing that Daniel was leaving, Merlin stopped him with one statement.

"You better hear this, Daniel."

"You mean now?" Daniel queried.

"Yes, now. You better sit down and hear me out."

The men sat down around Daniel's conference table.

"I just got a call from Tampa. We have a tap on Zuckowi's phone and there was a telephone call to his house. The answering machine answered the call. The agents had it set up to ring seven times, which gives them enough time to trace the call. The caller didn't leave a message but it was traced to a pay phone here in Maryland," Merlin reported.

"Where in Maryland, Wiz?" Daniel asked.

"Queenstown … across the bay."

"I know where it is. How long ago was the call made?"

"About an hour ago."

"Have you sent anyone there to check it out?" Daniel asked.

"Yes. Right now there is a team on the way there. They left about forty minutes ago and should be in Queenstown in about fifteen minutes. They have pictures of the one of the sisters that were taken at the airport. I told them to see if we can get a match."

Xi sat up in his chair. "This good. Sister look like sister … how say …"

"Twins?" Raul said helping Xi.

"Yes, twin. One there in Maryland. Know for sure."

"Let's go," Daniel said. "Wiz, have a suburban ready downstairs. We're going to Queenstown. Move!" Daniel said, getting up and going to his office closet.

Merlin and Raul ran out of Daniel's office while the Falcon Director put on a bullet-proof vest and grabbed two Beretta pistols. He tossed a vest to Xi and then a pistol.

"Xi no need. Have hands," he said tossing the pistol back to Daniel.

"You sure, Xi?"

"Xi sure."

Both men ran out of Daniel's office. Within five minutes, three suburbans escorted by two motorcycle police were on Highway 50 heading east toward Queenstown.

The drive to the small resort community was made in record time. When they arrived at the store where the phone call was made, the front group of agents that Merlin dispatched had already gathered information. Agents Dan Aibaya and Pat Scott were Co-Agents in Charge and greeted Daniel, Merlin and Raul upon their arrival.

"Hi, Pat ... Dan. What have you got?" Daniel asked as the group gathered in a circle.

"The owner of the store identified a Zuckowi sister. Her name is Jeannette Leclair. The same last name as Monique. The owner is right over there. Do you want to talk to her yourself?" Aibaya asked, as he pointed out the lady.

"Let's go," Daniel answered, walking to the owner's location.

"Hi, my name is Daniel White. I'm the Director of Falcon Agency. You may not have heard of us but we are a government agency that oversees all intelligence for the government, something like the FBI and CIA.

"Hi, Mr. White. I'm Donna Martin and I own this place."

"Pleasure to meet you, Donna," Daniel answered, while extending his hand to shake hers.

"Do you know this lady, Donna," he asked while showing her the photo.

"Yes. Her name is Jeannette Leclair."

"How long have you known her?" Daniel asked.

"She bought my parent's house about a year ago. My mom and dad used to own this grocery store. Actually they still own a piece of it. Last year they retired, sold their house and moved to Destin, Florida. Jeanette bought the house from them and paid cash.

She seems to be a nice lady but I don't see her that much. That's not unusual for people that live in this area though. Most just want to be alone and a lot of them have regular homes around DC and come here to get away."

"Does she live alone or is there someone else with her?" Daniel asked.

"I'm sure she lives alone but occasionally she has guests."

"Have you met any of them ... the guests?"

"Not really. I do know she has a sister that looks exactly like her."

"How do you know that, Donna?"

"One time Jeannette came in and filled up with gas. Her sister pumped the gas while Jeannette came in to pay. I asked her who her friend was and she said it was her sister from Canada. After she paid for the gas, I saw the sister getting into the SUV. I was amazed how she was identical looking. If they didn't have different clothes on, I would have never known the difference."

"Anyone else?" Daniel asked, continuing the questioning.

"Her father was here once, but I never saw him. Jeannette just said her father was in town."

"When was that, Donna?"

"When she first moved in. About a year ago, like I said."

"Okay. Is there anyone else that you can think of?"

Donna thought for a few seconds and then spoke. "You know, whenever she would head to the DC area, I'd ask if she was going to do anything special. I never go to DC and I'm always curious about what is going on. She mentioned a couple of times she was going to see CJ. I have no idea who CJ is, but I remember that about six months ago, Jeannette stopped in to get groceries and mentioned that CJ was at the cottage."

"You never saw this CJ?" Merlin asked.

"No. Never."

"Did Jeannette ever say whether CJ was man or woman?" Daniel queried.

"I just assumed it was a man by the way she talked. I'm not sure though."

Daniel and Merlin looked at each other, confirming that maybe this was the lead they were looking for. CJ and Scorpio could be one and the same person.

"Is there anything else you remember about Jeannette Leclair?" Daniel asked.

"That's about it. Like I said, most people keep to themselves."

"Thanks, Donna. You've been a big help. If we have any other questions for you, can we find you here?"

"Mr. White, I live and work here. My house is right next door. If I'm not there, I'm in the store," the helpful owner said smiling.

Daniel and his team walked away to talk in private.

"Okay, gang. Show me on the map exactly where this cottage is," Daniel said to the group.

After seeing the exact location of Jeannette Leclair's house, Daniel quickly formulated a plan.

"I want Merlin and Dan to go south of the house with a team."

"I already sent six agents down there, Daniel. Three are on the road south of the house and three on the north," Agent Scott said.

"You guys are ahead of me," Daniel said with a smile. "I like that. Okay, Merlin and Dan join up with the south group and form a perimeter on the south side of the house. Raul and Pat, you do the same on the north side. Make sure you have some people in place to cover the possibility of her trying to escape to the west.

I'll take the east side and move in by the driveway. Radio me when you are all in place and don't do anything without checking with me first.

One more thing. I want her taken alive, so don't shoot to kill. She has to know where Monique and this CJ are. Questions anyone?"

Everyone understood what had to be done.

"Okay, let's head out and stay in radio contact," Daniel ordered.

As the men were walking to the vehicles, Daniel told Dan to have one of his men stay at the grocery store.

"I'm ordering a chopper and have your guy tell the chopper to land over there in the parking lot. Make sure he directs the pilot in and keeps looky-loos away," Daniel ordered as he pointed to the large parking lot.

He wanted to make sure he had all the bases covered. There was always the chance that something could go wrong on a mission. He had plenty of experience in that area and it was better to be overly prepared for the unexpected than to assume nothing would go wrong.

Daniel got into the front seat of a suburban and called Kathy at headquarters as the driver started the vehicle. He gave her the instructions on the chopper allocation and also updated her on what was happening. They were the last vehicle in line as the trail of vehicles sped south on Highway 50.

Three miles down the road, Daniel's vehicle passed three black suburbans parked along the side of the road. Raul had just gotten out of the one he was riding in. Daniel's driver began to slow down as they approached a large black, mailbox and seashell-gravel driveway on the right side of the road. Two other suburbans in front of them slowed down and parked on each side of the driveway.

"This is it, Daniel," the driver said.

"Pull in just enough to get off the road," Daniel ordered.

As his vehicle pulled into the drive, Daniel saw the remaining three suburbans on the highway in front of his, slow down and pull to the gravel edge of the road. It wouldn't take long for Raul and Merlin to get their teams in place.

Daniel exited the vehicle and looked down the driveway. He couldn't see the cottage and told his men to spread out to his flanks. Once they were in place, the line moved toward the direction of the house. Daniel's team all had military M-16 rifles in their hands and Daniel had his Beretta pistol. Xi had his hands. Cautiously, the line moved forward. When they reached the bottom of the hill that hid the cottage, they all crouched down as they moved up the small incline.

Lying on his stomach, Daniel peaked over the hill's crest and saw the rustic, Cape Cod-style house. Parked in front of the cottage was a gray SUV. Daniel got his binoculars and searched the area. There was no movement that he could detect. He then looked south and saw the Wiz and his team encircling the south side. Daniel then focused on the north side and saw Raul's team doing the same.

"Write this down," Daniel said to one of the agents and he read off the numbers on the Maryland license plate.

When he finished, he told the agent to call the plate in and confirm who it was licensed to. Xi was on Daniel's right side.

"Do you want to take a look," Daniel asked, offering the glasses to Xi.

"No need. Know she there. This lady not know we here. She dangerous and when find out, get mad. Must be careful, Daniel," Xi said looking at his close friend, the Master.

"Any dreams about what will happen?" Daniel asked.

"See fire," Xi answered.

"Me, too, Xi. A ball of fire," Daniel answered as he checked to see the progress of the other two teams.

"Page 31," message entered Daniel's mind.

Merlin's and Raul's teams were in place and the team leaders radioed that they were in position.

"In five seconds I'm going to get on the bullhorn. Don't shoot unless it is life threatening and then only shoot to wound the suspect," was Daniel's order.

The agent on his left handed Daniel the bullhorn.

"Jeannette Leclair, this is the Federal government. We have you surrounded. Come out with your hands in the air. Jeannette Leclair, come out with your hands in the air."

Atiya had returned home from dropping off Azzah and put the groceries away. She again checked the email mailbox for messages. There weren't any. Discouraged and worried, she began getting things in order. Bored with nothing to do, she decided to begin packing her personal belongings. She packed only those items that could fit into two suitcases. Atiya was to give the appearance of being a tourist when she arrived at the airport. Everything else would be burned when she torched the cottage in the middle of the following night.

After making decisions on what would stay and go, she sat down and ate a tuna sandwich with a cup of tea. While savoring the meal, she saw that it was now almost two o'clock in the afternoon. Atiya cleaned up the kitchen and, out of force of habit, checked the email address again. There was a message. Her heart began to pound as she moved the mouse pointer to the email icon and clicked once. The email opened and she saw it was from her sister, Azzah. Happy to hear from her sister, she smiled, but was disappointed it wasn't from her father.

"No news. I'm safe in the right place. Will talk tomorrow. Azzah," was the brief message.

Atiya sat back in the chair and sighed.

"This is not good," she thought.

"Jeannette Leclair, this is the Federal government. We have you surrounded. Come out with your hands in the air. Jeannette Leclair, come out with your hands in the air."

The noise startled Atiya. It was a weird sound, not a normal voice.

"Jeannette Leclair, this is the Federal government. We have you surrounded. Come out with your hands in the air. Jeannette Leclair, come out with your hands in the air. You have one minute to come out with your hands raised."

Atiya jumped out of the chair and ran to the living room window. She looked out and saw no one. Then she ran to each window on each side of the cottage, searching where the noise was coming from.

"Jeannette Leclair, Atiya Zuckowi, we have you surrounded. We have captured your father Said Zuckowi. Come out with your hands in the air. Jeannette Leclair, come out with your hands in the air now."

Atiya sat down on the edge of her bed. "They have father. They have my father," she said to herself.

The message kept repeating itself from outside. "Come out with your hands in the air."

"They mean surrender," Atiya said.

That would not happen. She would never surrender to the Americans. She jumped off the bed and began throwing clothes onto the floor. Then she grabbed the bedding and threw them onto the floor in the living room.

"I will not surrender to you pigs. You killed my mother and brother. Screw you, Americans," she yelled, as she continued to pile clothing from the closets and dresser onto the floor.

"Jeannette Leclair, this is the Federal government. Come out with your hands in the air. Jeannette Leclair, come out with your hands in the air. This is your last warning," the voice said.

"Last warning … last warning. What are you going to do? Last warning," she yelled in a hysterical voice.

Jeannette Leclair then went to the kitchen and grabbed the two cans of gasoline that were by the back door. They were heavy but she carried them to the piles of clothes in the living room and bedroom. After pouring the gas on the heap of clothes in the bedroom and emptying the remaining flammable fuel around the room, she returned to the living room and did the same to the pile of clothing and linen in the living room with the second container of flammable fuel.

"Anybody see anything," Daniel asked into the radio.

"I see someone running from room to room," Raul answered.

"Same here, Daniel," Merlin answered.

"Hold your fire," Daniel ordered.

"There's a lot of activity, Daniel," Merlin said. "She's running from room to room."

"Tell her to come out with her hands in the air," Daniel said to the agent on his left as he handed him the bull horn.

Daniel looked through the binoculars, focusing on each window on his side of the house.

"Jeannette Leclair, come out with your hands in the air."

He could see movement. Someone was in a panic, running to different rooms throwing what looked like clothing around.

"Jeannette Leclair, come out with your hands in the air," the agent repeated.

Daniel kept looking and then he couldn't see any movement.

"Anyone see any movement?" he asked into the radio.

"Not anymore," Merlin said.

"I don't see any," Raul said. "Do you think she's coming out?"

"Keep an eye out," Daniel advised.

All the assault team members kept a close vigil on the cottage and after no sign of movement or activity for at least sixty seconds, a warning sign appeared from the house.

Daniel kept his eyes on the cottage and suddenly smoke started to seep out the cracks from the doorway and windows.

"I've got smoke," Raul said. "Daniel, there is smoke coming from the house. I think she started a fire."

"I see it also," Merlin confirmed into his radio.

The smoke intensified and then there was an explosion. The cottage erupted into a ball of flames and black smoke billowed from where the roof joined the side walls. In a matter of seconds, towering red flames shot through the old house's roof.

Daniel then heard what he thought was a single gunshot. The once cute Cape Cod house was now totally engulfed in towering flames. Seeing the fire erupt, Daniel stood up and the rest of the assault team that surrounded the burning inferno also stood, shocked at what they were witnessing. There was no way anyone could survive the hot flames.

Smoke billowed from the fire, sending black oily smoke high into the clear blue sky. Small explosions began to blow holes through the dry shake siding, sending hot cinders onto the ground. The old house, consisting of decades-old dry timber, went up like tinder in a forest fire. More explosions sent balls of fire mixed with cobalt black, oily smoke higher into the sky.

Daniel knew it was too late to call the fire department. Atiya Leclair, aka Jeannette Leclair, had to be dead. Off in the distance, he heard sirens. Someone must have seen the smoke and called in the alarm.

"Damn," was all he said as he walked toward the fire.

"There is no way I'm going to surrender," Leclair yelled and then struck a wooden match. She walked to the bedroom and threw the lit incendiary onto the pile of clothing that was soaked with gasoline. The pile exploded into a fireball, sending a wall of flames and scorching heat in her direction. Atiya raised her arm to protect her face and ran out of the bedroom into the living room.

She struck another match and threw it onto the pile. The blast of the combustion and flames scorched her hair and eyebrows. This time she didn't try to protect herself and calmly walked into the kitchen. The sniper, the killer of six innocent individuals around the United States, sat down at the kitchen table facing the growing inferno. Flames had spread throughout the living room and were working their blazing fingers of death into the kitchen. The heat was becoming unbearable and thick smoke enveloped the kitchen.

Calmly, Atiya reached for the Walther pistol and raised it to her head. The heat from the fire now burned her hair and the pain became excruciating. The assassin put the pistol's barrel into her mouth and gently squeezed the trigger, sending a 9mm projectile through her brain and out the back of her charred head. Atiya Zuckowi had committed her last assassination.

Daniel gathered his team together and told them to move the grey SUV away from the house. He also sent an agent back to the suburban blocking the driveway, to move it out of the way of the approaching vehicles with siren's wailing their eerie warning.

Merlin, Raul and the others walked from their posts to where Daniel was standing, staring at the bonfire.

"Who would have guessed she would torch the place. Damn, what a way to die," Merlin said, when he got to Daniel's location.

"She dead before fire kill her. She shoot self in head," Xi said calmly, as if he witnessed the suicide first hand.

Daniel looked at the Master. "I heard the shot, Xi. Did you, too?"

"No hear shot. Tell her to kill self. Use gun. She get message," the Master answered, then turned and retreated back up the driveway. He moved to the side as a fast-moving, bright, red fire truck with its white strobe and red flashing lights crested the hill of the driveway. Xi looked over his shoulder. The cottage roof and walls had collapsed and all the firemen had to save was a pile of burning rubble.

Daniel turned to Agents Pat Scott and Dan Aibaya. "You two are in charge. This is to be considered a crime scene. Wrap up everything with the local police and fire departments. I want the coroner's report on my desk tomorrow morning.

Search her SUV and see if you can find anything. Be careful and have the vehicle fingerprinted. We might get lucky and get prints on this CJ person. I'm taking Merlin, Xi and Raul back to DC with me."

"The chopper landed about five minutes ago in Queenstown, Daniel," Scott said.

"Then we'll have someone drive us there and he can return back here to help you out. Okay guys, we're out of here," Daniel said and began walking up the driveway.

When he, Raul and Merlin reached the crest of the hill on the driveway, all three turned to look at what was left of the crime scene. There wasn't much left. They turned in unison and slowly disappeared from sight.

"What a lousy day," Merlin said.

"Yeah, only two more to go. Monique Leclair and Scorpio," Raul said.

"They probably will be the toughest two to get," Daniel added.

As they walked quietly side by side, Daniel heard the familiar message again.

"The answer is "page 31"."

"I know … but where?" Daniel said out loud.

Both Merlin and Raul heard Daniel's words. As all three continued walking, they looked at him. Neither said a word.

Author W. Robb Robichaud

244

Chapter XXVII

Street Lady

On the seventh floor room of a luxury Georgetown hotel, Azzah Zuckowi sat in front of the large window enjoying the scenic view of the historical district and skyline of Washington, DC. In an hour she would meet Scorpio in a park near the hotel and finalize the plan. CJ, a freshman at John Hopkins University, was eager to complete the mission and also elated that the only bloodline left in the young adult's life would be killed. The senator had abandoned his child and mother years ago and wouldn't acknowledge that he had a child out of wedlock. He would pay the ultimate price for his denial.

Azzah got ready to go. She knew that the Federal authorities were looking for her. Monique had barely escaped capture in Oklahoma City and had seen her picture on the evening news. Nothing surprised the hardened lady any more and, when she saw her photo on the prime time television newscast, she took it in stride. Monique had the attitude that she was more intelligent than the Feds and she had proved it over the past month. In two more days, the plan that she had formulated herself would be completed and the United States, the most powerful country in the world, would be reduced by her, a single individual, to a conglomeration of floundering idiots.

Monique broke away from her thoughts and began to get ready for her rendezvous with Scorpio. She would have to be careful not to be recognized. On the bed, she had laid out her disguise. The attire she chose would give others the impression that she was a middle-aged, lower class lady, who bordered on being a street person. She undressed and put on a full-length, loose dress with a frayed and tattered hemline that she purchased at a second hand store. Next, she put on soiled, long white tube socks and then a pair of dirty, worn out tennis shoes with holes in the canvas tops. To compliment the outfit's appearance, she donned an oversized, stained sweatshirt and a cheap, dark blue ski jacket that was torn, exposing the white insulation fabric.

After putting everything on, she looked at herself in the full-length mirror and smiled at what she saw. No one in their right mind would ever suspect her of being a sniper and serial killer. She walked back to the bed and picked up the two final touches to her disguise, a soiled brunette wig and a black stocking hat. Standing in front of the mirror, Azzah put on the wig and ruffled it up even more than it originally was. Then she pulled the oversized, black knitted cap over her head and folded up the front. Azzah smiled at what she saw in the mirror. She looked like a street lady.

As she was leaving the hotel room, Monique put on a pair of large sunglasses that were scratched and grabbed a grungy canvas bag filled with rags. The last item she picked up from the dresser was a Walther 9mm pistol. Carefully she slid the weapon in the coat's large side pocket. She was now ready to meet CJ in the park.

Opening the room's door, she looked out into the hallway. No one was there. Quietly she closed the door and walked to the emergency exit stairwell. She couldn't take the elevator to the lobby. Her appearance would definitely create a stir with the hotel management and security staff. Azzah descended eight flights of stairs and opened the door to the underground parking facilities. She cracked open the steel door and looked for anyone in the area. It was quiet and no one was around.

Feeling confident, Azzah, the street woman walked quickly to the exit. With a slight limp, the street lady began walking to the park that was a half mile away.

Azzah played her role as a street person very well. Occasionally, she would stop at a trash can and look inside as if she was searching for something of value. Pedestrians made efforts to avoid. Her. When she approached them, they would walk on the outer edges of the sidewalk as if she were contagious disease on the move.

Monique entered the park and slyly searched the area for police and also for CJ. There were no officers present. A short distance away, she saw CJ sitting on a park bench. Monique slowly limped toward the young student who was reading a book. As she neared the park bench, Scorpio looked up and saw a bedraggled, possibly homeless, female approaching. CJ paid no attention to the lady and went back to reading.

Monique sat down on the opposite end of the bench and looked around once more. When she was positive that they were alone, she spoke.

"Don't look up and continue reading your book, CJ."

The voice was familiar to Scorpio but the person wasn't.

"It's Azzah. Keep reading and act as if you are ignoring me," Azzah said, as she looked into her canvas bag.

"It is good to see you, CJ. We have to be very careful," the street lady said.

"I know. I saw the picture of you or Atiya on the television. They are looking everywhere for you," Scorpio said.

"They'll never catch me. Look at me. Do I look like a wanted person?" she said giggling.

"You look like a bum."

"So the disguise works. That's good. I will make this quick. Where is the vial?"

"Behind my locker ... wrapped in a towel. No one will find it."

"Good. You are scheduled to work the night of the function?"

"Yes. I'm on the schedule. I checked on Friday. Everything is okay."

"Now, we won't go over what you have to do unless you have questions."

"I'm fine, Azzah. Five minutes after he begins speaking, I'll take the vial out of my pocket and drop it onto the floor. Then, all I have to do is smash the glass tube with the heal of my shoe and walk out of the chamber. I take the back stairwell to the street, get a taxi to the airport, and meet you at the ticket counter. I already have my bags packed.

Azzah, I'm so excited and looking forward to our vacation in the Bahamas."

After CJ smashed the vial, the only connection to Azzah, Atiya and their father would be dead in less than five seconds along with the rest of the people in the large hall. Scorpio had no idea that the sacrifice about to be made by the young adult was the right to continue living.

"We will have a wonderful time. Now, I must go. We've spent too much time together," Azzah said, as she looked around for any suspicious people.

"You are going to take care of my father?" Scorpio asked.

"He will be dead by the time we meet at the airport. I promised you that and I will not break my word."

"Thank you. You are a true sister."

"Thank you also. I will see you at the airport. Be careful. We are depending on you. Don't let your family down," Monique said as she rose from the bench.

"I promise. You are too important to me. I'll see you at the airport."

Monique looked at Scorpio for the last time, then turned and hobbled away in the direction from which she had come.

Scorpio looked at the bedraggled, homeless person as she limped down the concrete walkway. It was nice to have a family like Azzah, Atiya and Said Zuckowi.

"I do love you," Scorpio said softly, as Azzah disappeared around the corner.

Chapter XXVIII

Tightened Security

*D*aniel, *Merlin, Raul and Xi arrived back at Falcon* Agency's headquarters at 3:45 p.m. and went directly to the conference room. Daniel had called Kathy when they were being driven to the waiting helicopter in Queenstown, instructing her to have everyone who was supposed to be present at the postponed 2:00 meeting, there when he arrived.

The foursome walked into the room and everyone was present. The men and Kathy took their seats and Daniel took control of the meeting.

"Has everyone been briefed on what transpired this afternoon?" he asked.

"I just finished giving an update of everything you've told me," Kathy, Falcon's operation coordinator, answered.

"Good and thanks. We've got three of the five targets we were after. Kaleem Mushowui is dead and so is Atiya Zuckowi ... aka Jeannette Leclair. Said Zuckowi is in our custody and that leaves Monique Leclair, also know as Azzah Zuckowi, and Scorpio on the loose. All we know about Scorpio is that he or she goes by the surname CJ. We have no idea if Scorpio is male or female.

Right now, I suspect both are still in the Washington, DC area, maybe in Virginia or Maryland or right here in DC somewhere.

We are entering the time period of the zodiac sign Scorpio tomorrow. With everything that has happened, I also feel that whatever they have planned will happen very soon, especially now that one of the twins is dead and the remaining two haven't heard from the father, Said.

Have we found anything regarding "page 31" yet?" Daniel asked, as his eyes looked at each individual seated at the large conference table.

CIA Director Bill Angus volunteered to speak first. "Daniel, we've got nothing so far. I've got the CIA's resources stretched to the limit on this. We've eliminated all the religious books and congressional records going back five years. Every East Coast newspaper edition for the past year has been searched.

Daniel, I'm sorry to question you on this, but are you sure, absolutely positive, that the answer to "page 31" is in a book, magazine or something in print? Could "page 31" mean something else, like a code, derivative or connotation of something else? It is so broad and could mean anything and cover any areas," Angus said, looking a little flustered.

Daniel looked at Xi for assurance and the Master stood up and addressed the group.

"I not say much for long time, but now Xi must talk. There many thing that happen in this world and people have many power that don't use. I have many power that you don't use. It gift from Supreme Master.

Many know that when Xi have dream … vision, it come true. Xi never say have vision and not believe that it be true. That why some say that people have ESP. Not ESP, but true message from other world," Xi said, looking at Daniel as he smiled. The Master continued speaking.

"Some think people like Xi very different and some say crazy. Not crazy but spiritual and have gift. Xi learn from Masters how to … develop power God give everybody. That why people like Xi called Master. Same for Daniel. Daniel White Master also. He learn how to make powers better."

Everyone stared at the Chinese man, knowing that his words were true and coming from his heart.

"Xi say this and it stay in this room. When Daniel say "page 31", he not make up in mind. Daniel receive message from almighty Master. Xi get same message from Master and answer always in message. Answer is "page 31" but we not know where "page 31" is.

Sometime answer at feet and we step over question or answer. But, you must trust Daniel. He not crazy. Xi not crazy either. Well ... maybe sometime Xi crazy," he said and laughed.

The others all smiled, dumbfounded at what they had just heard.

"Xi think maybe this hardest answer ever get. Too much to think about but Xi know that answer always in message and never hard to understand. I not think answer in book. I think answer different ... but easy.

Now, all must think different and look inside self for what "page 31" really mean. Sorry Daniel, but that must be said," Xi said, looking at Daniel who was seated at the head of the table.

Xi continued. "I know that soon Scorpio try to kill many important people."

Getting a mental message, Xi stopped for a few seconds and held his hand in the air so people wouldn't talk.

"Scorpio is "page 31". Xi know for sure. Thank you." Xi sat down to a quiet audience.

Everyone was in awe of what they just heard and sat back in their chairs and looked around. Daniel left them to their thoughts for a few minutes. He looked at each individual present and saw in their faces that Xi's unplanned oration had hit home.

"Those were some powerful words, Xi. Thank you," Daniel said, as he stood up and looked at his friend and mentor.

Suddenly, Merlin started clapping his hands and stood up. The others joined in and stood also in appreciation and recognition of the humble Chinese Master. Xi remained seated, feeling a sense of embarrassment, and nodded once in acknowledgement to his associates.

"Maybe we forget who we are at times. Being who and what we are, everyone in this room has an obligation to their country to protect every person on America's soil. That is our commitment.

There is only one person or suspect that we are investigating who we have ... or, should I say, doesn't fit into the puzzle as far as I'm concerned. That's Senator Nigel Mason. I don't see the connection even though Said Zuckowi had his home phone number in his possession. Anyone got any ideas on this?" Daniel asked the attentive group.

"Our guys still have him under surveillance. So far, nothing has turned up. He goes about his daily routine with no deviations," Director Angus said. "Let me read what he does.

He's up every morning at 5:30 and goes for a two-mile jog through Georgetown. He runs about a six-minute mile. Not bad. He's out of the house at 6:30 sharp and drives directly to his office on the hill (the Capital Building), has lunch at 11:15 in the cafeteria and is back in his office or the Senate chamber for votes the rest of the day. He usually leaves his office between 6:00 and 6:30 p.m. and drives to his house back in Georgetown. Occasionally, he will stop at the same grocery store on the way home and then he goes straight to the house.

Around 8:00 p.m. he jogs another two miles using the same route he runs in the morning. He never stops when he's jogging. It's lights out at 11:30 p.m. That's it. Every day it's the same routine. On the weekends he may go out for breakfast at a little restaurant, alone. He never meets anyone there. That's it. Boring as it may seem, Senator Mason is clean so far.

Oh … we have a tap on his phone and check his cell calls every two days. Nothing unusual. Just phone calls to his wife and kids and maybe other Senators. No one else."

"What about activity around where he lives, Bill?" Daniel asked.

"Same thing. Everyone goes about their own business and don't really socialize with one another."

"Have you checked to see who else lives in the townhouse project?"

"Yes, and I have the list right here. There is only one place rented. The rest are owner-occupied. Let's see. There are two other senators and four congressmen living there. Six other Federal government employees and two judges. The rental is occupied by an FBI agent who was recently transferred back here from Chicago. He has an option to buy the place. That's it, sixteen town homes."

"Sounds like a nice group of professionals," Daniel answered. "What about upcoming functions or conventions here in the DC area?"

"I can answer that question, Daniel," Kathy said standing up. "Nothing happening this weekend. On Tuesday there is an AARP convention and the attendance is expected to be about twenty-five thousand people. On Thursday there are two conventions. One is the national convention for realtors, 15,000 people anticipated to attend, and a lawyer convention, about 6,000 people. That's it for the week," she said and sat down.

"Any of those trigger anyone's hot button," Daniel asked the group.

No one answered and some shook their heads no.

"What about New York, Daniel?" FBI Director Lambert asked.

"I don't think New York is the target. My gut feeling is that it will happen here in DC. The Atiya Zuckowi deal gave me that feeling. If they were planning something in New York soon, she would have been there or a lot closer to New York than Maryland," Daniel answered.

"I agree," Merlin interjected. "My intuition is that they want to do something that we would never expect to happen, like hit the White House or Langley. Something on that level."

"Security is so tight at those places. Unless they have an insider working for them, I can't see how they would get in. Tours of the White House have been suspended until further notice and to get into CIA headquarters at Langley is virtually impossible. Damn, I'm the director and gate security treats me like I'm a mad bomber," Bill Angus said.

"They're doing their job, Bill. You look like a bomber," Merlin answered, which got everyone laughing.

After everyone quieted down, Daniel asked another question. "You know, that brings up an interesting scenario. What about the FBI, NSA, DEA, Secret Service headquarters? How tight is their security?"

"Tight as the rest, Daniel. Every agency is tighter than a drum," FBI Director John Ebersole answered.

"Okay. Let's tighten all the agencies' security even tighter for the next two weeks," Daniel answered. "I want every government location's security patrols increased. If you need more manpower, pull them in from the mid-west offices. Let's get on this after the meeting.

Our number one priority now is to find Monique Leclair and Scorpio."

"What about the "page 31" search? I thought that was number one," Raul asked.

"It was, but it isn't anymore. We've been beating our heads against the wall on that. Not any more. Like Xi said, Scorpio is "page 31" and "page 31" is Scorpio. Find one and you have the other. That was my mistake.

If anyone has any questions, ask them now. Otherwise, let's get to work."

There weren't any questions and everyone left the conference room with the exception of Falcon members. When the room cleared, Merlin closed the doors and walked up behind Xi.

"Thanks for getting us in line, Xi," the Wizard said.

"Welcome, Wizard," the Master answered.

"Have you heard from Agents Scott or Aibaya, Kathy?"

"Yes. They have everything taken care of and Pat said you'll have a coroner's report on your desk late tonight. He saw the body and said that the back of the suspect's head had a large hole. Pat said it looks like she blew her brains out.

They've taken care of the local authorities and are maintaining Federal jurisdiction over the crime scene and investigation."

"Those guys are good. It's late and it's been one hell of a day. Anyone have anything else?"

No one had anything to add.

"Let's get out of this chicken coop and go home. Great job as usual, people. I'll see everyone on Monday morning," Daniel said and everyone gladly went home.

Chapter XXIX

The Last Sniper

*I*t was early morning and the city lights emitted their reflective yellow glow in the clear, black night sky of the District of Columbia. Included in the geographic boundaries of Washington is the small community of Georgetown, located northwest of the capital. Its claim to fame is the well-known Georgetown University. What most people don't know is that this neighborhood of tree-lined streets and handsome brick houses is the oldest part of the District of Columbia. It is also where many of Washington's "Who's Who" reside. The main thorough-fare is M street and is lined with upscale boutiques, stores, restaurants and bars. Large crowds visit the historical community on weekends.

Located on a small street off M street is a grouping of old brick townhomes, many of which are occupied by government officials. Two CIA undercover agents had one of the townhomes under a 24-7 surveillance. It was a boring operation because the subject under their scrutiny had the same daily routine. Senator Nigel Mason may be a good politician and senator, but he lived a boring life.

At 5:05 a.m., the sun still hadn't cast its light over the horizon and the street lights on the narrow street were still lit. The two agents were sitting in their unmarked black vehicle watching the home. A light shining in the bedroom could be seen through the closed shades. They knew it was the Senator's bedroom. The highlight for the balance of the agent's shift was about to happen. They knew the Senator was getting ready to go for his morning jog.

Both agents sat up in their seats and kept their eyes trained on the townhome. They played a game with each other to kill time. Every morning the Senator would come out the front door of the home and stretch his body, legs and arms, using the concrete front steps as a leverage base. The game to guess how many total minutes and seconds it would take to do his stretching routine.

The agents saw the upstairs bedroom light go off. They even timed from when the lights went out until the moment he emerged in the doorway. It was usually four minutes and ten seconds. Both men started their stop watches when the bedroom lights went off.

The agent in the passenger seat saw a movement up the street. He couldn't recognize if it was a person or animal, but he was sure that he saw movement.

"Let me see the night-vision goggles, John," he said to his partner John Gibson.

"You see something?" John asked.

"I'm not sure … but I thought I saw something move near one of the houses up the street."

Agent Frank Moore looked through the night-vision goggles, searching where he thought he saw the unidentified movement.

"See anything?" Gibson asked in a whisper.

"I'm not sure. What ever I think it is … is all in black." Moore said, still scanning the area.

"Maybe it's a dog out roaming the neighborhood."

"No … I don't think it was a dog," Moore answered.

He continued looking through the goggles, moving them carefully and slowly in small increments, trying to pick up an unusual object.

"Got it. It's against the wall of the house. The third house down from the end," Moore said keeping the goggles on the hard-to-see-object.

"What is it?" John asked.

"I can't make it out. It's blending into the walls and I can barely make out a profile."

"Keep your eyes trained on it. I'm getting out of the car and will work my way up to it. Turn your headset on."

"It is on. Keep a low profile. I don't want you to spook it. How long before Mason comes out?" Agent Moore asked his partner.

Gibson looked at his watch. "Lights went out one minute and twenty seconds ago."

John opened the car door; the inside lights didn't illuminate. Standard procedure for surveillance situations was to remove all interior light bulbs in case a door accidentally was opened, thereby revealing the agents. He quietly closed the door, removed his hidden pistol from the shoulder case under his sport coat. In a crouched position, began moving slowly up the street.

Moore saw the shadow move down to the ground and then it was even harder to see the black object. If he moved the night-vision goggles away to look with his naked eyes, he would never be able to find it again. He kept the goggles trained on the location.

On the opposite side of the street a front porch light came on and John crouched down next to a car. A man appeared in the doorway in his striped pajamas and dark bathrobe. John watched the male step onto the cement porch and stretch his arms while yawning. The man with the disheveled white hair bent over as if to pick something up.

"The newspaper," John said to himself.

Suddenly, the early riser tumbled forward and fell down the cement stairs. John watched to see if he would get up.

"John, the shadow is on the move and is running. I'm going after him in the car," Moore said into his microphone.

John heard the car start up. When he looked back to where Moore was he saw Senator Nigel Mason opening the front door to his house and begin to step outside.

"Get back into the house and lock the doors," Agent Gibson yelled, as he heard the screeching of tires from the agent's vehicle.

Mason slammed the door shut and John turned and began running up the street. He saw the figure running and it was human. The agent also saw that the suspect was carrying what appeared to be a rifle.

When John reached where the man in the pajamas was lying, he saw a pool of blood beginning to spread on the gray concrete. Quickly, he reached down to feel a pulse from the neck's main artery on the lifeless body. There was no pulse. Knowing that he couldn't help the dead man, he continued his foot pursuit up the street. Agent Moore and the powerful V-8 engine vehicle went speeding by John, as he ran in a full sprint. He saw the figure now near the end of the street and the car was very close to the black figure's location. Moore saw the small human dressed all in black trying to run fast, but was having difficulties because it was carrying a large rifle.

Seeing the black vehicle approaching fast, the shadow dropped the rifle and pulled a pistol equipped with a silencer from its waist belt. The shadow turned and fired two quick shots at the car, hoping to get lucky and maybe slow the vehicle down.

Frank saw the shadow drop the rifle and then turn and point something at him. The car windshield shattered and he turned the vehicle toward the black figure. When he was twenty-five feet away, Frank locked up the brakes, coming to a screeching stop. In one motion he drew his pistol and opened the vehicle door. The windshield shattered again and then the door window exploded, sending sharp shards of glass onto Frank. He felt pieces of glass imbed into his face. That didn't stop the CIA agent and he shot at the black figure as it turned to run. Frank's 38 revolver made a loud explosion. The shooter stumbled and fell to the ground. Frank wasn't sure if he had hit it when he fired or if the person had just stumbled and fell.

The shadow rolled on the ground and pointed its pistol at the figure that was running in its direction. The human on the ground raised the pistol and took careful aim. It never fired the shot.

John caught up to where the battle was happening and saw the figure dressed in black running and then turn and point something at the vehicle. He never heard the sound of a shot but did see his partner turn the car toward the figure.

Frank stopped the vehicle and opened the door. John then saw the driver's door window explode. He looked toward the human figure as it turned and began to run away. A loud repercussion sound from a gun firing broke the eerie silence. The shadowy figure stumbled and fell to the ground. In the same motion, the person rolled and then pointed an object at his partner.

John reacted swiftly. He aimed his 38 pistol at the prone human being and squeezed off two shots. The noise from Frank's first shot had to have awakened the neighborhood. His two shots confirmed that there was trouble in the streets of Georgetown.

The figure lying on the grass didn't move.

"You alright, Frank," Gibson yelled to his partner.

"Yeah, I think I've got some glass cuts. Cover me," Frank yelled back, as he moved to the motionless figure on the ground while keeping his pistol pointed at the black body.

He was about five feet away when the body suddenly moved, raising the pistol. Frank fired twice and the assailant's arm and pistol dropped to the ground. He continued walking forward. When he reached the body, he kicked the black clothed body's pistol away.

John ran up beside his partner also with his pistol pointed at the shooter. Seeing his partner beside him, Frank knelt down to the body that was lying face down and felt for a pulse. There was none. He searched the lifeless body for other weapons and then rolled the dead body over onto its back. Its head was covered by a tight fitting wool hat with holes for its eyes. He also saw that it had on leather gloves with one finger cut off, exposing the trigger finger.

John still had his pistol pointed at the figure, not willing to take any chances. Frank reached for the hood and pulled it up, exposing the body's face. It was a woman's face staring up at him with her eyes closed. Blood was dripping from a hole in her forehead.

"She's dead," Frank said, as he looked up at his partner with blood dripping all over his face. He looked like something from a monster movie,

"Holy shit. You're shot Frank," Gibson said reaching for his partner.

"No. It's just glass cuts from the window she shot out. I'm okay. Call headquarters and get some help here. The local cops will be screaming here in a little bit."

John ran to the car and placed the emergency call to Langley. While his friend was radioing the call, Frank completely removed the hood from the woman's head and searched her body for any ID. Off in the distance, he heard the wailing of sirens. The locals were on the way.

A blood-curdling scream cut through the air. Frank and John looked back down the street. A woman was screaming from an open doorway.

"Oh, shit," John said, and began running toward the hysterical woman who was standing over the dead man on the front steps of their home.

Frank stayed behind with the dead sniper. The police sirens wailed their warning and were closer.

Chapter XXX

Interview

*D*aniel and Xi rose early Saturday morning and worked out. After their run, they sat down on the patio of the house.

"Quite a week, my friend," Daniel said.

"Much happen and not done yet. Time for Xi to go home. I leave tomorrow. You no need me here now. You do okay."

"That's all right. It is time for you to go back to Colorado and be with your family. I think that whatever Scorpio is planning will happen this week. I wish I knew what the hell … or where they are going to strike."

"I think part of answer is "page 31". Other part missing and should know soon."

"Any idea if Scorpio is a male or female?"

"Not know. Sometime think man … sometime think lady."

"Well, whatever it is, we'll find out soon. Listen, Susan and the kids and I are going to look at dogs this morning. I think Susan found the type they're looking for. Do you want to go with us?" Daniel asked.

"Ah … you go get Charlie today."

"I won't ask how you knew that, Master Xi," Daniel said laughing.

"Ali and Lance tell me. No message," Xi answered and laughed hard.

After they finished laughing, Xi answered Daniel's original question.

"I not go with you to get Charlie. That family business. Important that only family go and have fun. Better balance."

"I definitely need balance Xi," Daniel answered, and they went into the house to get cleaned up.

Around 8:30 a.m. under the protection of a Secret Service escort, the White family left the observatory via the Massachusetts Avenue exit. The military style convoy headed northwest until the Wisconsin Avenue intersection and then turned north toward Chevy Chase.

Susan and the children had searched the newspapers and internet for yellow Labrador retrievers and found two families whose female Labs had litters eight weeks ago. The puppies were ready to be placed in homes and the owners were interviewing prospective buyers of the puppies.

"Interviewing prospective owners?" Daniel said, when Susan told him the news. "Since when do you have to be interviewed to buy a dog? Now that's a bunch of crap."

"Well, that's the way it's done here in yuppie land, my dear," Susan answered with a wide smile.

"How many interviews do we have?"

"Two. One at nine and the other is at ten."

"Okay. Get the kids and let's leave here at 8:30 a.m. That should give us ample time to make OUR interviews," Daniel answered sarcastically.

"We'll be ready. You better be also or the wrath of Ali and Lance will haunt you for the rest of your life," his beautiful wife answer while giggling.

"Interview," Daniel said under his breath as he walked away to let his security team know the plans. "I'll fix those interviewers," he said in a conniving way and then laughed.

When everyone was ready to leave, they walked out the front door. In front of them were five black SUV's and four motorcycle cops.

Seeing all the vehicles, Susan stopped in her tracks and looked at her husband. "Daniel, what are all these vehicles doing here. Is someone important coming or already here?"

"Nope. The White family is going to be interviewed so THEY CAN BUY A DOG! Well, they want to interview us, so I figured we'll just scare the hell out of the interviewers. This should be great. C'mon. Let's go," Daniel said, leading Susan by the hand.

"Daniel?" was Susan's response and she knew that anything she said wouldn't matter. When Daniel White sets his mind to something, look out.

"It will be fun," she thought and laughed.

They arrived at their first appointment with all the vehicles flashing their lights. Daniel told the security supervisor not to use their sirens. He wanted to make an impression but not scare the interviewers to death. The fleet drove down a long driveway and stopped in front of the house. Two children opened the front door and saw the black suburbans and motorcycle cops. Their eyes opened wide and they slammed the door shut.

Seeing the kids' reactions, Daniel roared with devious laughter.

"Oh, this is great."

Agents poured out of the vehicles and took up guard positions. The front door of the Victorian house opened and a man and wife in their early forties walked slowly out onto the porch. The two children stayed cowering behind their parents. Daniel put on his straight face and helped Susan and the kids out of the suburban.

"Hi, I'm Daniel White and this is my wife, Susan. And these are our two children, Ali and Lance. I guess we have a nine o'clock appointment for an interview."

The owners were very apprehensive to speak.

"Ahh …hi, Mr. White. I … I'm Christopher Boatwright and … and this is my wife, Barbara. Oh … and these are our children, Kathleen Marie and Thomas. Pleasure to meet you, sir," Christopher said very nervously.

"Well, let's get this over with. We have another appointment to go to, Chris," Daniel said, with authority, and very conscious that he used the nickname for Christopher.

"Sure, Mr. White. May I ask what you do?"

"I'm with the government and everything I do is top secret. You can't ask me any questions regarding my occupation. You need special security clearances to ask. If I tell you anything, I'll have to kill you. Now, next question," Daniel said, trying to keep a straight face.

The Boatwright family didn't know what to say as they looked at the security staff and the Falcon Agency decals on the doors of the vehicles.

"I don't think there is any need for more questions, Mr. White. The kennel is out back. Why don't you follow me?"

"Great. C'mon kids. Let's go look at the puppies," Daniel said and they followed the Boatwright family into the house.

Four security staff also entered the house. Susan felt embarrassed but didn't say a word. Daniel was in his prime and it really was hilarious.

There were six puppies in the kennel with the mother. All were wagging their tails, happy to see visitors. Christopher Boatwright opened the gate and the puppies all made a dash to freedom. Lance and Ali laughed as the dogs jumped on each of them, vying for attention. Boatwright explained the linage of the litter and emphasized the background of the parents to Daniel and Susan. The children were enjoying the companionship and happy dogs. Susan smiled as she watched them play.

Daniel walked over to the kids and squatted down. The puppies saw they had a new admirer and rushed over to him.

"Well, guys, see any you like?" he asked.

"I like all of them, daddy," Ali said.

"That's good, Ali. But we can only take one."

"What about you, Lance. See any that you like?"

Lance, being the oldest, felt like it was his decision. "Hm … you know, dad, if we only get one, it might get lonely without a buddy dog to play with. How about we get two. Then they can be friends."

Daniel knew he was dead meat now. He fell into the kid-dog trap. "That's a good thought, Lance. But maybe we should get one here and another at the other place. What do you think about that idea?"

"That sounds fine. What do you think, Ali?" Lance asked his sister.

"Okay. We will take this one … Charlie … and you can pick out the other one at the other house," Ali answered her brother as she picked up a male puppy in her arms. The dog kept kissing her face as if to say, "Thank you for choosing me."

Susan, a veterinarian, examined the Lab and, after the examination, told Daniel that the dog was healthy.

"Well, Christopher. Looks like they've made a decision. What's next?" Daniel said standing up.

"All I have to do is prepare the papers and that's it."

"How much for the dog?"

"Normally, they go for eight-hundred dollars, Mr. White, but in your case, is four-hundred okay?"

"Nope. Eight-hundred is just right. I wouldn't want to have to arrest you for bribing a government official, Chris. So let's get this done. I don't want to be late for our next appointment."

271

"I wasn't trying to …"

"It's okay, Chris. Let's get this done," Daniel said, turning, and walked toward the house.

"Yes, sir, Mr. White," Boatwright said and ran to Daniel's side like one of the puppies in the litter. "I have all the papers in my studio library. A check would be fine."

"Nah. I'll slap eight hundred dollar bills on the table. You do take cash, don't you Chris?"

"Cash is fine, sir. Just fine."

Daniel completed the transaction and everyone loaded into the suburbans. Lance, Ali and Charlie got in another black vehicle with the Falcon Agency logo on the doors.

Once the convoy started to roll down the driveway, Susan turned to Daniel and burst out laughing.

"Daniel White, you are such a jerk sometimes."

Both laughed hard and then kissed each other.

"Let's do it again at the next place," Susan suggested.

"Interviewing to buy a freaking dog. How stupid can people get?" he said and laughed again. "What a great day!"

At the next appointment, Daniel did the same routine to a pompous yuppie couple. It didn't take Daniel long to have them eating out of his hands. Lance selected a female and named her Mattie. When Daniel asked his son why the name Mattie, Lance answered that the puppy jumped around like a kangaroo and kangaroos are always called Matilda.

"I think Mattie is a nickname for Matilda, dad. It's a cool name for a girl dog, anyway," the young man said.

Daniel knew that the White's future, when it came to animals, wasn't over. He envisioned puppies all over the place. Luckily, they had a veterinarian in the family and Susan was happy, that in a few years, she could resume her career in the animal medical practice.

On the way back home, Daniel received a phone call on the special phone in the vehicle. The agent in the passenger seat answered the phone and handed it back to Daniel.

"This is Daniel."

"Daniel, Merlin here. They got Monique Leclair. I know you're with the kids and Susan, so I won't say anymore."

"I'll meet you at Falcon in about an hour. We're on our way home right now. Get Raul, Bill Angus, John Ebersole, Pat Scott and Dan Aibaya to meet us there."

"What about Kathy and Xi?"

"Let her enjoy the weekend. She's worked her tail off and needs a break. Xi's going back to Colorado tomorrow. Let's let him relax also."

"Okay. See you in about an hour." Merlin and Daniel disconnected the call.

"Who was that, Daniel?" Susan asked.

"Merlin. I've got to go into the office for a bit."

"Anything serious?"

"Everything I'm involved with is serious, Susan."

"I know," she answered softly, reflecting back to the times Daniel was gone overseas for long periods of time.

Daniel had the convoy pull off the road and Susan got into the suburban the children were in. Daniel's and one other vehicle sped down Massachusetts Avenue toward Falcon Agency's headquarters. He sat alone behind the Secret Service driver and the other agent in the passenger seat.

"Page 31," the message said.

Chapter XXXI

What is the Question

Merlin called in the people Daniel had requested and they were all seated in the quiet conference room when the Director of Falcon Agency arrived. Everyone was dressed in weekend casual clothing and relaxed at the table. Daniel walked into the room and looked at his watch. It was 11:45 a.m. on Saturday, October 23rd.

"Good morning, all. I guess we have some good news. Merlin, why don't you start," Daniel said

"I yield the floor to Bill Angus, Daniel. He has the report and it was his men that got her."

"Okay, Bill. The floor is yours," Daniel said, acknowledging Merlin's request.

"It was a hell of a night, people, but we got Monique Leclair," Bill said with a smile.

He gave a detailed explanation of what had happened with the two CIA agents, Frank Moore and John Gibson, while they were watching Senator Nigel Mason's house.

"Do you have confirmation that it was Monique Leclair … Azzah Zuckowi, Bill?" Daniel asked.

"Yes, Daniel. I got the fingerprint results about an hour ago. We ran them through the international database. The Canadians had them on file under Azzah Zuckowi and Monique Leclair."

"Where is the body now?" Daniel queried.

"In the DC morgue."

"I want pictures of her laid out on the coroner's table."

"What's up, Daniel," Raul asked.

"We're going to show them to Said Zuckowi and also the pictures of the burnt cottage. I want to rattle his brain and scare the shit out of him. Maybe he'll give us information on Scorpio.

Now, what's the story on the person Leclair killed?"

"It was Senator Byron Matheson. He was shot in the head," Director Angus answered.

"One shot ... one kill?" Daniel said softly.

"One shot ... one kill, Daniel," Angus answered.

"Damn ... Matheson. Do you think Leclair made a mistake and shot the wrong senator? I mean, isn't it ironic that a senator who lives on the same street as Senator Nigel Mason is killed? Are there any ties to Matheson, Bill?" Daniel asked.

"Right now, we have no idea, Daniel. We're talking to Matheson's wife to see if there are any links with Zuckowi's or al Qaeda. I called the agent-in-charge at the scene. So far, there is nothing that ties him with anything.

They've also talked to Senator Mason and he has no idea what this is all about. When he was questioned about Said Zuckowi and why he would have the Senator's telephone number hidden in his wallet, he didn't have any idea who any of the Zuckowi's were. This is really strange, Daniel. Really weird."

"For some reason, I don't think it was a random killing. Monique Leclair was too smart to try anything like that. Everything they've done has been well planned," Daniel said, while trying to think of a connection or what they had missed.

"Where is Said Zuckowi now, Bill?"

"We've got him locked up in the county jail and have two agents posted there at all times."

"Wiz, set up an appointment for you, Raul and me to visit him."

"When and what time?" Merlin answered.

"The sooner, the better, Wiz. We're on a super fast track now. Scorpio is the only one alive and we have no freaking idea who it is."

At that moment, the familiar words entered Daniel's mind, "page 31".

"Bill, use our phone to get those pictures. That's it. Let's get moving. I'll be in my office."

Daniel read the coroner's report on Atiya Zuckowi that was on his desk. She did commit suicide with a shot in the head. Xi was right again.

Two hours later, Daniel, Raul, Merlin and Bill Angus walked into the county jail's interrogation room. Said Zuckowi was seated in a chair with his handcuffed hands on the table in front of him. He was dressed in a loose fitting, orange top that had COUNTY JAIL in bold black letters on the back of the shirt. Said looked up as the men walked into the barren, dull-gray room. All the men sat across the table from Zuckowi and Daniel was seated directly across from Said.

"I'm Daniel White and these are my associates. I'm the Director of Falcon Agency and we're here to ask you some questions."

"I don't have anything to say to you," Zuckowi answered.

"That's fine. Bill, hand me that envelope please," Daniel said.

He opened the manila envelope and removed a stack of photographs, making sure that Zuckowi couldn't see them.

"When was the last time you saw your daughter, Atiya?"

"I have no answer."

"Well, we saw her yesterday at her cottage south of Queenstown."

Zuckowi looked at Daniel.

"Got your interest now, Said. Atiya is dead. Here are the last pictures of her at the cottage," Daniel said and tossed four photos of a burnt, unrecognizable body lying on a pile of charred rubble.

"Now you may not be able to recognize her because she was burnt to death in her rustic cottage south of Queenstown. She set the fire herself. It's an ugly sight to see one of your children burnt. Isn't it Said?"

Zuckowi studied the pictures, thinking it was a trap.

"That's not Atiya. That could be anyone. Nice try," he answered.

"Well, here are a couple more pictures of the home with her car out front and a beautiful view of the sand dunes. Look familiar?" Daniel asked, as he tossed two more pictures at Said.

As he looked at the pictures, they could see that he recognized the location.

"Now, when was the last time you saw Azzah, or should I say Monique?"

Zuckowi didn't answer and kept looking at the photos.

"Our men saw her early this morning in Georgetown. You are familiar with where Georgetown is, right?"

He still didn't answer and kept looking at the pictures.

"Georgetown is northwest of Washington, DC. It's a small community and there are a lot of important people who live there. One person who lives in a townhouse is a United States Senator. Do you know Senator Byron Matheson, Said?"

"No, I don't."

"Hmm ... well Monique must have, because she killed him this morning."

Daniel looked at Zuckowi's reaction to his statement. A brief smile appeared on his face.

"Our men saw her shoot the Senator and then guess what happened. C'mon, Said. Help me out here. Guess what happened?"

Said looked up at Daniel with an angry look on his face.

"Let me help you out with this tough question. The men that saw her kill the senator, killed Azzah," Daniel answered, and threw the pictures of Zuckowi daughter's body lying naked on a stainless steel table.

"These pictures were taken at the coroner's office before he started cutting up her beautiful body to perform an autopsy. That is Azzah, Said," Daniel said.

Said snapped when he saw the pictures of Azzah's dead body.

"You fucking assholes. You killed both of my daughters," he yelled, trying to cross the table to grab Daniel. In one quick move, Daniel's right arm extended and the palm of his hand hit Said on the forehead, snapping his head back, followed by his body. Zuckowi went flying backwards and fell back over his chair.

Merlin and Raul ran around the table, grabbed Said by each arm and sat him back down into the chair. They then took two steps back and stood guard over the terrorist.

"That wasn't a good thing to do, Said. You could get seriously hurt trying stupid tricks like that. Now, I'm going to ask you once more. Why did Monique kill Senator Matheson?" Daniel asked.

Zuckowi was still angry and spit at Daniel, missing him.

"Look you asshole. I'm just about had it with you. Both of your daughters are dead. You're either going to prison for life or will be executed. Frankly, I don't give a fuck what happens to you."

Said Zuckowi looked down at the horrible pictures of his dead daughters and closed his eyes. He realized now that they really were dead.

"Matheson is Scorpio's dad. That's all I have to say. You're so fucking smart, so you figure the rest out for yourself," Zuckowi answered.

"Scorpio's father?" Daniel asked in amazement. It was a twist that he never expected. He looked at the others in the room. They also had amazed looks on their faces.

"Scorpio is an American citizen?"

"I said that Matheson is Scorpio's father, asshole."

"And who is Scorpio? Let me rephrase that question. Who is CJ?" Daniel asked hitting Zuckowi with another surprise.

"I don't know," he answered, while wondering how they found out Scorpio's name.

"What do you mean, you don't know. You know who CJ's father is, and now you're telling me you don't know who CJ is?

Now Said, that doesn't make any sense. We know that Scorpio and CJ are the same person. That wasn't hard for us to figure out. Where does CJ live?"

"I have no idea where she ..." Zuckowi slipped up and he realized it.

Scorpio was a she.

"She lives where?" Daniel immediately asked keeping the pressure on, and slapped the table hard with his hand to emphasize the question.

"Fuck you. I'm not saying another fucking word."

"We're going to get CJ and she will end up just like your daughters, in a body bag. Look at those pictures of your daughters. It has to be hard seeing your children dead. Why don't you tell us where she is and her last name? Save her life,

Zuckowi. For once in your life, do something good," Daniel said, trying to tap into Zuckowi's emotions.

He only answered, "Fuck you."

"That's not a good attitude to have, Said. If you want to see CJ dead, it's okay with me. I'll just stop by one day and give you some more pictures to look at, dead naked pictures of CJ.

Now, will you answer my question? What is CJ's last name and where does she live?"

"Fuck you."

Daniel stopped his barrage of questions and looked at his associates. Merlin, who was standing behind Zuckowi, smiled and winked at Daniel.

"Well, guys. I guess we're done here. If you decide to answer my questions after thinking about how your daughters died, just tell the CIA men that are guarding your cell and they will get the message to me. I'll even come here to visit with you."

"Fuck you."

"Okay, we're out of here. Oh, one more thing Zuckowi. You should work on your anger management and vocabulary. It really sucks," Daniel said and walked to the door, followed by the rest of his friends.

When Raul closed the door behind him, they all stood at the two-way window and watched Zuckowi sitting at the table, alone, with the pictures of his dead children scattered on the table. He then broke down and cried as the jailers entered the room to return him to his cell. He left the gruesome pictures on the table. He didn't need them because those images were imbedded in his mind forever.

"Jeeze, Daniel. Great job," Merlin said, patting Daniel on the back.

"You tore him up," Raul added.

"Good job, Daniel. If you ever need a job interrogating, let me know," Bill said, smiling.

"Damn. What a stubborn son of a bitch! You would think he would try to at least save Scorpio," Daniel said, as Zuckowi was led out the back door.

"Maybe it will sink in and he'll want to talk later. I bet he won't sleep a wink tonight or maybe longer," Raul added.

"Maybe," Daniel answered.

He snapped out of his thoughts and composed himself.

"We now know that Scorpio, CJ, is a she and I'm sure that she lives somewhere is the vicinity. We've got some work to do."

They all left the building and Bill Angus went separately to CIA-Langley while Daniel, Raul and Merlin returned to Falcon headquarters. When they arrived at Falcon, everyone went to Daniel's office.

"Well. guys, what do you think?" Daniel asked as they all sat down.

"I'm going to get the weekend staff to search all DMV records for any female whose goes by CJ. Then search Canadian passport records, border records and visas. They should have a list by Monday morning," Merlin explained.

"I'm going over to FBI headquarters and get them to search Federal and government employees in the Maryland and Virginia area.

We're getting close to getting Scorpio," Raul said.

"I agree with us getting close but damn … we were getting close to the Zuckowi's but didn't get them until it was too late.

In the searches, try the names CJ Zuckowi, CJ Leclair and the other names they used when they traveled. And just for the hell of it, try CJ Scorpio and CJ Page," Daniel suggested.

"I feel we are so close and are missing something obvious. I can't put my finger on it, but I know we're very close," the Wizard said.

"I have the same feeling," Raul added.

Daniel looked at his best friends and thought the same thing. He just wished he could get or understand the key to Scorpio, "page 31". It was the answer to the question.

"Help me out here, guys. We've been looking for what "page 31" is and the specific message I keep getting is "page 31". Now, if that is the answer to the question, what is the question?" Daniel asked.

"*Who is Scorpio*, is the question and the answer is on *page 31*, is my thought," Raul said.

"Let's change things around. Xi taught me that the answer is always in the messages I get. But like he said in the meeting, "Sometime answer at feet and we step over question or answer."

Maybe we are stepping over the question and not the answer. What if the question is: Who is Scorpio and the answer is "page 31" instead of on "page 31".

Who is CJ? CJ is Scorpio, who is "page 31". Therefore, CJ is "page 31". See what I mean?" Daniel said.

Both Merlin and Raul perked up.

"You know, you might have something there, Daniel," Merlin said as he thought of different ways to ask the question to the answer.

"Damn … if that is true, then what is "page 31"?" Raul asked.

"I think we should rule the answer "page 31" out of our thought process and just work on different questions. Let's go home and think about it for the rest of the weekend," Daniel suggested.

"Sounds good to me," Merlin answered.

"I've got a kennel at the house now and I better get home. This should be great."

"Kennel? What do you mean kennel?" Raul asked.

Daniel explained about the new members of the White family, Charlie and Mattie, as they walked out of his office to their waiting vehicles. He also told the story of both "interviews". Raul and Merlin busted out laughing as they visualized Daniel's explanation.

"You had to have those people totally stressed out. I bet they would have given you the dogs just to get you off their property," Wiz said, still laughing.

"Yeah, and then come back the next day and accuse them of bribing a Federal employee," Raul added. "That would have given them all heart attacks."

That got all three laughing again.

The men then left for their respective homes to relax for what was left of the weekend.

Chapter XXXII

Identification of Scorpio

*D*aniel *arrived home and walked into a world of bedlam.* Lance and Ali were screaming and chasing Charlie and Mattie, who were continually barking, all over the house. It sounded like a riot. He laughed and went looking for Susan.

"Where is mom?" he asked, as the kids and litter ran by him.

"Outside on the patio," was the retort from Lance.

He walked through the dining room out to the patio and saw Susan sitting on a chaise lounge.

"Hi," Daniel said, as he walked over and kissed her on the forehead.

"Hi. How did everything go?" Susan asked.

"Okay. How are you doing?"

"Okay, I guess. We have got to get these dogs and kids under control. I figured I'd wait until you got home."

"What's the problem? Everything is real quiet inside," he asked and laughed.

"It has been utter chaos since we got home. The dogs think they rule the house and, of course, Ali and Lance don't know any better. They've never had dogs."

"You're the vet."

"You're the father. We better set down some rules. I'll train the dogs. That will be no problem. Labs are really smart animals. You train the kids. This is a joint effort, my dear."

"I've got no problem with that. Let's get started, trainer," he said, extending his hand to help her up.

"Okay. Off on a new adventure."

They walked into the house and the dogs and children were in the living room. One of the dogs had pooped on the oak hardwood floor.

Seeing the mess, Daniel yelled, "Time out."

Lance and Ali stopped in their tracks. Daniel never had raised his voice. Both dogs also stopped and looked at where the loud noise came from.

"Thank you. Now, the dogs are going outside with mom. Lance, you go and get something to clean up that mess. Ali, you sit on the sofa and don't move."

Daniel helped his son clean up the feces and then Susan, Ali, Lance and Daniel sat down and listened to what the rules were. After Daniel's kind words of law were delivered, the house returned to normal and there was never an outbreak of craziness with the dogs vs. children again.

They spent a quiet evening watching a movie and the White family, including Mattie and Charlie, went to bed.

Sunday morning and afternoon were spent playing, training the dogs and having fun at the observatory home. Daniel called into Falcon headquarters and checked with the weekend agent-in-charge for any updates. Everything was quiet and running smoothly. He also called Raul and Merlin and they hadn't heard any news.

At 4:30 p.m. Susan went into the living room where Daniel was alone watching a football game. She was glad to see him relax alone. He had been putting in long hours and even with the few days that he took off to Montana, he still looked tired. Daniel had explained where he went and the changes that were happening, both mentally and spiritually, to him and his life. That was a great thing about Daniel. There were no secrets kept from his wife, other than what was happening at Falcon Agency. That was the promise he made to Susan and he would never break it.

They all needed a vacation and she suggested they take off for their home in Grand Lake, Colorado, for a couple of weeks. Daniel was all for it, but told Susan that it would have to wait until the project he was working on was finished.

"It's 4:30, Daniel. You better get ready."

Daniel had been so engrossed in the football game that he forgot about time.

"Boy, the time flew. It's 4:30?" he answered as he looked at his watch. "I better get ready. It starts at 6:00 p.m. sharp. Do me a favor, Susan. Would you please call Raul and Merlin and tell them I'll meet them outside the building?"

"Sure."

Daniel jumped off the sofa and went upstairs to the master bedroom, took a shower, dressed in his black Armani suit, white shirt and red and black silk striped tie. He looked at himself in the mirror.

"You look like the Director of Falcon Agency," he said quietly.

As he was leaving the bedroom, he stopped. He had forgotten one more important item. Since the 9-11 attack and multiple threats and killings of high ranking government officials, the president had given direct orders to all intelligent and security directors and their assistant directors to carry weapons at all times, when they leave their residences. Daniel, Merlin and Raul were not exempt from this direct order. He went to the walk-in closet and opened the large safe in the corner, removing his shoulder holster and Beretta pistol. No matter when he arrived home, he always stored the weapon in the vault, keeping it safely out of harm's way.

He put the holster on and then removed two clips of 9mm bullets from the safe, checking to make sure that each clip was full to capacity. Once he was satisfied that they were, he checked the safety on the pistol and saw it was on. Daniel inserted one clip into the pistol, put the backup into the small pouch on the shoulder harness and the pistol in the holster. He then put on his suit coat and closed the safe.

Walking back into the bedroom, he stopped once more at the full-length mirror and buttoned his suit coat. There was no evidence he was armed. Satisfied, he checked his watch and it was now 5:25 p.m.

Susan met him at the bottom of the wide spiral staircase.

"My, don't you look handsome, Director Daniel White," she said smiling.

"Thanks. I really don't like going to these things. It's all political. But, it is part of the job. Merlin and Raul don't like these functions either, but if I have to go, I make them go also. That pisses them off," he said, with a devious smirk.

Susan moved toward her handsome husband and wrapped her arms around his upper torso. She felt a hard object under Daniel's left arm pit area. She knew what it was.

"I wish you didn't have to carry a gun, but I understand. Maybe someday you won't have to."

"I know. Every day when I put it on, I feel like I'm going off to war. I've got to go. I should be home early, around nine or so."

They kissed and Susan walked with Daniel to the door. He opened one of the French style doors and outside was his waiting security team, standing next to three shiny, black suburbans with the Falcon Agency government seals on the front doors. Daniel kissed Susan goodbye and entered the vehicle's rear seat. The driver closed the door and spoke into the small microphone in his left hand. He gave the orders that they were leaving the Old Naval Observatory with the VIP, Daniel White, call sign Falcon One.

All three black, bulletproof vehicles drove slowly down the driveway with their lights flashing. As they approached the electronic gate with four armed Marine guards at their posts, the gate opened automatically. The guards saluted as the vehicle passed and the three-vehicle convoy drove onto Massachusetts Avenue NW and headed southeast toward Capital Hill.

It was an election year and both the Democrat and Republican conventions were over. Being the seated president, he decided to address the Joint Session of Congress. It was a political move on the president's part and had never happened before, prior to an election. Usually the president gave his State of the Union address at the Joint Session of Congress in January. The election was nine days away and it was a very tight race. The president and his staff secretly made the decision two months ago, knowing that speaking to the joint session would have maximum prime time media coverage.

The public announcement wasn't made until four days ago, but the plans were leaked out, to those in positions that had to prepare and attend, three weeks prior. The president wanted to make sure that all the Senate, Congress, U.S. department heads and directors were in attendance.

As Daniel's small procession of vehicles approached Capital Hill, he saw the many television news vehicles, with their towering antennas and dishes, parked along the roadside. His suburban pulled up to the stairway and the driver got out and opened the door for Daniel. He looked around for Merlin and Raul. They were twenty feet away and walking toward their boss. Daniel looked at his watch. It was now 5:48 p.m.

"Hi, Daniel, we'd better get in there. The president is already here and they'll start this shindig right on time," Merlin said.

"Okay. Let's get going," Daniel answered, as the made their way up the stairs with the rest of the crowd.

"I want to thank you also for inviting us. We really appreciate it," Raul said meaning the statement to be sarcastic.

"Part of the bullshit and position, my friends," Daniel answered, smiling.

"I want to be demoted to janitor," Merlin said, also smiling.

"Okay, but I will still order your ass to attend these things," Daniel laughed.

"No way around it, is there?" Wiz said.

"Nope," Daniel responded. "I own you."

All three laughed again as they approached the security entrance. Only those with special credentials could enter via this entrance because they were carrying hidden weapons. The rest of the attendees were required to enter through another entry way.

Merlin opened the door for his friends and Daniel walked in first, pulling out his credentials. A Marine guard, with six other armed Marines behind him, inspected the identification documents carefully and let Daniel pass while saluting him. Merlin and Raul went through the identical procedure.

After all three cleared security, Daniel looked at his watch. It was 5:59 and the president was standing ten feet behind the tall, highly-polished double doors, waiting for the man in front of him to open the doors and announce the president to Congress and all the other dignitaries in attendance.

Daniel, followed by his two close associates, started walking toward the side door they were to enter and he walked up to a young man who was handing out a press release on what the president was going to speak about. The young adult was dressed in a white shirt and tie with a dark-blue blazer. On the coat's breast pocket was the Seal of the United States Congress. Daniel took the paper and then received the message, "page 31". He looked back at the man's chest.

Above the seal was a name tag, identifying him. Daniel read the tag. In front of him was Brent Thompson and below the name was Page 87. Daniel froze and tensed up. He now knew what the question to the answer was. Who is Scorpio and CJ? Answer: "page 31".

He looked up at Page 87, "Where is your supervisor, son?"

The young man saw the look on Daniel's face and thought he had done something wrong.

"Is there something wrong, sir?"

"Where is your supervisor?" Daniel repeated more harshly.

The man nervously looked around and pointed to a tall man dressed in the similar style to his.

"That's him over there. Mr. Austin."

Daniel ran to the man followed by Merlin and Raul, who had no idea what was happening, but knew by Daniel's actions that something was seriously wrong.

The wide, wood doors opened to the large congressional room.

"Mr. Speaker, the President of the United States," the short man yelled and stepped aside as the president entered the chamber to a rousing, cheering crowd who were applauding.

"You Austin?" Daniel asked, when he reached the page supervisor.

"Yes, sir."

Daniel showed him his ID and Falcon government badge. "I'm Daniel White, the Director of Falcon Agency. Do you have a "page 31" here? Her name is CJ."

Austin reached into his inside coat pocket and removed a stapled, folded piece of paper.

"I don't know of a CJ, but let me check. Is there something wrong, Mr. White?"

Merlin and Raul were on each side of Daniel and the Falcon Director rudely grabbed the papers from Austin.

""Page 31". The kids that are runners and do errands here at the capital are called pages," Daniel answered and walked away from Austin. He opened the folded document exposing a list.

The crowd in the chamber was still applauding as the president made his way down the wide isle that was packed with senators, congress people and other dignitaries.

On the top of the entitled document, PAGE STAFF, in bold letters, were the column headings. Daniel looked at the headings: Page Name, Page Number and Posting Location. The list was two pages long and in alphabetical order by last name first, then first name. He moved his finger down the column titled Page Number and came to "page 31". He then moved his finger to the left, where the name identifying the respective person was typed.

Charlayne Jean Monet.

"CJ Monet. Scorpio is Charlayne Jean Monet," Daniel said out loud to Merlin and Raul, who were also looking where Daniel's finger was pointed.

The doors to the congressional chamber closed.

Daniel slid his finger to the column labeled Posting Location: Door 6, Second Level.

Daniel turned and briskly walked back to the nervous Mr. Austin.

"Where is door six, second level?" Daniel asked.

"Take those stairs up one flight and go down the hall to the sixth door. The first door at the top of the stairs is door one, sir. Can I help you?" Austin asked.

"You just did. Are the pages posted inside the doors or outside?"

"Once they close the doors through which the president enters, the pages close the doors they are posted and stand inside, sir."

"Keep your mouth shut and stay right here. Don't you move one step. If you do, I'll have you arrested. Understand? Don't you move, Austin."

"Yes, sir."

Daniel turned and walked in the direction of the wide, brass railed, marble staircase and stopped at the base.

"Okay, this is what we do. Scorpio is posted at the sixth door. Merlin, you go to the seventh door and, Raul, you to the sixth. I'll be at the fifth. Don't let anyone out the doors.

When you're in position, I'll go in the fifth door."

"Do you think we should get backup?" Raul whispered.

"That's the last thing we need. They'll sound the alarm and we'll lose the element of surprise; there will be pandemonium. Right now, we don't need chaos," Daniel answered and began climbing the stairs, taking them two at a time.

Wiz and Raul were right behind him.

At the top of the staircase, Daniel stopped and once more said, "Remember. Don't let anyone open the doors and leave. You'll know when to open them."

Both nodded the affirmative and the threesome walked down the hallway. Once Raul and Merlin were in position, Daniel looked at both.

Inside, Scorpio looked at her watch. Three minutes had passed and she had mixed emotions of impatience and excitement.

Chapter XXXIII

Chamber Terrorist

Charlayne Jean Monet attended *John Hopkins University* and enjoyed the college life. The Zuckowi family was graciously paying for her expensive education and living expenses. But she felt some obligation to work part-time and, during the early summer, she found out about working as an intern for the government. Even though she despised the United States and all that it stood for, CJ figured it would be good experience to learn about what people do.

She applied in person for a job as a page on Capital Hill. After thirty days of waiting, she received a letter of acceptance and was asked to report for training two days later. The position was better than what she had expected. It was part-time and the hours were flexible because she was a college student. During training, CJ designed her schedule to work three days a week. If any special events were scheduled on the weekends, she would volunteer.

After the first week as a page, she told Atiya what she was doing. At first, Atiya was upset that CJ was working for the United States. When Atiya told Azzah what CJ had done, Azzah was surprisingly calm about the situation.

"That's good, Atiya. CJ is showing initiative and maturity," Azzah had told her sister.

The real reason Azzah wasn't upset when she heard the news was her mind immediately realized that they now had someone inside the government she hated. It would work to their advantage.

Azzah incorporated CJ's situation into her already-developed terrorist attack against the United States. A few days later, Azzah also was informed by Kaleem Mushowui that a special biological chemical was on its way to Canada on a French freighter. Everything was on schedule and better than Azzah had expected. All she would have to do now was wait for the right opportunity to attack the U.S. in the right place and time. Time was definitely on their side and now, with Scorpio working on Capital Hill as a page, the plan was even better.

At one meeting in late summer, Azzah asked CJ to let her know when any special event was scheduled to occur in the capital building. She also explained to Scorpio that she would be the most important individual in destroying the United States of America. CJ was excited and one-hundred percent cooperative.

When CJ was told about a special event coming up by her supervisor, Mr. Austin, she volunteered to work the function. She called Atiya with the news and she in turn informed her sister. Azzah started to formulate a plan to get the chemical, which would soon arrive, into the United States and to Scorpio.

When Scorpio was informed about Azzah's plan, she also formulated her own scheme to get the chemical into the well-securitized, government facility. Azzah had told Scorpio that the QD-9 was in a sealed glass tube, similar to a laboratory's test tube. One day she went to a laboratory classroom at John Hopkins and stole one of the glass ceramic test tubes.

The following morning, she filled it with a gel shampoo, sealed the tube and put it in her backpack. That afternoon she went to work at the capital and when she reached the employee's security entrance, she passed through easily. She was now inside the high security building with the vial.

That evening she called Atiya and told her the news. Again, Atiya relayed the information to her twin sister. "What a child," Azzah had responded. "We never asked her to do that and she has the smarts to do it herself. We are now ready."

Several times Scorpio walked through the security station with the test tube filled with different liquids and once with pebbles. Then she passed through the checkpoint with the tube filled with QD-9. Disaster was now inside the halls of the United States government.

CJ arrived two hours before the event where the President of the United States would speak to all of America as well as the top government officials on Capital Hill. After the meeting with Mr. Austin and her fellow pages, Scorpio went to her locker in the basement area. She checked and made sure no one else was present. When Scorpio was satisfied she was alone, she removed a rag from behind the lockers and carefully unfolded the cloth. She put the tube that contained the most deadly chemical known to man into the inside breast pocket of her blue blazer.

The instruction from her guardian, Azzah, was to wait until the president had been speaking at least five minutes because he then would have the audience's full attention. At that time, she was to remove the vial from her pocket, drop it onto the carpeted floor, smash it with her shoe and casually leave the chamber. If anyone asked her where she was going, she was to answer, "the restroom".

The smiling president was at the podium and raising his hands to the noisy crowd, asking them to quiet down. The audience quieted and the president began to speak. Scorpio looked at her wristwatch. The time clock was running. For self assurance, she reached up and pressed her hand against the left breast pocket of her blazer. She felt the tube and smiled.

"You ready?" Daniel asked as he pulled his Beretta out of the hidden shoulder case.

Raul and Merlin did the same and answered in unison, "Ready."

Daniel waited until he heard the audience begin applauding. When the noise and cheers resounded loudly, he grabbed the brass handle and opened the mahogany door. Stepping partially inside the door, the noise from inside the chamber escaped into the hallway, creating an echo reverberation.

A page positioned at the doorway that Daniel opened, turned and looked at the tall, handsome man entering. Daniel put his finger to his lips, indicating for the young page to be quiet and then gave a finger signal to come here. The page followed the well-dressed man's silent instructions and stepped out into the hallway.

"Stay here and see those two men there by those doors; watch them because they are government agents looking for someone. Don't let anyone come in this door. Is CJ still down at door six?"

"Who?"

"Charlayne Monet," Daniel answered.

"Oh, Charlayne ... yes, sir. That's her post and she can't leave until this is over," the page answered.

Daniel entered the doorway again and looked toward door number six. Standing in her assigned position was a petite female dressed in the same style blazer, shirt and tie as the rest of her fellow associates. She was staring straight ahead as the applauding crowd cheered the most powerful person in America.

Daniel fully entered the chamber and waited until the door closed behind him. With his Beretta hidden behind his back, he started to walk toward Scorpio. CJ was nothing like he expected. She had long flowing black hair and was a very attractive young lady.

Scorpio saw movement out of the corner of her left eye and turned in that direction to see what it was. Walking toward her was a tall, well-dressed man who was staring at her. She sensed danger. While staring back at the stranger, she began to raise her right arm toward the left inside pocket of the blazer.

Daniel saw the movement as the crowd began to quiet. He kept moving forward toward Scorpio and revealed the Beretta pistol in his right hand. Scorpio's eyes widened and she moved her arm up faster. At the same time, Daniel raised his pistol.

"Don't move, CJ. Drop your arm now," Daniel yelled.

His loud warning carried throughout the chamber and then he yelled the one word he knew would signal an alarm to all security personnel, who were trained to respond to it immediately.

"GUN!"

The crowd's heads began to turn when they heard the loud shout.

Daniel yelled again as Scorpio put her hand inside her blue blazer.

"Don't do it, Charlayne."

Scorpio had indicated that the tube was in her coat. There was only one place to aim at where the bullet would not hit the vial. Scorpio didn't stop and Daniel, with the Beretta aimed at her head, had no recourse. He squeezed the trigger of the 9mm Beretta. The projectile traveled at high speed and entered the young lady's head, knocking her sideways as her hand inside her coat fell out. Daniel saw that the hand didn't have anything in it.

The loud explosion from the Beretta was louder than any sound ever heard in the hallowed chamber and sent the audience into shock. Scorpio was falling to the carpeted floor as Raul and Merlin opened their doors. Daniel continued walking toward the terrorist, with his pistol still aimed at the prone body.

"I've got you covered, Raul. Check her pulse," Daniel ordered, as members of the audience began to stand, scream and panic.

Raul reached down and placed his finger tips against the main artery on Scorpio's thin neck. At first, he felt a slight pulse and then none. He looked down at Scorpio and saw a red hole in her head, then a pool of blood blending into the plush red carpet.

Raul looked at Daniel and yelled over the screaming crowd's noise, "She's dead."

Daniel walked up to where the young, dead terrorist lay, put his Beretta into his shoulder holster and knelt down on one knee as Merlin came rushing up.

"Put your guns away," Daniel ordered.

He then unbuttoned the dead Scorpio's Blazer and reached into the inside breast pocket. He felt a long thin tube inside and carefully removed it.

"You guys stay here and handle the heat. I've got to get this out of here, now. Call our drivers downstairs and tell them we have a code red. We're going to the CIA lab and get this shit quarantined. I want a fully armed escort," Daniel said, as he put the vial into his inside suit jacket pocket. At that moment, Daniel gave new meaning to being the most dangerous person on earth.

He looked down to the main chamber floor and saw Secret Service agents ushering the president out of the room. Television cameras turned toward the second floor balcony, trying to get pictures of what happened for the evening news. He walked calmly out door six and down the hall. Security people and news reporters, followed by remote camera men, were trying to get up the stairway.

Daniel stopped one Secret Service agent in the hallway.

"I'm Daniel White, the Director of Falcon Agency. Seal this floor and don't let any unauthorized civilians up here. There are two of my top directors inside door six. They'll give you full instructions. Their names are Merlin and Raul and they are the agents-in-charge. Now, go."

He then dialed CIA Director Bill Angus' cellphone. Bill answered on the first ring.

"Bill Angus," the director answered.

Daniel could hear the loud voices on his cellphone.

"Bill, Daniel White. Where are you?"

"I'm in the rotunda. Where are you"

"At the top of the stairwell on the second floor. I need some help. I just killed Scorpio and I need you to get your men and some FBI agents up there to help Merlin and Raul seal the area. It would also be good if you went up there and took charge."

"What the hell happened, Daniel?"

"Scorpio was "page 31". That was her ID number. She was a page here?"

"Holy shit. I see you now at the top of the stairs. Hold on, Daniel."

Daniel could see Angus in the confused crowd. Bill had turned to two of his agent guards and snapped orders. They got on their radios and, suddenly, there was a rush of ten agents moving toward the stairwell.

"I got my men on the way, Daniel."

"Good. Listen Bill. I have the tube of QD-9 on me. I need a protective wall around me to the outside. My team of Secret

Service guards is waiting for me. I'm taking the vial to the Langley lab."

"Start coming down the stairs. I'll meet you at the bottom; Lambert is with me. Hold on."

"Lamb, get some of your agents over by the stairs. Daniel is coming down and he needs a wall of protection to get to his team outside," Bill said to FBI Director John Lambert.

"I'm back, Daniel."

"I see you and Lamb now. I'm on my way. Hey, call Langley and let them know I'm coming. I need direct access to the lab. No bullshit security stops, Bill. We'll be in Falcon suburbans and have an escort."

"Done. Now come down the stairs. Lamb and I will take care of everything," Bill said and disconnected the call.

Daniel walked down the stairwell. About half way down, six agents gathered around him.

"We've got eight more of us at the bottom of the stairs, sir," an agent said to Daniel.

At the bottom, Daniel saw Bill and Lamb.

"I don't got time to fart around. Help Merlin and Raul upstairs. I'll call you after the package has been delivered. C'mon. Let's go," he ordered the group of agents surrounding him. The pack moved toward the exit.

The procession began with five vehicles and grew in size as Daniel traveled to McLean, Virginia, better known as "Langley", which is the name of the McLean neighborhood where the CIA headquarters is located. The trip was made in record time and they passed through the gates with no stops. Once they had entered, another CIA vehicle led the motorcade directly to a remote building. Daniel delivered the tube of QD-9 to a scientist who was waiting for him.

Daniel was never so happy to get rid of the vial and told the driver to take him back to Washington.

"Back to Capital Hill, sir?" the driver asked.

"No, the White House," Daniel answered.

He called ahead to the president's office and Jennifer York, the president's assistant, answered the phone.

"Jennifer, Daniel White. Is he in the office?"

"Yes, Daniel," she answered.

"Tell him I'm on my way there. I should get there in about fifteen to twenty minutes."

"Okay, Daniel. He's pretty rattled right now."

"Tell him everything is safe."

"I will. Thanks, Daniel."

The line went dead.

Chapter XXXIV

President's Brief

D*aniel's vehicle procession drove to the White House and,* as they sped down the avenue, he called Merlin for an update.

"This is Merlin Miles."

"Wiz, Daniel. The package is safe at Langley. What's going on there?"

"We have everything under control here. Angus and Lambert really helped a lot. Everyone who has a badge wanted in on the investigation. Bill kicked everyone out but the special team of his agents and the ones Lamb selected. Right now, the coroner is here.

All the press and cameras were kicked out of the building. They're all gathered outside like a heard of cattle, speculating on what happened. We haven't leaked anything so far. They will have a field day with this."

"Get some pictures before they remove the body and tell the coroner I want some of Scorpio on the slab. I'll use the same procedure on Zuckowi that we used before. He'll have no reason not to tell us everything."

"Where are you now?" Wiz asked.

"On my way to the White House. I better brief the president on what happened. I'm sure he will go on the air and explain to the American people what happened and assure the citizens they are safe. What a place for them to hit. I was just thinking that if Scorpio had been successful, all of our leadership would have been wiped out on television. That is one hell of a scary thought," Merlin said and then continued explaining additional aspects of what was happening at Capital Hill.

"They came real close. One hell of a job, Daniel," the Wizard complimented.

"Thanks. I'll call you after I brief the president."

"One more thing. I think I'll stay on as the assistant director. Don't demote me to a janitor," Wiz laughed.

Daniel laughed also.

"I was thinking of moving you up to take over my job."

"No damn way. I'll talk to you later. I've got some pictures to take. Bye."

"Hi, Daniel. Go right in," Jennifer York said when Daniel arrived at the oval office.

He walked into the president's office where he was seated in his favorite leather chair. With the Commander-in-Chief were his national security advisor and Admiral Boryla, Chairman of the Joint Chiefs of Staff.

"Evening, Mr. President."

"Daniel, come on in and have a seat. How are you?" he asked with sincere concern.

"I'm fine, sir. A little tired, but fine. I thought I'd better brief you as soon as I could. Hi, Mike and Bob," he said, acknowledging the other two guests.

"How are you doing, sir?" Daniel asked the president as he took his seat next to him.

"That was one hell of a scare. I'm okay. So, what the hell happened?"

"This is going to take a while. So here goes," Daniel answered and it took forty minutes to explain the whole story.

"Damn, Daniel, that was so close. One hell of a job … Daniel, one damn hell of a job," the president said, looking proudly at his Director of Falcon Agency.

"Thank you, Mr. President."

"What about Senator Nigel Mason? Is he cleared of any wrong doing?"

"He's cleared. Bill Angus talked to him afterwards and what we have on his relationship with Scorpio is that she loved working for him. He had no idea what was going on behind the scene.

He remembered telling her one day when she told him about her stepfather, Said Zuckowi, to have him call him if he ever got to DC and the senator would arrange a tour of Capital Hill. That's the only thing he could remember telling her and he gave his home number to CJ."

"Weird how this has all transpired. At least America is somewhat safe now."

"Our government and you are safe, Mr. President. That's the most important thing."

"America is safe, Daniel. I'm replaceable and might be replaced in a few days. We'll see. I've got to do a national telecast in about fifteen minutes. America is waiting for an explanation. You want to stick around for it?" the president asked.

"Thanks for the invitation sir, but I'm beat."

"Daniel, why don't you head home and then take a couple of weeks off. Hell, you deserve a year off after all of this."

"I've got to wrap this up next week. After it's in the can, I will take a couple of weeks off."

They all stood up and shook Daniel's hand, again complimenting him for an awesome job for his country.

Daniel left alone by the side exit of the White House. As he was walking toward the vehicles, a reporter and cameraman spotted him and ran up, hoping to get an interview.

"Director White, Pamela Francis with CNN. Do you have a moment?" she asked, as the cameraman turned on the bright lights.

"Turn that off and I'll talk to you. Otherwise no deal."

"Shut it off, Tony," she ordered.

"And put it over there. I don't trust you guys. I've heard that you let the sound tape run and record unauthorized conversations," Daniel said.

"Do as he says," Francis said to Tony.

After the cameraman moved out of ear shot with the camera, Daniel looked at the reporter and spoke.

"Here are the ground rules and don't give me any of the first amendment stuff. I'll answer some of your questions, but you can't put it on the air until after the president's talk tonight. That's the deal, Pamela. I don't want to upstage the president."

"It's a deal, I promise, Mr. White. Can we film it?"

"Yes, but if you go against your word, I'll see to it that you'll never work within five-hundred miles of DC. That I promise you."

"I never break my word. I have a good reputation in this business and want to keep it."

"Okay. You have three minutes. Tony, come over here and bring your camera," Daniel ordered.

Tony came running over and turned the equipment on.

"We're rolling, Mr. White," she said.

Daniel nodded his head.

"I'm with Falcon Agency Director, Mr. Daniel White, who was present tonight at the president's address to the Joint Session of Congress.

Director White. Rumors are that you were involved in the shooting tonight. Were you involved?"

"I was in the building tonight when the shooting took place. Right now, because of security reasons, I'm not at liberty to discuss the details of what happened. I can assure the American people, that as of right now, we are a lot safer than a week ago."

"Was this a terrorist attack, Mr. White?"

"I can't answer that because of the ongoing investigation."

Seeing that her line of questioning was not going in the right direction, Francis changed topics.

"As the Intelligence Czar for the United States, what is the intelligence community doing to stop the threat of terrorism here in the United States?"

"I'm sure that America will agree that using the term czar to describe any member of our government is not what America is about. I'm Director Daniel White, who works with a fine group of individuals at Falcon Agency. Falcon Agency's mission is to help, in any way possible, the CIA, FBI, NSA, Secret Service and every other agency to fulfill their mission to protect the soil and citizens of the United States.

A czar rules and I don't rule anyone. We now have an awesome team of agencies that have finally been brought together for one united cause, protecting America. They are not separate entities as they once were, who considered themselves as independent empires. America's intelligence community and I say community, because we all work as one, is the best the United States has ever had, and we're getting even better each and every day.

I am just one person helping others so please, don't refer to me as a czar. It really is very rude and offensive."

Pamela Francis was put in her place. Her calling Daniel an Intelligence Czar was typical of what the news media does.

They hope to be the first to coin a phrase, making them the original author.

"One more question, Director White. The election is next week. If the president loses, will you stay on as the Director of Falcon Agency?"

"I have sworn an oath to serve, protect and be loyal to the President of the United States and its citizens, no matter who the president is. The president is my Commander-in-Chief. I have no plans of retiring, but those plans can change at any time. I have no term limit as the director."

"Do you have time for one more question, Director White?" she asked.

"Last one, then I have to go."

'Thank you. Do you have any future political aspirations? There are a lot of people who want you to run for public office. Would you consider running for Congress, the Senate or taking a cabinet position?"

"Interesting question, Pamela. I have been approached and asked that question before. Right now, I have my hands full with helping Falcon Agency. I have given it some thought and will continue thinking about it.

If the right opportunity comes along, I will discuss it with my family and close friends. They are very important to me. To honestly answer your question Pamela, if I was asked today, I would decline."

"Thank you, Mr. White. I and America appreciate your honesty. Now, back to our studio in Washington. Pamela Francis, CNN News."

"Don't leave, Mr. White," she pleaded as the camera lights went out. "The camera is off. I'm sorry about calling you a czar. It is offensive and I will try to correct anyone who uses it. You are a kind person and it was a pleasure to meet you, sir."

"You may ask for an interview anytime, Pamela, on one condition."

"What's that, sir?"

"You don't call me sir or Mr. White when we are not doing an interview. Call me Daniel," he said extending his hand.

Reporter Francis shook Daniel's hand. "Thank you, Daniel. It's been a pleasure. Run for office. You're a shoo-in."

"Maybe someday. Thanks and good night, Pamela."

"Good night, Daniel."

Daniel walked to the waiting suburban. He was exhausted and wanted to go home and fall into his beautiful wife Susan's arms and fall asleep. On the drive home he made two calls. The first was to Susan, letting her know he was on his way and he would talk about what happened when he got there. The next was to Merlin.

"Wiz, Daniel. How's everything going?"

"Hey, buddy. Everything is wrapped up and I'm on my way home. How did it go with the president?"

"Everything went fine. He should be on the television right now addressing what happened tonight."

"Shit, I hope he's not telling everything?"

"No. Just the items that will assure Americans that they are safe tonight."

"We are safe, Daniel, thanks to you."

"Thanks, Wiz. See you tomorrow morning at the office. I want to talk to you about something."

"Okay. See you in the morning. Night."

"Night, Wiz."

As Daniel's vehicle procession turned into the Naval Observatory, he received a message.

"Good evening, Master Daniel."

"Good evening, Master Xi," Daniel answered in his mind.

"Answer alway in message Daniel. You do as Master should. You learn good. See you in Colorado. Good night, Master Daniel White."

"Good night, Master Xi. Thank you."

"Welcome."

Epilogue

November, 2004

*T*he squad of eight elite Army Green Beret was resting in a small canyon in Afghanistan. Their mission was to locate al Qaeda insurgents who were reported to be in the area. It was now 0345 hours. In the past seven hours, they had seen no evidence or activity of any al Qaeda terrorists.

Early that evening the squad had been dropped off by an Apache helicopter on the southeast side of the Tora Bora White Mountain range. The area was known to have many terrorist hideouts, but detecting them was very difficult because they were deeply imbedded in cave complexes. This particular area had many hidden caverns in the rugged mountainous terrain and the militant groups kept their activities to a minimum. Travel from their secret locations was always under the cover of darkness and they usually traveled only in pairs.

Weather conditions the past few weeks provided evidence that winter was quickly approaching. The temperature was close to freezing and snow showers, accompanied by freezing rain, were frequent occurrences. This evening was free of any precipitation and the dark sky was clear of any clouds, revealing the millions of bright stars in the galaxy above.

It was time to move out from the Beret's rest area and the staff sergeant whispered his order. The point soldier began to move around a large boulder and immediately stopped in his tracks. Through his night-vision goggles, he saw human movement approximately 200 hundred meters to the northeast. After giving a warning hand signal to the others to hold their positions, he studied the two dark human silhouettes. They were moving slowly, trying to stay close to the base of a mountain and conceal their movement by hiding behind large rocks and boulders. For a few seconds, they disappeared behind a large pile of stones and then reappeared. The two suspected terrorists suddenly stopped and turned toward the west. One of them pointed up the high mountain and both individuals began to climb up the mountain.

The area was close to the Pakistan border and was designated hostile territory. Prior patrols had made contact with al Qaeda in the area and many severe firefights engagements had occurred. Several American soldiers and coalition forces had been wounded and killed in this specific area.

After the invasion of Afghanistan and the removal of the Taliban's leader, Mullah Omar, Taliban and al Qaeda members and supporters escaped across the border seeking sanctuary in Pakistan. They traveled back and forth across the imaginary line bringing supplies and trained terrorists, who continually ambushed the coalition forces.

The E-5 sergeant kept his eyes trained on the two men until they disappeared from sight. He moved out of his hiding position, trying to locate the climbers and saw them again, hunched over while climbing a steep incline. Again, they disappeared from sight.

What the Green Beret sergeant saw were two al Qaeda members returning to the unfriendly location. The squad leader knew that if there was one terrorist seen in the area, there was the probability of many more. He returned to where the rest of his squad was concealed and reported his findings to the squad's leader. They had made contact with insurgents.

Both the observer and the squad leader left the safety of the rest area and moved east in hopes of getting a better angle and view of the mountain. When they were two hundred meters perpendicular to where the soldier last saw the two unidentified individuals, the highly trained soldiers concealed themselves behind a wide clump of bushes. Both scanned the side of the mountain, looking for either the two insurgents or a cave location. At this time, patience was very important. They systematically searched small quadrants at a time, looking for any evidence of movement or openings.

After fifteen minutes of intense searching, the leader saw the upper torso of a human behind a boulder, half way up the mountainside. He shared his findings with the other Green Beret and both men trained their night-vision goggles on the location. Two other men appeared and joined the others. It looked like they were talking to each other The sergeant leader now knew that the location had more than one person and could possibly be an undiscovered, concealed hideaway.

The new policy, incorporated when discoveries such as this happened, was to call in air strikes. The command center had revised previous procedures in an attempt to eliminate injuries and deaths to the coalition forces. The tactic was working. After the air attacks, ground troops went in and assessed the damage. Often, they did encounter surviving enemy and battles would happen.

The leader sent his partner back to where the other members of the squad were and told him to lead them back to his position. Where they currently were, was too close to the targeted area and he wanted them safely out of the area. When the E-5 left, he got on his radio and called the information into the command center and ordered an air strike.

Usamah bin Laden was not in a good mood. He had been living in the grotto ever since he survived the attack on his cave complex three years ago. Very few al Qaeda members knew that he was still alive. For his own safety, he maintained that secrecy. Only ten close members of his scattered organization knew of his existence.

From his command center in the Tora Bora cave, he sent out orders via his trusted comrades. He still had command of al Qaeda. Several times his location was almost discovered but no attacks had occurred. The entrance to the cavern was virtually undetectable from the air because of the small entrance way, which was always sealed after anyone entered the cave.

Recently, there was a lot more activity from the American and coalition forces in the area. Their continual persistence in searching for him was on the rise. Usamah had considered moving to another location but, under the current circumstance, the move would be too dangerous.

He was very upset with the news he had received the previous evening. The plan he had designed many years ago, and patiently waited for the right opportunity to integrate, had failed. A secret cell in Canada and the United States consisting of a childhood friend, his two daughters and a young female orphan had failed at the last minute in destroying America's government infrastructure. Millions of dollars had been spent on this project, all for naught. He didn't care about the deaths of the terrorists. People were an expendable commodity in his eyes. It was the loss of the only two vials of QD-9 in the world that most disappointed him. The formula was destroyed by Saddam Hussein's scientists. Usamah bin Laden had paid Saddam Hussein fifteen million American dollars for the two small test tubes containing the most dangerous chemical ever invented. Overall, his total expenditure for the entire project over five years had exceeded thirty-five million dollars and now he had nothing to show for it.

Two visitors had just arrived from their hideout in Pakistan. When they arrived, he sent his sleeping guard outside to join the only other sentry that was his protection force. He didn't even want those two men protecting him, but his trusted associates insisted on it.

The visitors brought a limited amount of supplies and updated information on what was being reported in the news media around the world regarding the thwarted attack against the U.S. government.

The information disclosed the name of the leading United States agency that foiled the attack. Led by Director Daniel White of Falcon Agency, the combined intelligence community consisting of the FBI, CIA, NSA and the Secret Service were the ones who killed three of the four of Usamah bin Laden's best terrorists.

"This Daniel White has been a big obstacle in my life. I have seen his picture and he is the one who shot me, thinking he was leaving me to die in the cave above. And now he is a leader in the United States government. I want him dead," bin Laden told his close friends.

At King Khalid Military Airport in Saudi Arabia, a 117-A Stealth bomber and two F-18 cover aircraft were scrambled for a secret mission in Afghanistan. The target was unknown and all the pilots were concerned about were the coordinates for the target or targets. Because of the urgency, the aircraft's pilots went to maximum airspeed and broke the sound barrier of Mach One after takeoff. At that speed, they would arrive at the assigned coordinates in 1 hour and 23 minutes.

The squad of Green Berets was lying on the ground behind whatever cover they could conceal themselves with and were spread out with twenty feet between each of the men. The soldiers on the ends were responsible for guarding their comrades. The remaining six soldiers kept close surveillance on the mountainside target area. If one or two took a break, there was always someone observing the mountainside hideout.

It had been a little over an hour since the squad leader had called in the request for air power. He knew that contact with the aircraft would be coming soon. As he looked through his night-vision goggles, he saw only one individual guarding the target.

"Crimson 6 … this is Vulture 1, how do you read?"

The squad leader, Crimson 6 heard the radio call in his ear set and smiled. Help had arrived.

"Vulture 1, this is Crimson 6. I have you five by five."

"Good morning, Crimson 6. We are now on location and ready for you to target the objective. Call when ready," Vulture 1 radioed.

"Roger, Vulture 1. Standby."

The sergeant smiled and got the laser aiming device out. He would direct the sophisticated laser beam device at the target. When he was locked in on the target, Vulture 1 would fire a rocket. The explosive projectile would begin to fly toward the preprogrammed coordinates. Within seconds after launch, the rocket's computer would detect the laser beam, change course and track toward the targeted impact location where the laser beam was aimed. Advanced laser technology was so precise and accurate that the guided rockets impacted targets within two feet of the laser's aimed destination.

"Vulture 1, Crimson 6. Target is ready," the squad leader radioed.

"Roger, Crimson 6. Will fire one and then three more in ten second intervals. The first one is on the way, Crimson 6."

"Roger, Vulture 1."

Crimson 6 listened for the aircraft. All he could hear was the wind moving through the bushes. Otherwise, it was eerie quiet.

Fifteen seconds later, the side of the mountain exploded. As he looked through the laser sight, he saw the guard one second and then, in the next, nothing but a huge explosion ball of fire. Ten seconds later another rocket exploded, then the third. All three rockets impacted at the exact focal point. The sergeant knew that at that moment the al Qaeda guard was no more than small bits and pieces of scattered flesh.

"Vulture 1, Crimson 6. All three impacted. Target destroyed."

"Roger, Crimson 6. We're going to get a drink. Spartan 1 and 2 are on location. If you need help, radio them. I'll be back in fifteen. Good luck."

"Thanks, Vulture 1. Talk to you in a few. Out."

Now the hard part was to begin. The squad had to climb up the mountainside and assess the damage.

"We have to make a plan to get this Daniel White," Usamah bin Laden said to his trusted confidants. "This man has become the one major obstacle to our jihad success."

As soon as bin Laden finished that statement, the cave entrance that had rocks concealing the opening exploded, sending sharp, devastating projectiles flying into the cavern. Usamah was knocked to the stone floor and his two al Qaeda associates, whose backs were to the exit, took the brunt of the flying shards of rocks. They were torn to shreds and dead as they sat. Dust filled the grotto. Usamah bin Laden was lying on the floor, severely injured. The injuries were the worst that he had ever received. Lying on the cold floor when the second and third rockets impacted at the same point as the first, the unconscious terrorist was now in a sealed black hole and bleeding to death.

The Green Beret squad scrambled up the mountainside and when they arrived at the target zone, there was nothing to see. The mountain had caved in and created a landslide covering what they couldn't see from below. There might have been a cave entrance at one time but now there was nothing but smoke rising from the ground and piles of rocks.

"Vulture 1 … Crimson 6."

"Crimson 6, Vulture 1."

"Target assessment. Destroyed. No bodies identifiable. Thanks, Vulture 1."

"Roger, Crimson 6. Stay safe. Spartan 1 and 2, let's go home."

"Roger, Vulture 1. We're at your six o'clock one mile back," Spartan 1 acknowledged.

It was Friday and Daniel was having his last meeting for the week. It would also be his last meeting for the next three weeks. He was going home to Grand Lake, Colorado, with his family to relax and get his life back in balance.

"The interview or should I say the interrogation of Said Zuckowi went well. He broke down and spilled his guts after he saw the pictures of Scorpio. The Senator Nigel Mason's telephone number that was in Zuckowi's wallet was for emergency purposes in case Scorpio got into trouble. He also said he had never talked to or met the Senator.

Now, the Senator Byron Matheson story is different. Matheson was the father of Scorpio. When he was young, he worked for the U.S. Embassy in Beirut, Lebanon. About a month after he arrived on his assignment, he met Scorpio's mother and she got pregnant. After the bombing of the embassy, Matheson was reassigned back to the U.S. Scorpio's mother was left deserted and was killed during the Lebanon civil war. The only surviving relative was Scorpio's uncle. He and Scorpio immigrated to France. He eventually was shot in Paris and CJ was totally orphaned.

She ended up on the streets of Paris as a pickpocket and thief. One day she stole Azzah Zuckowi's purse outside Notre Dame cathedral and Said Zuckowi saw the caper. He caught CJ. When he and his daughters learned she was a street urchin, they took her under their wings and brought her to Canada, where she became a Canadian citizen.

The Zuckowi family brainwashed Scorpio into thinking that her father, the senator, was responsible for her mother's death. They made contact with Matheson a couple of times. He denied he was the father and made threats against them. The rest you know about."

"I'll bet Scorpio had no idea of the real potential of QD-9," Merlin said.

"She had no idea according to Said. She was told that it was a poison and all she had to do was smash it on the floor and walk away. Because she was an orphan, she was expendable."

"Well, it's over now. The good thing is we got them all," Bill Angus said.

"According to Zuckowi, they were the only ones involved here. Interesting thing though, he said he was a friend of Usamah bin Laden. Usamah was the one who initially planned the whole thing years ago.

The picture of Usamah and threat written on the back was sent by Atiya. She was a big supporter and fan of bin Laden. Both the sisters had met him several times in Afghanistan when they were training as snipers," Daniel explained.

"We've changed the procedures for all people applying for government jobs, especially here in DC and no matter what the position is. It should kick in within thirty days. I also have all the agencies conducting complete background checks on every Federal employee," Merlin added.

"I hope I don't have any skeletons in my closets," Bill Angus added, with a serious look on his face.

They all laughed.

"Good job, people," Daniel said.

"I have one thing to add," Raul said. "Did everyone see the television interview of Daniel the other night? That was one hell of an interview, Daniel. You put her in her place. Intelligence Czar. That pissed me off using the word czar. What a slam."

Everyone agreed.

"I think we should call Daniel the Intelligence King," the Wizard said.

Daniel looked at his good friend with a scowl on his face.

"Holy shit, Daniel, I was just kidding. Someone grab his gun before he shoots me," Merlin responded with his hands in the air.

Again they all laughed.

"I'm just Daniel White who has the best damn group of people working with him. That's all I am.

Now, I'm off to Colorado for three weeks and Merlin and Raul are in charge. I need a break, so if no one has any questions or anything to add, that's all I've got."

There were no questions. Everyone spent a little time congratulating Daniel and wishing him and his family well.

On the drive to the observatory, he received a message from Xi. Not a written one but mental.

"Hello, Master Daniel. It Xi. You come now to Colorado. Xi teach you how travel different place like Xi did in Montana. You now ready for next step in Master. See you soon, Master Daniel."

He smiled and answered, "Yes, Master Xi. See you soon." Daniel was now prepared to learn the art of transfiguration, the next step in the world of the Masters.

Other Novels

by

Author

W. Robb Robichaud

The Executive Order 211 Trilogy

Executive Order 211 al Qaeda

Executive Order 211 Afghanistan

Executive Order 211 Falcon Agency

Nonfiction

Knowing You – Mind, Body and Soul

Author's Bio

W. Robb Robichaud was a private commercial pilot for 17 years, Owner/CEO/President of various corporations, Chairman of Board of Directors, Realtor, Banker, Real Estate Appraiser, author of five novels and a Vietnam Veteran.

He worked in the Middle East for many years, traveled and lived all over the world the past 40 years. Robb has capitalized off of his life's experiences by authoring five novels during the past seven years. The modern day fiction novels, Executive Order 211 trilogy, followed by The Scorpio File, are action/adventure/political genre. Knowing You-Mind, Body and Soul is a true message of spiritual enlightenment. Robb's passion for writing good novels with twists, turns, dead end paths and underlying messages, has become his life's obsession.

He and his spouse Roseann of 36 years; have four sons, a grandson and a granddaughter. They reside in Colorado. He received his college education at the University of Wisconsin-Platteville, continues to write, travel extensively and does speaking engagements.

Printed in the United States
22424LVS00001BC/14